Bryan Forbes

the choice

Matador
9 De Montfort Mews
Leicester LE1 7FW, UK
Tel: (+44) 116 255 9311 / 9312
Email: books@troubador.co.uk
Web: www.troubador.co.uk/matador

ISBN: 978-1905886-722

Typeset in 11pt Stempel Garamond by Troubador Publishing Ltd, Leicester, UK
Printed in the UK by The Cromwell Press Ltd, Trowbridge, Wilts, UK

Matador is an imprint of Troubador Publishing Ltd

Once again
for
Nanette
with all my love

ONE

I could begin by saying that this is just a story of lost illusions, of wrong choices made, but that would be too simple. Human experience, I was once told, is only understandable as a state of transition. Whether or not that's true, I'm not clever enough to decide. All I know is that, years ago, in a foreign country, I lived through events and a love that, ever since, I have struggled to justify. How odd it is we can be so certain of the rightness of all our actions except those that stem from affairs of the heart. None of us are rich enough to buy back our pasts.

Nothing was clear-cut in Hamburg that merciless winter of 1946 in the stale aftermath of a long war. I slept fully clothed under my British Army greatcoat, in a ruined hotel bedroom with shards of glass from the broken window still lodged in the walls as though a circus knife-thrower had occupied it before me. Waking every morning semi-frozen, I shaved in icy water before facing our surly German waiters in the Mess; the only time I ever saw them smile was the morning they got the news that Goering had cheated the hangman at Nuremberg.

Until then I had had a lucky war, crossing to France as part of a Field Security unit on D+5 after the beaches had been secured, thus missing the carnage, true descriptions of which were deliberately concealed from the general public. Newsreel footage edited out the true horrors – men hosed down by MG-42 machine guns as, crapping themselves, they jumped from the landing craft and were taken out, pierced through the eyes or testicles, their faces blown off, heads disintegrating into myriad red dots, the sea around them lapping a tide of frothy blood: the actuality had to be sanitized, preserving the fiction of men going bravely to their deaths, cleanly and surgically killed by bullets, not atomised by shell and mortar fire. I came through with nothing more serious than temporary deafness when a sapper ahead of me stepped on a Schu mine that blew his foot off, the severed extremity hitting me on the side of my head.

The other members of my unit were an easygoing lot. We had survived the war together more or less intact, only losing our CSM to a sniper's bullet in the battle for Abbeville, which resulted in my being promoted in the field. Our commanding officer was an Lt.Colonel Machell, an amiable, middle-aged old-Harrovian, ex-Indian Army, fluent in fourteen languages. His favourite tipple was heroic slugs of neat Scotch which he termed 'mahoganies', for he took his poison neat and once, when pissed, confessed to me that he had left behind a love child in the Punjab ('The Monsoons always made me randy, dear boy.'). He referred to us as his 'Battersea Dogs Home' with some justification because we were certainly a mongrel bunch drawn from widely different backgrounds and thrown together in the haphazard way the Army did these things.

No stickler for discipline, he was content to sit back and leave most operational matters to his second in command, Lt. Grable, a much younger man who let everybody know he had a Cambridge degree in modern history, was generally regarded as a pedant and nicknamed, inevitably, 'Betty'. The chain of command then descended from me to Sergeant Armstrong, a regular who had survived Dunkirk, and two Corporals: Groves, a ponderous character who endlessly whistled Bach, and Sasdy, a Czech who had escaped to England after Munich.

Since he valued his own creature comforts, Machell had

always commandeered a series of reasonable billets as we progressed deeper into Germany. When we finally arrived in the gutted nightmare of Hamburg and set up a permanent base he pulled strings and obtained quarters in the Hotel zum Kronprinzen, which fronted onto the battered Haupt-Bahnhof Platz. The hotel had partially survived Operation Gomorrah, the great firestorm raid that blotted out the sun for four days and left thirty thousand of the inhabitants incinerated beyond recognition. It was definitely superior to most of our previous habitats. I had a room to myself on the third floor, which, despite the broken window, was an unaccustomed luxury. Outside, those that had survived the bombing existed like troglodytes, emerging every day to trundle their remaining possessions through rubbled streets to barter for bare essentials. That winter many starved; many froze to death. It was an uneasy peace belonging neither to the victors nor the vanquished.

Now as part of the Army of Occupation our time was spent sifting through the lies of a Third Reich that hadn't lasted for a thousand years. For the most part we went our own way and made our own rules. Unlike Eisenhower who ensured he got his oats throughout the campaign, prior to us crossing the Rhine our celibate Monty issued one of his famous edicts, spelling out a code of behaviour we were to obey once in the enemy's home territory. "It is too soon for you to distinguish between good and bad Germans. In streets, houses, cafes, cinemas etc, you must keep clear of the Germans, man, woman and child. You must not walk out with them, or shake hands, or visit their homes, or make them gifts, or take gifts from them. In short, you must not fraternise with Germans."

The ban was more or less adhered to while the fighting lasted, but within a few weeks of VE Day a vast army deprived of female company saw no reason to settle for a monastic existence. Brothels soon flourished, but most men took up with compliant German girls – hate was difficult to sustain when long-dormant gonads stirred again. In any case, German women proved just as amenable as the women of France, Holland and Belgium. If sex wasn't the panacea for post victory angst, some took solace by soaking their brains in wood alcohol that sent them blind. The Yanks had their own tipple called Swipe, just as lethal, while other foolhardy souls left this life asshole drunk on captured buzz-bomb fuel. Like everybody else I found the everyday misery of barbequed cities like Hamburg difficult to live in without compassion. Back home the new Labour Government promised a welfare state flowing with milk, honey and free dentures to return to, but it was hard to believe in a rosy future when nothing but reminders of recent horrors stared at us from every street corner.

When hostilities ended a barter system immediately sprang up. With the official exchange rate around 13 old Reich marks to the pound sterling, a single cigarette commanded 20 marks, a bag of coffee beans would get you a Leica or Rolleiflex, a bar of soap got your laundry done for a month. Non-smokers could hoard the weekly free cigarette issue until they had saved enough to acquire a Volkswagen. Those lucky enough to be invited to visit a Yank PX and buy some nylon stockings could count on getting laid. For entertainment we made do with the welcome, if basic, comforts of the Salvation Army and Nuffield canteens; occasionally ENSA concert parties arrived to demonstrate that variety was on the way out – there was usually a soubrette in every party ironically giving a rendition of Lily Marlene, a lament purloined from the Africa Corps. When ENSA was disbanded, the Ministry of Defence devised 'Combined Services Entertainment Units' made up of officers and other ranks from all three Services who had some connection, however tenuous, with show business. Officers were not allowed to perform, only other ranks, so that the class status quo was kept inviolate.

It was at a production of *Charley's Aunt* given by an Army and ATS cast in the local Opera House (which had miraculously escaped total destruction), that I first came across a character named Chivers who was destined to become my nemesis. He was seated in the row in front of me with a very beddable Wren officer – the Senior Service always recruited the best lookers – wearing the uniform of the newly-established Control Commission with the equivalent rank of Major and had his arm around the Wren, from time to time possessively stroking her neck.

The play's creaky plot and stilted dialogue from a by-gone age bored rather than amused me – my humour that year was more graveyard. Staring at the Wren's delectable neck rather than following the play I felt an irrational resentment. Some of the Control Commission types took the superior attitude of 'Well, you brown jobs have done your stint and now you can move over and leave it to us to bring some order.' We who had come through the whole shooting match took it for granted that some of them had sat out the war in cushy civvy street jobs and, now that the danger had passed, wanted their share of the spoils, though the majority were probably motivated by a genuine desire to administer a conquered country fairly.

My first impressions of Chivers grated. His brand new uniform and insignia, his clean-shaven, almost babyish face and neatly styled hair, in contrast to my statutory Army-shorn-back-and-sides, put me in a lower social order. I judged him to be in his middle thirties, some ten years older than me. At the interval he got up to stretch his legs and gave me a smug look as he and the Wren edged along the row of seats. "Enjoying it, soldier?" he said.

I heard the Wren whisper to him as they left. Returning for the second act Chivers leaned back over his seat to say: "Sorry for the mistake in not addressing you by your correct rank, CSM. Still learning, but Babs here put me right. Can I make amends by offering you a snifter after the show? Come and share a dram of Johnny Walker with us back at my hotel."

I felt an urge to reply: 'people kill for real Scotch in this town' but instead I thought, Why Not? A free drink was a free drink and there was always the chance Babs might be persuaded to switch partners by the end of the evening. "Thanks," I said, "I'll take you up on that."

"Splendid." His plumy upper-class accent slipped occasionally, betraying the fact it was probably assumed. "Good fun, didn't you think?" he said, as we filed out at the finale. "Very droll. I thought the chappie who played the Aunt was top hole, considering the programme says he's only a Corporal in the Green Howard's. Granted a bit downmarket from Olivier and Gielgud, but we can't have everything, can we? Sorry. Haven't introduced ourselves. This is First Officer Wilson, known as Babs to a privileged few, and I'm Major Kenneth Chivers. And your name?"

"Seaton. Alex Seaton."

"Company Sergeant Major Seaton that is. Get it right this time, Kenneth."

"Alex will do."

"I thought all Sergeant Majors were meant to look fearsome," Babs said with a sidelong smile I felt held promise.

"Only those in the infantry," I said.

While we walked to his billet Chivers remarked, "I'm told there's going to be a classical symphony concert here next week. I like a bit of Beethoven, much more my bag. He was a good German."

"How would you know?"

"Sorry?"

"Nothing," I said. "Just a joke."

Chivers' billet was in an officer-only hotel which had

been smartened up and the windows of his room were intact. He even had his own bathroom and a wardrobe, though there was only one chair. Producing three odd glasses he poured generous tots. I sat beside Babs on the lumpy bed. Close to she smelled delicious, her French perfume doubtless courtesy of some Yank. Girls like Babs always knew the ropes and where to find long denied luxuries.

"So, here's to life to come on the ocean waves," Chivers toasted with a knowing grin. "I think I'm going to enjoy living here."

"Well, time will tell. When did you arrive?"

"Got into Flensburg a couple of weeks ago. Still finding my feet. From the first look of this place, I've got a big job to do. A big job." He made it sound as though he alone had the responsibility for putting Germany back on its feet. "Of course, you know who we've got to be on our guard against, don't you?"

"Tell me."

"The Soviets."

"You think so?"

"I know so. Don't be blinkered. Nazi Germany may be finished, but the enemy is still the Russian bear."

"What makes you say that?"

"Hiroshima. That was a big loss of face for them. Basically, of course they have an Oriental mentality as you may or may not know. To have America steal the march didn't go down well. Suddenly they're behind in the race for world domination. Not a good omen." He imparted this wisdom as though he alone had the inside track.

"I hope you're wrong. I don't fancy starting again."

"I hope I'm wrong, sport. But I always take the cynical view."

Going to the wardrobe, he produced a full tin of Players cigarettes, authentic coffin nails, and offered them around, lighting them for Babs and me with an American Zippo. "Bit

7

of Lend Lease in reverse," he said. "About time we got something back from the Yanks." Abruptly he switched to ask: "What's the going rate for cigarettes? They're the official currency, I understand."

"A tin like that will get you a Rolleiflex," I said. "Or a quick trip home if you aren't careful, but I'll let you off with a caution."

He blinked and then recovered. "Oh, I'm careful. Careful is my middle name. I'm told that what really makes the Krauts salivate is a pound of coffee beans, so I packed a few."

"Wouldn't you salivate, if you'd been drinking roasted acorns for years?"

"I suppose so, but mind you the brew at the Savoy Grill, my favourite watering hole by the way, wasn't anything to write home about during the jolly old krieg."

"Really? How was your krieg?"

"Can't complain, sport, though to my lasting regret I never saw action. Desperate to be a fighter pilot, but failed the medical. Dickey eyesight. They only took you with 20-20 vision."

Or maybe you shaved your armpits, I thought.

"So because of my background," he continued, his free hand resting on Babs' thigh, "They put me into Bletchley."

"Bletchley? What's that?"

"Hush-hush outfit, still on the secret list, so I can't say much. It'll all come out one day. Until then, mum's the word. Careless talk can still cost lives."

"What was your background?"

"Academic. Senior Wrangler."

"Really?" I had no idea what a Senior Wrangler was, though it suggested something to do with horses.

"When the show was over, felt I ought to do my bit over here. They were looking for chaps of my calibre and I guess we're thin on the ground. What are you going back to?"

"Going back to?"

"Yes, what career?"

"No idea. Never had the chance to start one."

"Going to be rich pickings if you keep your eyes open for the main chance."

His self-satisfaction began to depress me and I regretted having accepted his hospitality, although the thin possibility of being able to shag the delectable Babs kept me there. I wished I had the nerve to make a pass at her, but she was savvy enough to know Chivers had more to offer. I turned to her. "How long before you're demobbed, Babs?"

"Oh, I've volunteered to stay on and take a short commission. Anything rather than face going back to dreary old England. Everybody I saw on my last leave was so dowdy and depressing," she said. "All those pinched, grey faces and hideous fashions. Plus the ghastly government. Daddy's still in shock. You didn't vote Labour, I hope?"

"Yes, as a matter of fact."

"Oh, are we sharing a drink with the proletariat?" Chivers said. "We've got you to thank for them, have we? You'll live to regret it, because they'll fuck up, given time. Pardon my French, Babs. That awful little creep Attlee looks like Hitler in a Trilby hat. And I couldn't agree more about the women. Can't wait for them look sexy again. Present company excepted of course."

"Watch it, Major," Babs replied. "You nearly blotted your copy book then."

She gave me a knowing smile and for a brief moment I fancied my chances, but given her general air of superiority she probably didn't rate me. Chivers topped up her glass. He's welcome to her, I thought, and then changed my mind again as she removed her uniform jacket, revealing good breasts straining against the crisp, regulation white shirt. I didn't want to imagine the ubiquitous Chivers pasturing on that body when I left. There are few things more depressing than being in the company of potential lovers. I downed the remainder of my drink and stood up. "Thanks for the drink. It's nice to see how the other half live. Excuse me if I call it day, I have to be on the road early tomorrow."

"What does your work entail?" Chivers enquired.

"Seeking out past corruption."

"Only 'past'?"

"For the moment, though you never know."

"I hope we don't make the same mistake as last time. Be too harsh on them, I mean. No more Versailles. They lost in a straight fight and now we must get them back on their feet."

"You thought it was 'straight', did you?"

Chivers flushed and I knew I had finally scored a point.

"I meant we traded blow for blow."

"Did we? Maybe eventually. Most of the war we were boxing above our weight. If you'd been here you'd have known it was often touch and go."

"Yes, well unfortunately I missed it doing another vital job else where."

As I put my glass down I brushed against Babs. "Always a pleasure to meet the Senior Service. Be careful going back to your billet, there are some ugly characters around, out for only one thing," I said pointedly. "But I'm sure you can take care of yourself. Nice to have met you, Babs."

She merely smiled. "We must meet up again," Chivers said.

"I expect we will. This is a small place."

As I left, Babs was kicking off her shoes. I walked back to my own hotel with the safety catch off on my Walter. An elderly couple pushing a wooden cart stepped off the pavement into the roadway as I approached. The man bowed, removed his hat and whispered 'Guten Abend', then waited, his expression fearful, expecting to be questioned. The homeless and tarts often took their chances and ignored the curfew. I walked on. Outside my hotel two Military Police with blanched belts almost florescent white were frisking a youth.

Inside the Sergeant's Mess a three-piece German band was attempting to play one of the current American hits to a sparse audience of drunks. I ordered a beer but after Chivers' whisky it tasted like weak piss and I left it unfinished and went upstairs to my room feeling deflated. I thought of all the things I could have said to counter Chivers' insufferable air of superiority, but most of all I thought what Babs would look like naked.

TWO

The next morning I began a journey that was to take me all the way to Graz in Austria, charged with a no-win mission. Group HQ had passed on evidence that the British Brigadier commanding the Graz salient was deeply involved in an ingenious black market scam, masterminded by a similar high-ranking Yank officer in charge of the marshalling yards at Antwerp docks. The scam was simplicity itself: from every new shipment of booze, cigarettes and nylons arriving for American PX stores, one truckload would be immediately diverted and disappear. That wasn't difficult, given the vast quantities being handled. If the loss was reported, it was put down to a highjack by one of the many marauding gangs still at large. The booty would be quickly disposed of to a chain of willing customers. The beauty of the scheme was in the final stage: all proceeds were used to buy Dutch tulip bulbs, which were then shipped to an England deprived of them for five years where they fetched a high price. To all appearances they were legitimate transactions paid for in sterling. The major players, including our Brigadier who ran the Austrian end of the operation, were getting very rich. The break only came when one of the contraband trucks was involved in an autobahn pile up and the GI driver sang to save his skin. His story was quickly traced to source.

My brief was to face down our erstwhile war hero and offer him a deal: in return for turning King's evidence and revealing how the scam operated, he was to be allowed to resign with an honourable discharge and draw his pension from a grateful nation. That was the way it worked in those days and maybe still does, for all I know: it was a case of 'don't, in the flush of victory, humiliate the good and the great for the sake of a headline. How the Yanks handled their end was their concern.

I was savvy enough to know why I had been picked for the assignment. Sending a Warrant Officer instead of somebody of comparable rank ensured the top brass could wash their hands of it if something went wrong – any snafu could be put down to me. I was expendable.

My Jeep driver that morning was a Corporal Charlie Boag. He wasn't in the Intelligence Corps, but it was the form to use drivers seconded from REME once hostilities ended. Charlie was a loquacious character of mongrel extraction, part Maltese, part North African on his mother's side. Squat and muscular, with a face that was seldom without a smile, I frequently chose him over others. He had volunteered to join the British Army at the outbreak of the war, fought his way through Italy and had twice been recommended for bravery. History not being his strong point, he constantly pumped me about the rise of Nazi Germany, punctuating his responses with his favourite expression of "Mine bloody godfathers, you don't say?" Fanatically patriotic, his hero was Churchill, his one ambition to get to England and open a restaurant. I enjoyed his company. He wasn't the greatest driver, but he could fix anything mechanical and was always cheerful.

We had been on the road for about five hours and making good progress, only stopping once to refuel and eat a packed meal. During our break the weather shut in, slanting sleet reduced visibility and the route became treacherous. The maps we had were unreliable and we found ourselves on a road pitted with bomb craters that necessitated back-tracking on a complicated diversion.

Afterwards, neither of us remembered much about the

skid. I vaguely recalled us turning a concealed corner and the shape of an oncoming car coming at us very fast well over on the wrong side. Charlie swung the wheel violently, but there wasn't enough room to avoid the other vehicle and we sideswiped it, ending up with our Jeep on its side in a ditch. Both of us had been smoking and my first instinctive reaction was to grope for the ignition key and kill the engine.

We disentangled ourselves, helped each other out and took stock of the damage. Charlie walked up and down cursing. He had a cut on his forehand, but refused my offer of a field dressing. I had a few minor abrasions and the odd bruise but was otherwise unscathed. "Try and get it back on the road," I told him, then went to see how the other vehicle had fared. It was a Mercedes with chrome exterior super-chargers, a model historically favoured by high-ranking Nazi officers, and had come to rest sideways across the road, with the driver's side panel crumpled and a front wheel tyre guard hanging loose. A burly, uniformed GI was standing by it inspecting the damage. He swung around and came straight for me.

"You the driver?" he said.

"No. I have a driver."

"You don't say? Well, I'm gonna to kick him in the crotch. What outfit you both with?"

"I'm British Intelligence."

"But not intelligent enough to drive straight."

"Let's not get personal," I said. "You were coming too fast and we couldn't avoid you. It was fifty-fifty."

"You hear that, honey? This asshole's saying it was my fault."

"No, I'm not. I'm saying we share the blame." I saw 'honey' for the first time as she got out of the front passenger seat. She was auburn-haired, petite, wearing a WAC uniform and ignored my tentative smile. "Is your girlfriend okay?"

"She ain't my girlfriend, asshole, she's my wife and she's

14

pregnant, that's what," he said. "We were on our way to the boat and then Stateside. If she loses the baby I'm gonna start another war. Jesus fucking wept!"

"Look, we both should have been more careful. These icy roads are a death trap, so calm down and first make sure your wife's okay."

"I'll take care of my bride, don't you worry." He looked me up and down. "You an officer?"

"Warrant Officer. Top Sergeant in your army."

"What's your name?"

"Seaton."

"I'm Steinmetz, 12th Army Group. You ever killed anybody?"

"What's that got to do with it?

"Well, have you?"

"I wasn't Infantry."

"That figures. You don't look man enough. Well, I killed plenty, so don't get in my way because I'm going to kick your driver's brains in."

"I don't think you're going to do that," I replied flatly. "If you lay a hand on him, I'll arrest you, you're in our sector and it's my call." I rested a hand on my revolver holster and edged into the centre of the road to put myself between him and Charlie who had managed to right the Jeep and was revving the engine. "Let's not trade threats. We're supposed to be allies, so let's act the part. We both got off lightly, considering, could have been a lot worse. Why don't we take a look at your vehicle and see if it still works? if it doesn't, I've got a field telephone and I'll send for help."

The offer seemed to calm him momentarily. He hesitated, and then walked back to the Merc. I followed him. "Try it," I said.

"Don't tell me what to do." Despite his continued show of truculence, he got in behind the wheel and tried the ignition. The engine spluttered a few times before it fired, then ticked over quietly. "There are some things which aren't too bad about Germany," I said," They make decent cars."

"They make shit!" Steinmetz killed and then restarted the engine. Looking under the chassis, I couldn't see any sign of petrol leaking.

"So far so good," I said.

At that moment Charlie joined us and straight away lay down on the slushy road and began straightening the crumpled mudguard. Steinmetz was out of the Merc in a flash and kicked him in the groin before I could do anything. Charlie doubled up and lay with his head drawn in and almost touching his knees, rocking backwards and forwards with the pain of the blow. As Steinmetz moved to aim another kick, I drew my Walther out and fired a shot into the air. Steinmetz froze, squinting at me and for a second he seemed angry enough to risk anything.

"Back off." I said and ordered Charlie to return to our Jeep. He belly-crabbed a few yards on the icy road before he recovered enough to get to his feet.

"You won't get away with this, I'll make sure of that." Steinmetz said. "I'll have you busted, you fucking British piece of crud."

"What are you going to bust me for?"

"Shooting at me, that's what."

"Well this fucking piece of British crud didn't shoot at you. He fired a warning shot in the air to stop you kicking his driver's brains in as you threatened. That wouldn't look too good on your charge sheet. So don't push your luck any further, soldier. Let's both leave it at that and get ourselves back on the road."

"Yeah, let's go," his wife, said. "Don't waste your time talking to him."

"How are you, Hon?" Steinmetz said, finally putting the question to her.

"I'm fine, just cold, let's go"

16

For a second he seemed about to prolong the debate, but his wife repeated, "Let's go! I'm frozen," and he surrendered to her. I stood my ground until they both got back into the Merc and, after spinning the wheels, he managed to get it pointing in the right direction and drove off.

Charlie was bent over the bonnet, nursing his groin, when I rejoined him.

"Get in, I'll drive."

Charlie protested, but without much conviction. I dropped a bar of chocolate in his lap. "Eat that. Sugar's good for shock."

The steering on the Jeep was a little dodgy and I tested the brakes a couple of times before setting off, taking it slowly for the first few miles until the diversion ended and we were able to rejoin the autobahn.

For half an hour Charlie said nothing, then it all burst out of him. "Why the fuck did he do that? Mine bloody Godfathers, we're fucking supposed to be on the same fucking side, for fuck'sake."

" The war's over, Charlie. Things are getting back to normal."

"I was only fucking trying to help," Charlie said finally, baffled, as ever, by a world of inconsistencies.

THREE

Because of the accident we didn't reach Graz that night, and were forced to stop in a small village where there was a transit hostel for Allied personnel run by the Church Army. A crucifix and religious inscription over the main door denoted the building had once been a convent.

Charlie usually liked to be left to his own devices, so I gave him a pack of cigarettes, knowing he would use them to find a bed somewhere – he was never down for long. "I might test the love muscles if I get lucky," he said.

"Just be careful. You've had all your luck for one day. And be ready to move off at seven tomorrow after you've checked the Jeep."

Everything in the hostel was utilitarian, but it was warm and the comfort food they provided reminded me of my mother's cooking. That night I slept without my greatcoat over me for once, and slipped into one of those recurring, confused dreams from which there is no escape. When I finally managed to drag myself awake it was still dark, but I found a bathroom and showered in hot water, a real luxury. Going downstairs I found a middle-aged woman already at work in the kitchen – one of those easily recognisable, middle class, typical English characters from the Shires, the kind who sold homemade jam and tea cosies at village fetes, often derided, but who could always be relied upon to come up trumps in an emergency. She told me to call her Audrey, and confided that she was having the time of her life. "It took a war to get me out of Cheltenham, don't know how I'll settle down again when eventually I return home. Do you know Cheltenham?"

"No, 'fraid not."

"Nice, but stuffy. Some people call it God's waiting room. Haven't got a husband and the children fled the nest as soon as they could. Couldn't blame them. You married?"

"No."

"I had a good marriage, but he was killed early on. One of those who didn't benefit from the miracle of Dunkirk. Nice man, smoked a pipe and collected stamps. Such a boring hobby, I always thought, but he was passionate about his stamps, bless him. Sticking them in, taking them out with his tweezers. Could have been worse, I suppose. He could have taken up growing dahlias. Vulgar flowers, to my mind. Too many garish colours. One of these days I must try and find his grave. That is if he has one. Now, stop it, Audrey, don't get maudlin in your old age. How d'you like your eggs?"

"Eggs, plural?"

"Yes."

"Fried, please."

"Sunny side up or easy over?"

"What's that mean?"

"Expression the doughboys taught me."

"I'll leave it to you."

I ate the best breakfast I had had in months. When I said goodbye she produced a bottle of brandy. "Can't vouch for it, don't touch it myself, gin's my ruin, but I'm told it warms your toes in this weather."

"You're spoiling me, Audrey."

"Got to spoil somebody," she said and kissed me. She smelt of lavender.

Outside, Charlie had the Jeep's engine running. "Doesn't seem to have done any damage, boss," he said.

"Good. How was your night?"

"No problem, boss, everything in working order, and it only cost me ten fags."

"How d'you manage to score every time, Charlie? Let me in on your secret."

"I laugh them into bed. I reckon they haven't had too many laughs around here recently."

Austria, in contrast to Germany, was remarkably unscathed, the farms we passed were laid out like Dinky displays in a toy shop – geometrically neat, smoke rising straight from chimneys, wood stacked with military precision in a near-deserted, pristine landscape, pale beige cows looking as though they had been freshly polished. "Mine bloody Godfathers," Charlie observed. "Like they never had a war."

We made the outskirts of Graz before nightfall, and found the local Field Security based in a large farmhouse. A portly Sergeant named Hargreaves with a pronounced North Country accent greeted me. "We were expecting you yesterday, Warrant."

"Yes, unfortunately we ran into a bit of bother with one of our American friends. Quite ugly while it lasted."

"Funny lot, the Yanks. Nice as pie until they suddenly turn. Must be their diet. Too much red meat. Talking of which, I'm sure you're famished. How would a steak sit with you?"

"You kidding?"

"Oh, no. We don't do things by halves here. What's the point of winning a war if you can't live well? Come over to the Mess. Not much but we're proud of it."

"This place reminds me of home," I said.

"Where's home?"

"A farm in Lincolnshire."

He led me to an adjacent stable block that had been roughly converted and made habitable with odds and ends of rustic furniture. There was a framed picture of the King and Queen on one of the walls, hung alongside a Nazi flag with bullet holes in it. Hargreaves introduced me to two other sergeants, Mathews and Lewis, who were helping themselves to a beer from a keg on top of a makeshift bar, behind which was an imposing array of wines. Seeing my eye goes to them, Hargreaves explained: "We had a bit of luck when we first got here. The local Gestapo had acquired quite a cellar, which we helped ourselves to. Some nice French reds, which go down a treat with a steak."

"Sounds good to me. You choose, I'm no expert."

He selected a bottle of 1940 Margaux. "A good year for Margaux if not for the French army."

We killed a second bottle over a relaxed meal, during which I remained deliberately vague about the real purpose of my visit, but pumped the other three for local information. "What's the Brigadier here like?"

"Hirst? What would you say, Bert?" Hargreaves said, turning to Mathews.

"Bit of a martinet. Well, definitely a martinet."

"Yes, definitely. Pre-war professional soldier, took the honour sword at Sandhurst in his year, collected an MC at Anzio, well connected, friends in high places, played polo with the Prince of Wales, so I'm told."

"D'you see much of him?"

"No more than we have to. He's not our number one fan. We usually deal with Wadham, his Adjutant."

"He's a pompous prick," Lewis said. "Together they run this area like a personal fiefdom."

That night I slept soundly in a loft above the stables which smelt of musty hay. After a substantial breakfast I found Charlie hosing the dust off the Jeep. "How was your night?" I asked."

"Got my oats again, boss. No problem."

"What about your wife back In Malta? Don't you ever have a conscience?"

"I ain't seen the missus in four years, haven't had a letter from her in two, maybe she's gone walkabout. In any case

I'm not going back to Malta. No future there. England, that's where I'm heading after this."

Arriving at the camp our identity passes were closely scrutinised before we were allowed to proceed. Hargreaves was right about Hirst being a bullshit artist – the camp looked as though it was expecting a visit from royalty. I was directed to Wadham's office where, again, a sentry stood guard and I was required to produce my pass once more. Major Wadham turned out to be a dapper little individual with a trimmed toothbrush moustache and a clipped accent who immediately made me aware that my presence wasn't welcome.

"I fail to understand why Hamburg didn't inform us you were coming, Sergeant Major," he said after I'd thrown him a crisp salute. "What is the purpose of this visit?"

"We've had reports of Martin Bormann being sighted in this area," I lied, having decided this was a good opening ploy.

"So?"

"I was sent to check them out, sir. Amongst other things."

"You don't think we're capable of doing that ourselves?"

"Mine not to question orders, sir."

"You said 'other things'. What other things?" he snapped.

An orderly interrupted, bringing a cup of tea for Wadham who pointedly didn't offer me one. "What other things?" he repeated, stirring his cup and dumping in enough sugar to bring on instant diabetes.

"General security matters, sir. Making sure everybody's on their toes."

"That's a bloody impertinence. You can go back and inform Group that had Bormann been seen in this sector I would have known and dealt with it. Everything comes through my office, I make certain of that. You've had a wasted trip."

"You could be right, sir."

"I shall certainly take this up with Group and make my views known."

I began to get the distinct impression there was unease behind his bluster and suspected that somehow he had got wind of the true purpose for my visit.

"May I request a meeting with the Brigadier, sir?"

"That won't be necessary. You can get all you need from me."

"My orders were specific, sir, and were signed by the General commanding 30 Corps. Perhaps you'd like to see a copy?"

"I certainly would," Wadham said, his expression betraying the fact that this was something he had not allowed for. He studied the document and handed it back to me. "Well, Brigadier Hirst is not available today. He's in Vienna attending a tri-party conference on the refugee situation."

"My orders are to stay in the area until I have a personal meeting, sir, so will you be good enough to let me know when he returns? I'm contactable at local Field Security."

"I'll do that," Wadham said tersely and brought the meeting to an end. I saluted and withdrew.

"How did you make out?" Hargreaves asked.

"I didn't get very far because Hirst is away in Vienna, so you're going to have to put up with me for a while longer. I agree with you about Wadham. Puffed up little sod."

"I don't want to push you, but would I be right in guessing that this isn't a casual, routine visit?"

"No, it isn't. I'll explain when I've seen Hirst. In the meantime what d'you lot do for relaxation around here?"

"Usually we take a ride into a small village called Krumpendorf, not far from here where we discovered a very pleasant Gasthof, which we more or less take over. Pretty setting, overlooking the lake, good grub, lethal local cider and some female talent. War widows just looking for company and a free meal. Nothing heavy."

"Lead me to it," I said.

23

FOUR

I reported the lack of progress to Group and was told that on no account to return until Hirst had been confronted with the charges. Suddenly handed a few days unexpected French leave, I decided to move into the Gasthof at Krumpendorf and enjoy a complete change of scenery. After the dirt and squalor of Hamburg, to be able to recapture an almost forgotten freedom brought back the feeling of the first day after school broke up for the holidays.

The Gasthof nestled in a thickly wooded area of pine and had a quality about it, which reminded me of an illustration from a childhood fairytale book. The proprietor, Herr Walbrook, and his wife allocated me the best room, while Charlie was given one in the attic. The Walbrooks were hospitable without being servile, though I couldn't make up my mind whether their attitude was genuine or calculated as good for business. There was a photograph of a young soldier in Wehrmacht uniform on a table in the entrance hallway that I took to be a portrait of their dead son. A candle was always kept burning in front of it along with a vase of fresh flowers. The food they served was simple but good, with homemade rye bread and local wine. I felt compelled to make some gesture in return, and gave the wife two bars of soap and, to Walbrook, some pipe tobacco, having been nauseated by the odour of the herbal mixture he habitually smoked.

In the evenings half a dozen women of varying ages frequented the small bar. Hargreaves had described them accurately: they were just lonely, looking for companionship. Some of them came in traditional Austrian costumes, their scrubbed, peasant faces devoid of makeup reminding me of Lincolnshire girls at a village hop. I chatted in German with them, bought them drinks, but, unlike Mathews and Lewis, shied away from any further involvement.

During the three days I spent there Walbrook lit a fire in my bedroom. Pleasantly drunk but becalmed under the feather duvet, I retraced my life to date, thinking what a long journey it had been from the Normandy beaches to this moment. A line seemed to have been drawn between my childhood and maturity with everything in between a blank. I was a stranger to myself, unsure what was normal any more. I tried to imagine how others – Charlie, Hargreaves, Wadham – made sense of the lives they had been compelled to live. The scent of pine from the hissing logs in the tiled stove eventually lulled me to sleep and I awoke to the sound of distant cowbells.

After breakfast, having checked that there was no word of Hirst's return, I would go for long walks, taking the icy path that skirted the dark waters of the nearby lake – a black wound in a landscape blanketed by dazzling snow. Apart from the sound of my boots crunching the packed snow, I was alone in a country of stillness.

Then word came that Hirst had returned and would to grant me an interview. In preparation for the meeting I had folded my uniform every night and slept with it under the mattress to ensure that the trouser creases were straight. I spit-and-polished my boots, blanched my webbing and when satisfied that Charlie's appearance was likewise parade-ground perfect, drove to Brigade HQ, arriving ahead of the prescribed time.

Wadham greeted me with a curt, "The Brigadier will see you when he's finished with daily orders," and I was left to cool my heels for the best part of an hour before the phone on his desk rang and I was marched into the presence. Hirst's room was dominated by a partner's desk and other antique pieces, giving it the look of a successful lawyer's chambers rather than an Army office. My eye went to several silver photo frames displayed on the desk, one showing Hirst in polo gear receiving a cup from Edward VIII, another a family portrait of his wife and two young sons.

Hirst was a tall man, handsome in a period way, the sort of Anthony Eden good looks that found favour with pre-war debutants. He wore a well-tailored uniform with the MC ribbon on his chest. In contrast to Wadham he received me with a smile and from the start he conducted the meeting with studied politeness.

"At ease, Sergeant Major. Apologies for keeping you hanging about, rather heavy schedule this morning. However I did find time to make enquiries about you. You have an exemplary record so far." He gave a slight emphasis to 'so far'. "Always a good thing, don't you agree, to know who one's dealing with?"

"Yes, sir."

"The fact that you were promoted in the field speaks volumes. Where did that happen?"

"Outside Abbeville, sir," I replied, "When our previous CSM bought it."

"I wasn't at the Normandy party. From all reports a good show." Many of the top brass aped Montgomery's cricket-commentary-style of speech when talking about battles – "we're going to knock them for six." and so forth. "Not that Italy was a cakewalk," he added.

"No, I'm sure not, sir."

"I understand you were educated at grammar school and came away fluent in two languages."

"Wouldn't say fluent, sir. I get by."

There was something too studied about this opening exchange, as though from the outset he wanted to establish the social difference between us.

"Do stand at ease. Why weren't you ever considered for a commission?"

"No idea, sir."

"Obviously an oversight. I would have thought you're obvious officer material. Has anybody offered you any refreshment, by the way?"

"No, but I'm fine, sir."

"How old are you?"

"Twenty four, sir."

"Ever thought of staying on in the Army?"

"No, I haven't, sir."

"What are you going back to when you get demobbed? Got a job waiting?"

"In a way, sir. My people are farmers."

"Is that what you want to do?"

"It's sort of taken for granted, sir."

"Never take anything for granted. The Army can use intelligent officers of your calibre. If you're keen, I'd be happy to put forward a recommendation."

"That's kind of you, sir, but I'm looking forward to getting demobbed."

"Well, bear it in mind. The offer's there if you want it. And coming from me, it would carry weight. . . Now, I understand from my Adjutant you're here to see if we're up to scratch on security matters."

"It's part of my brief, yes, sir."

"Any particular area that you're concerned about?"

He was going out of his way to be pleasant to me, as though he had determined charm was his best defence, but as we edged closer to the crux of the matter, I was aware of a tightness in his voice.

"One of the leads I was asked to follow up concerns a reported sighting of Martin Bormann in your sector, sir," I answered.

"I thought he was presumed dead?"

"He can't be accounted dead, sir, until we've captured him or found his corpse. There are conflicting stories about his last days in Berlin and the Russians are not sharing any information they have."

"And you say he's been sighted around here? "

"Allegedly once in Villach, sir, and once in Werfen."

"Were we circulated?"

"I believe so, sir."

"Not to my knowledge." He frowned and scribbled something on a notepad. "I'll look into it straight away. Is that all?"

I took a deep breath and plunged. "There is another matter, sir, of a more personal nature."

"Personal?"

"Yes, sir."

"And what would that be?" His voice remained flat.

"You name has cropped up in connection with an ongoing investigation, sir."

There was the slightest of pauses. "What does that mean?"

"Well, sir, for some months now we've been involved in a combined operation between ourselves and the American special branch to crack a major scam."

"'Scam'? What does that mean?"

"An American expression, sir, for an illegal scheme. In this case it carries criminal charges," I added for emphasis.

"What have the Yanks got to do with it?"

"Their prime suspect was in charge of the marshalling yards at Antwerp where the chain originated."

"You said 'was' in charge."

"He's currently under arrest, sir, awaiting trial."

"I still don't understand what this has to do with me or my command."

"We have been given to believe, sir, that you form part of that chain."

Hirst did not flinch, or lose his thin smile. "That's a very serious allegation, Sergeant Major. In the circumstances, you'd better repeat it in front of Major Wadham."

"Of course, sir."

He pressed a button on his internal phone. "Come in please, Wadham."

Wadham entered immediately as though he had been listening for the summons on the other side of the door. "Brigadier?"

"The Sergeant Major here has just made an extraordinary allegation which I would like repeated in the presence of a witness. Continue, Sergeant Major."

"I am under orders to inform Brigadier Hirst, that he is implicated in a serious breach of King's Regulations which, if substantiated, would lead to a court martial."

Wadham's response had menace in it. "I hope you are aware of the gravity of that statement, Sergeant Major."

"I am, sir." The whole atmosphere in the room had undergone a change.

"Should you repeat it outside this room, you will leave here under arrest yourself," Wadham said.

"Well, let's not be too hasty," Hirst said, jumping in. "First of all I need to know how I am supposedly implicated." He still maintained a calm facade, though by now I was convinced that he and Wadham were in cahoots.

I began a carefully prepared speech, memorised from the full briefing I had been given in Hamburg. "Sir, a Yank GI truck driver was recently detained outside Vienna. Under interrogation he gave names and full details of a widespread scheme involving participants in both the American and British sectors. The consignment of cigarettes, liquor and other goods he was transporting were intended as stock for American PX stores, but would never find their way there. Instead, the goods would be diverted and disappear into the black market and quickly disposed of. A bogus trading company had been set up in Holland to handle the proceeds, the money fed to this company was then used to purchase and ship to England large quantities of tulip bulbs. The scheme was operated on a regular basis and the considerable profits generated could not be traced back to their source."

Hirst heard me out. "Yes," he said, "very ingenious, but I fail to see what it has to do with me." He took a cigarette from the silver box on his desk and lit it.

"The driver gave a number of names, sir. One of the names was yours."

I caught a quick glance between them. Wadham immediately responded with, "Are you telling us that this GI's word is the sole basis for a monstrous accusation against a senior British officer?"

"No, sir. It isn't just this man's word. At least a dozen others involved have already been rounded up, including an American Colonel. He also implicated Brigadier Hirst."

Hirst took his time before speaking again. "I take it you came with written authority to put these allegations before me?"

"Yes, sir. My authority was signed by the GOC 30 Corps. I have already shown it to Major Wadham."

"Let me see it."

I produced the document and he studied it, then got up from his desk and went to the window. There was an appreciable silence before he said: "Wadham, leave this with me, will you?" Wadham hesitated, seeming about to say something else before withdrawing as ordered. When we were alone once again, Hirst returned to his desk and slumped into his swivel chair, staring past me for a few moments before looking me in the face. "You appreciate, Sergeant Major Seaton, that I have no intention of responding to the charge you have laid against me. That will have to wait until I am dignified by a higher authority than you. But I would value talking to you off the record, as soldier to soldier."

"By all means, sir."

"Without prejudice."

"As you wish, sir."

Hirst began slowly, picking his words carefully. "We're living in turbulent times, Seaton, the best of times and the worst of times in many ways, times none of us could have envisaged a few years back. We're all at the end of a long war, fought against a terrible enemy. A terrible enemy," he repeated, "and many, too many, good men paid the ultimate sacrifice to put us where we are. But those of us lucky enough to come through it didn't escape unscarred. I know I didn't, and I suspect you didn't either. Or perhaps you did? Only you can decide that. There were many moments, especially when things were not going our way, when I tried to imagine how I would react to defeat. I never came up with an answer. All I did know was that if I came out unscathed I had no intention of letting myself be sold down the river like my father. The signs are already there. It's highly unlikely this new Labour government will retain a large standing army unless they've changed their spots. Chaps like me will soon be forgotten, despite this." He tapped the Military Cross ribbon on his chest. "My father won a DSO and bar at Ypres and a damn lot of good it did him. He died of his wounds and my mother had to sell his medals to put me through college. I long ago determined I would not condemn my own children to live on charity." He stopped and seemed at a loss to know how to conclude. "What I'm trying to say is, we've all had to reconcile ourselves to the fact that nothing is ever black and white. Wouldn't you agree?"

"I'm not sure that I follow you, sir," I said.

"Those who didn't go through what you and I went through, find it easy to make moral judgements about our behaviour. But they weren't there; they didn't see men die as we did. They think the annual laying of wreaths at the Cenotaph is repayment enough. Well, I beg to differ. They owe us, and if they choose to ignore us as before, then we have to take matters into our own hands."

"Sir, with respect, although I appreciate your views, I did not lay the charges against you, I'm only the messenger."

HIs mood changed abruptly. "Don't patronise me," he barked. "I know you're the bloody messenger and I've eaten types like you for breakfast. They sent small fry like you because those bloody desk wallets don't have the balls to face me themselves. What else were you instructed to say? I'm sure they didn't let you come empty-handed."

"I wasn't told the nuts and bolts, sir, but I was given to understand that, in return for your co-operation, a compromise could be reached."

"Compromise? What does that imply?"

"That the matter could be settled without dragging anybody down."

"Come on, man, be more explicit, spell it out."

"You'd be offered early retirement, with all charges dropped."

Much to my surprise, Hirst snorted with laughter. "Oh, that's rich. One of their typical stitch-ups. Push everything under the carpet. So, if I co-operate, as they put it, admit guilt, I can be shunted off into oblivion. And what if I don't accept their bloody compromise?"

"I can't answer that, sir."

He got up and walked around the room. " Well, so be it. You can report back that you put the charge, that I admitted nothing, nor agreed to anything, and that I will give my response when formal charges are lodged. Is that understood?"

"Understood, sir."

"Do you, do you? I doubt it. I doubt if you're capable of understanding my situation, given your background, Now, leave me with it."

I saluted and left the room. Wadham eyed me as I went through, but said nothing.

FIVE

My run in with Hirst left me angry. I suppose it was his parting shot about my background that really rankled. He was right, of course, I was unable fully to understand his way of the world. Certain rules of conduct had been instilled in him from birth as surely as coal dust is engrained in a miner's face, and he lived by them come what may.

That night, hunched beside the warmth of the tiled stove, I made an effort to remember every thing that he and Wadham had said before writing out my report. I put in I suspected Hirst had known the real purpose of my visit from the start, and had prepared his careful responses. I also included that I viewed his offer to obtain a commission for me as a not too subtle ploy to win me over to his side and I summed up by saying that I had come away convinced of his involvement.

The following morning after organising for the report to be couriered back to Group, I stopped Charlie preparing for our departure.

"We're not moving out just yet, Charlie. I have to wait here until I get further orders."

"Suits me, boss. Can I ask you something? Are you believing in love at first sight?"

"I suppose so, a lot of people claim it does happen. Why?"

"I've got it bad," Charlie said. "Mine bloody godfathers, have I got it bad. She's the real thing for me."

"What're you talking about?"

"Anna. I see her and suddenly I can't breathe."

"Charlie, wait a minute, you're going too fast for me. Who's Anna?" I was alarmed. I had never seen him so animated.

"My bride to be. This time it's the full works."

"How d'you mean, 'your bride to be?' Slow down. You're already married. You've got a wife back in Malta"

"Maybe. Maybe not, boss. "

"No, not maybe. You're marrIed, you silly sod."

"Okay, you're right, boss. But now I am not going back there. Next stop England, with Anna."

"Charlie, listen. Calm down and listen to me. Marriage, England, what the fuck are you talking about? You'd never met this Anna before we got here, for Christ'sake."

"A few days are plenty for the real thing."

"Who is this Anna?"

"Tonight, I show you her, then you understand."

"Is she Austrian?"

"No, she ain't anything right now, but after we marry she gets British papers like me."

"What d'you mean 'like you'? You don't have British papers. You're Maltese."

He grinned, shook his head and produced a British passport from his battledress pocket. "I buy this in Hamburg for just such an occasion."

"What about your Army documents? They show you as Maltese."

"You want to bet, boss?"

"I shouldn't be listening to this," I said. "You're going to end up in the slammer."

"I tell you, boss, my life up to now has been a bloody bummer, I need to change it before it's too late."

"A prison cell, that's what you'll change it for."

"I'll take my chances, boss," he said, but for the first time his voice betrayed the fact that his convictions had been dented.

"Well, I never heard this conversation. You're crazy."

"Ain't you ever been crazy, boss?"

"Not that crazy. Just think it through, that's my advice."

That evening he brought his prospective bride into the small dining room and introduced her. I've never been able to fathom what determines selection in the mating game. By any criteria Charlie and the girl he called Anna were worlds apart. Anna was in her twenties, Charlie approaching forty. She wasn't sexy, just pleasantly attractive with deep-set, dark eyes under auburn hair, a small Cupid's bow mouth. I saw history and tragedy in her wan face, the legacy that the war had etched into it. I did my best to put her at ease, since she was transparently awed by having to meet me. She carried the wariness of the dispossessed like a birthmark to anybody who showed kindness; kindness, she had learned, always had a price. I made some innocuous remarks to Charlie, complimenting him on his choice, which he accepted with eagerness, immediately telling me that he hoped he would allow him to pay for dinner with them. Anna made little or no conversation during the meal and it did not escape me that Walbrook served her with smaller portions. He was offended, I suppose, that I had permitted her to eat with me. There was no way of telling whether her feelings matched Charlie's; perhaps, like so many women in her situation she saw him as a lifebelt miraculously thrown her way. Aware that Charlie was desperate for me to be impressed, I went along with the charade.

Charlie frequently raised Anna's hand to his lips and kissed it. "All I don't sleep, boss," he said. "But love is a debt you got to pay, right? So I fix everything." He drained his wine glass. "Am I getting processed, boss?"

"I think so, just a bit."

"You can't have no idea what's going through my head. I have a big favour to ask, boss." He stood up. "I hope I put it to you right, because I got to do this. Although I've fixed it, I need two."

"Two what?"

"Witnesses. Right now I only got one, Anna's friend." From habit, he drew himself up to attention. "The favour is, boss, I need you to make it legit."

"Sit down, Charlie. Sit down and let's talk this through." I felt uneasy discussing the situation in front of Anna, whether she understood or not. "We've already been over the pros and cons and I've told you what I think. I accept you feel this way about Anna, and having met her, I agree she's a very nice girl. But taking it further until you're free isn't a good idea. It'll lead to nothing but trouble for you both." I shot a look at Anna and smiled at her.

"Boss, sir, with respect always, it's a matter of honour. I've given my word." He reached for Anna's hand again. "I have made the marriage proposal."

"I appreciate that, I appreciate you're acting with the best intentions, but sometimes best intentions aren't enough, even in matters of the heart . . . especially in matters of the heart . because sometimes we let our hearts rule our heads and we need to stop and think very carefully." I realised I had begun to sound like a bank manager discussing a dubious request for an overdraft. " You know it would be wrong of me to pretend I think this is a good move . . . " Seeing the look of hopelessness in both their faces, I faltered. "You say you've 'fixed everything', what exactly does that mean?"

"The time, the place, boss, for tomorrow."

"Tomorrow?"

"Yes, boss." His eyes pleaded.

Anna had the expression of somebody who had just been told of a death in the family and I could imagine that her future would be if Charlie's scheme fell apart. Life for the stateless was a living nightmare: without papers they didn't exist.

They both stared at me with the hurt eyes of dogs waiting to see if they would be put down, and I didn't have the heart to fight any longer.

36

"Okay," I said, "let's have another drink, you crazy characters. I don't know why I'm saying this, but I'll go along, I'll do it."

For a moment I thought CharlIe might throw his arms around me, but discipline kicked in and he hugged Anna instead. For the rest of the evening I tried to enter into the spirit of the thing and share their happiness, but it required an effort. I could see nothing but disaster ahead. The only way I reconciled myself to their madness was that, as far as I knew, nothing in King's Regulations forbade witnessing a marriage, albeit a bigamous one.

SIX

Hargreaves rang while I was having breakfast the next morning and said: "Has the news reached you yet?"

"What news?"

"About Hirst?"

"No."

"He's out of the reckoning."

"In what way?"

"Dead."

"Dead?"

"Found in his staff car with his brains splattered on the windscreen."

"Jesus!" I exclaimed. "Where?"

"Not far from you, on the road To Klagenfurt."

"Jesus!" I repeated.

"My bet is he pulled the trigger himself, but they're already covering their tracks. Word is the story we have to stick to is that he was ambushed and killed by a band of last-ditch SS."

"He was in deep shit, you know."

"I didn't, but I guessed as much. We figured your trip here wasn't a courtesy call. You didn't let on, but what was he facing, a wrist-slap or the chop?"

"The chop. But I thought he'd find a way of beating the rap."

"Well, I guess you could say he did in a way. But, watch this space. You wait, they'll bury him with full military honours. Tragic murder of decorated hero."

"You think?"

"I bloody know. Look, before you disappear let's all have a farewell dinner and you can tell us the full story."

My appetite gone, I pushed the rest of my breakfast to one side. Irrationally, I felt I was responsible for Hirst's end. 'We have to take matters into our own hands.' he had said as we parted company. Had he, by then, decided what to do?

I telephoned Wadham. "CSM Seaton, sir. I've just learned the tragic news about Brigadier Hirst and wanted to offer my sympathy and give any help I can.'

"I think we can get along without your help, Sergeant Major," he said tersely.

"Have you established what happened, sir?"

He hesitated before answering. "From what we've been able to piece together it would appear that he was struck down by enemy elements still at large. I have already mounted a full scale search and destroy operation."

"I hope you succeed, sir."

"I have no doubt we will."

"A great loss, sir."

"Yes. Do you have anything else you wish to discuss with me? I'm a busy man."

"No, sir."

"Good." The line went dead.

Hargreaves was right. The Establishment moved quickly to protect their own. Doubtless Wadham would stage manage the rest of the charade, arrange for the corpse to be flown home, a flag draped on the coffin for the full ceremonial funeral, ensure that any remaining evidence was destroyed, and eventually be rewarded with his own red tabs in return for keeping his mouth shut. Death was preferable to disgrace in the book they all read from.

It was only then that I remembered what I had to do that morning. I found the nervous bridegroom, and told him the news without elaboration, sticking to the official line.

Charlie took it philosophically, his mind on more pressing matters. "Poor fucker," he said. "That's bad news on my wedding day."

"You haven't had second thoughts then?"

"No, boss. Like I said, love is a debt you've got to honour." I wasn't sure what debt Charlie had to repay. He was prepared to risk his and Anna's future for a love that hadn't existed a week ago.

"How do I look, boss?" he asked me.

He was wearing his best battledress, his hair was slicked down and he had half a dozen shaving cuts dotted around his chin, each one stuck with a piece of toilet paper.

"Apart from the sabre wounds, you look fine."

"I want to be smooth for my wedding night."

"You're smooth all right, CharlIe." I said.

"Hey, boss, you think we could have a drink before we set off?"

"Meaning you want one? Okay, but just a small one."

"And, boss, one last favour. Teach me the German words I got to say. Anna went through them last night, but I forgot already."

Over the drink, I told him," You know what you're going to be after this, don't you? By the end of today you're going to be a Maltese citizen holding a fake British passport bigamously married under Austrian law to a stateless girl. That's some big shit list."

"Boss, how I look at it, if you're going to take a risk, take a big one." He produced a crumpled piece of paper from his breast pocket. "This is the stuff I have to say."

I did my best to teach him his responses which he repeated after me in halting German. There was no point any longer in persuading him against it; like Hirst he was determined to put a gun to his head and pull the trigger. He had an *amour fou* as the French put it.

There were only four people at the ceremony: the bride

and groom, me and the second witness – a drab, starved little woman, presumably recruited by Anna, who left the moment the proceedings were concluded. The knot was tied in a bare, first floor room in the Town Hall, conducted by the Burgermeister, Herr Kruger, who scowled at Charlie throughout. It was hardly a joyous occasion, more like applying for a driving licence. A section of ceiling plaster fell down just as Charlie and Anna were pronounced man and wife, which was as close as it got to a white wedding. We two witnesses signed the certificates and Register, then Kruger rubber-stamped everything, the only part of the proceedings he appeared to enjoy. Charlie slipped my fellow witness some money and she disappeared.

Back at the Gasthof, I treated the happy couple to what passed for a wedding breakfast. Throughout the meal Charlie repeatedly kissed his bride, leaving specks of blood on her face from his shaving cuts. "How could I be this lucky?" he said. "What did I do to deserve this angel?" He kept the marriage certificate beside his plate and from time to time studied it as though he couldn't quite believe it existed. As they nuzzled each, I began to feel like an intruder and excused myself. "May you both be very happy," I said.

"Boss," Charlie said, "I never forget what you do for me. I saw that he had tears in his eyes. "You always have a best friend in me and when I have my restaurant in London, every day you eat for free."

"You'd soon go broke. Have a great day, but don't forget we have to leave first thing in the morning."

It was only when I had left them that I realised he had never mentioned how Anna was going to live with him in Hamburg, or indeed how she was going to get to Hamburg. She couldn't travel back with us in an Army Jeep.

Next morning a tearful Anna saw us off and it wasn't until we had been on the road half an hour that I broached the question.

41

"I left money for her keep and the train ticket," Charlie said. "When I've found a place for her she'll join me. I've got contacts."

"Then what? What's the long term plan?"

He stared ahead, gripping the steering wheel. "That's going to take a bit of working out, boss. But I got it going round in my head. I ain't worried long term. Where there's a will there's a way, ain't that the British saying?"

But some of the old ebullience had gone out of his voice.

SEVEN

It was grim to be back in my cheerless Hamburg bedroom and having to resume the daily round of interrogations after those few days in the Gasthof. The onus of having to make spot decisions about the probability of innocence, the possibility of guilt, was never easy. If they were to be believed, few of those who came before me ever admitted to having supported Hitler: in their reckoning, the dead Fuehrer was a regretted genetic aberration thrown up by mistake. As the first chill winds of the Cold War started to blow across the political landscape, many denied they had ever wished to fight the British. Historically, they insisted, we are blood brothers who have always been allies. ('We were side by side at Waterloo, don't forget.' 'Your Royal family is German.' 'The real enemy is Bolshevism.')

Listening to the same pleadings day after day wore me down and what truly pissed me off was that we were under unwritten orders to operate double standards. On the one hand we were supposed to be ruthless in rooting out Nazis guilty of crimes against humanity, yet allowed to turn a blind eye if we thought any of them had the necessary qualifications to help get our part of Germany back on its feet. It was an open secret that the Yanks were shipping home the rocket scientists.

Whereas I had power over the lives of others, my own life was in what the airlines call a holding pattern. Many of us had been promised we would soon be demobbed, but somewhere, someone decided our services were too valuable to lose. Before the election we had been told ' Vote Labour and you'll go to the head of the queue' – a con which drove Grable into paroxysms, but which Machell accepted with his usual equanimity. "Rule one," he said. "Never believe anything that isn't written down in triplicate and signed by your mother. Have it framed and nail it above your bed." Unlike the rest of us he was quite content to be left in harness. "You lot may be anxious to see the back of me, but personally I'm quite happy to keep my head below the parapet until somebody wakes up to the fact that I am long overdue for putting out to pasture. What have I got to go back to? Just the prospect of joining a tribe of fellow geriatrics in some seaside guest house and boring them rigid with reminiscences of the glory days of the Raj."

Allied to his cheerful cynicism, I envied him having a past. My own as the only son of aged parents reared on a small Lincolnshire farm was hardly the stuff of legend. Schooling had ended for me at age sixteen, for then the war seemed destined to last forever and I could count on being called up in a year's time. Denied the chance to go to university, I was lucky in that Mr.Bennet, the headmaster, was passionate about literature and the English language. An odd character, crippled from a First World War wound so that he walked with a lopsided gait, unmarried, certainty not everybody's cup of tea, his temper was always on a short fuse. To most of my classmates he was an ogre, but curiously he was always prepared to take pains over me. I don't think I was particularly bright, maybe a little brighter than the rest, but, presumably, Bennet must have detected some potential because he gave me special tuition in French and German, a grounding later honed by Machell. He also allowed me the run of his eclectic library, which was manna in my eyes, my home being devoid of books. He lifted me out of the set school curriculum, and guided me towards authors such as Aldous Huxley, Aldington and D.H.Lawrence, instilling in me a reverence for the written word. I went to war with his well-thumbed copy of *Death of a Hero* in my knapsack. "Don't ever be fooled by what authority wants you to believe in," he told me, curiously anticipating Machell's advice. "Put not your faith in politicians, question everything, never become the passive cannon fodder they want you to be." I suppose the fact that he gave me special attention would be immediately suspect nowadays – currently you can't approach a lost child in a supermarket without being taken for a paedophile.

On the long haul from the Normandy beaches I could endure most privations providing I had a book to read; occasionally I was lucky enough to come across an odd volume in the debris of a bombed-out house, but it wasn't until the unit had a base in Hamburg that I had the opportunity to seek out the few bookshops that remained in business.

Chance so often changes the compass bearings of our lives, pointing us in directions we would otherwise never have taken. Who knows what led me one afternoon to the shabby exterior of a small backstreet shop where I spied an English copy of *The Scarlet Letter* which had somehow, escaped the Nazi burnings? There was another customer in the dim interior when I went in to enquire the price and was quoted the equivalent of one-pound sterling. "I'll take it," I said. While my purchase was being retrieved from the window, the other customer, a middle-aged man of unprepossessing appearance, addressed me deferentially in English: "You have made a good purchase, sir. I myself was tempted, but alas the price was beyond my means."

My trained, suspicious mind noted his ingratiating smile and command of English, and I took him to be another black market operator, albeit more cultivated than average, since most did not frequent antiquarian bookshops. I waited for the inevitable – 'Do you by any chance have cigarettes for sale?' – but he surprised me by saying: " Allow me to introduce myself. Professor Grundwall."

I shook his proffered hand. "A professor of literature?"

"A lover of literature, a professor of philosophy," he answered.

"Here in Hamburg?"

"Yes, at the University. The faculty is gradually getting back to normal. Well, as normal as can be expected in the circumstances."

After I had paid for my purchase, he left the shop with me. "It's not usual to find British soldiers in a bookshop," he said.

"We're not all philistines."

"Of course, forgive me, I had not intended to be rude. Just an observation." Now that we were outside in the daylight I saw that his shabby suit seemed a size too large for his frame and his shirt collar was frayed. He seemed anxious to keep me in conversation.

"The novel you have just purchased created a stir, I believe, when it was first published."

"Yes," I said, "I believe it did. The branding of sinners was a shameful stigma." I decided to test him closer to home. "In the same way that forcing Jews to wear the Yellow star was."

He took this. "Indeed. A blot which can never be written out of our history." There was a pause before he asked: "Do you write, by any chance?"

"No. I don't have any talent in that direction. But I love books."

"Well, to make amends for my rudeness just now, perhaps you will allow me to lend you some from my own, modest library? I know what it is to be deprived of reading matter, even though I was fortunate and came through the war with most of my collection more or less intact."

"That's kind of you. I remember seeing newsreel footage of books being burnt."

"Ah, yes, another event we would like to expunge. Destruction of the printed word is always one of the first acts of a dictatorship."

"Were you still teaching at the university throughout the war?"

"No. I had to serve in the forces like everybody else. Not as a fighting soldier I'm happy to say. I was in communications, monitoring foreign broadcasts like your BBC."

"That must have given you different slant on the news compared to that put out by Goebbels. "

"Totally different, but too dangerous to share with my fellow citizens."

"Well, it was a pleasure to meet you," I said.

"The pleasure is mine. Again, should you ever wish to look at my library, allow me to give you my address." He wrote it down on a scrap of paper and handed it to me. "Like most people, my family has to share a house now, but you'd be very welcome."

Because of pressure of work, the address lay forgotten in my pocket for a couple of weeks, then, finding myself at a loose end one day, I had Charlie find the location on the map and drive me there. The exterior of the house was smoke blackened still and stood isolated, with gutted shells on either side. The front door swung open on damaged hinges and the first thing that struck me as I stepped over the threshold was the scent of charred wood as though the very walls had been impregnated. There was also the smell, too, of boiled cabbage, taking me back to childhood visits to an elderly aunt.

The Grundwall's only had the use of three rooms on the first floor. The door was opened by a small bird-like woman, dressed in old clothes that hung loose on her sparse frame.

"Frau Grundwall?" I asked.

Confronted by an unexpected caller in uniform, her expression was immediately fearful.

"Ja, mein Herr."

"Is Professor Grundwall at home?"

"Ja, mein Herr."

Behind her Grundwall came into view and peered at me, his expression likewise wary until he recognised me. "It's all right, Gerta, the officer is somebody I met. Please, sir, do come in. I'm sorry, but I don't know your name or rank."

"My rank doesn't matter. My name's Alex."

I stepped straight into the dimly lit main room, which was crammed with ill-assorted furniture as though, in their reduced circumstances, they had retained the sentimental rather than the functional. Three odd chairs were grouped around a central table covered with a moquette cloth and strewn with papers.

"I'm glad I found you in," I said. "I just called on the off chance."

"Then we are both lucky," he replied. "This is the day in the week when I stay at home and mark test papers. Please, take a seat. May we offer you some refreshment? Gerta, can you?" He started to gather up the papers.

"Don't go to any trouble," I said.

"It is our pleasure."

His wife returned with an opened bottle of hock and a plate of plain cake slices. She served the wine in two odd glasses and then sat quietly in a corner of the room. The wine had little taste.

"There is my library, such as it is," Grundwall said, indicating a small, glass-fronted bookcase which also housed a few china ornaments. It could scarcely be termed a library, since there were fewer than fifty volumes in shabby bindings, of which only a score were in English. Grundwall took out a selection of these and laid them on the table for my inspection.

"As a teacher I was permitted to retain those not deemed subversive. At one time I had the complete works of

Shakespeare, but was forced to sell most of them."

Before starting to examine the books I took out a packet of cigarettes and offered one to him. He extracted it with care, and then turned it over and over between his fingers, studying it as he would some rare clinical specimen.

"Please do not be offended if I don't smoke it now, but save it for later."

"Don't save it. You're welcome to the whole packet."

He acquiesced and let me light it for him, inhaling deeply with an expression of bliss. We sat and talked about authors we both admired, though some names he mentioned were unknown to me.

"There are likewise many blanks in my own knowledge," he confessed. "We lived in a vacuum for a decade. You have no idea what it was like to be cut off from the world of culture. We had our own culture, of course, the one designed by Speer. A Utopia built on sand."

I discovered that poets were his great love, especially Rilke and Heine, and he waxed lyrical about "your all-but-forgotten Edward Young whom Johnson described as a genius. Does anybody read him now?"

"I can't say. Certainly I haven't."

"Then, bitte, borrow my copy because he won't disappoint you. And if I may presume further, please have this too." He handed me a slim volume. The title on the spine was *Wanderschaft* but gave no clue as to the author. It wasn't until I opened it and turned to the title page that I saw it bore his name.

"Privately printed for friends," he said. "You will find it is the ramblings of a once romantic young man. My only opus. Wasn't it your great novelist, Forster, who said, 'write one book and rest on your oars forever? I took his advice."

"I hadn't heard that before, although he didn't take his own advice, did he? Are you sure you can spare this?"

"Oh, yes. I still have a few more copies."

Sitting there I felt relaxed and happy. Not since the days when old Bennet had taken me under his wing, had I spent an afternoon talking of things other than Army matters. A few days later I paid a second visit and this time went armed with a small collection of luxuries – a tin of corned beef, a packet of coffee, a tablet of soap, a bar of chocolate, some razor blades, and two ragged Penguin paperbacks I was finished with. Grundwall and his wife spread the gifts out on the table and regarded them with reverence.

"The razor blades are especially welcome," Grundwall said. "The one I have been using is a year old, carefully sharpened every day on a piece of leather. This and the soap will make my mornings a joy."

Frau Grundwall immediately wanted to brew the coffee. "Please," I said," save it for yourselves," but she insisted. As she busied herself I complimented her husband on his poems. "I've read them twice, they're so fresh and lyrical."

"Perhaps that's because when I wrote them, I was fresh and lyrical. Alas, no longer."

"Nonsense, you still are, Karl," his wife called from the small kitchen.

"Perhaps to you, my dear," he replied.

It was at this moment a young girl entered the apartment. "This is our only daughter, Lisa," Grundwall said. "Lisa, please meet our new British friend, Alex."

Like her mother Lisa wore nondescript clothes that made her look older than her years for I guessed she was on the brink of leaving adolescence. She looked at me with bright, questioning eyes, surprised, I thought, to be confronted by a strange visitor. I had to make a conscious effort not to gape, for her delicate beauty had taken me unawares. There was a raw pallor to her cheeks, a familiar sign of under-nourishment at that time, only her full mouth, although devoid of lipstick, had colour. When we had greeted each other, her eyes flicked past me to the gifts on the table.

"Chocolate," she said. "Is it real Mutti?"

"Oh, yes, my dear, it's real."

"Have some, " I said. "It's there to be eaten."

"Can I?" she appealed to her parent.

"Of course, of course," her father said.

Lisa handled the bar of chocolate as though it might suddenly slip through her fingers and vanish. Carefully removing the wrapper she broke off a single portion, looking at it closely before putting it in her mouth and savouring the moment. "Oh, it's just wonderful."

"Eat it all, "I said. "I can always bring you some more." I offered my cigarettes. "Bitte, I don't smoke," she said.

"You speak such good English. Are you a student at your father's university?"

"She is an actress," Grundwall answered.

"Really? Are you acting anywhere at the moment?"

"Now we are still rehearing."

"What play is it?"

"Not a play, an operetta. *The White Horse Inn*. We open in about ten days in the Stadt Opera House."

"I'll make sure I'm there on the first night," I said, perhaps a shade too quickly for I caught the look that passed between her parents. Did they think I was just another soldier on the make for their precious daughter? My gifts suddenly took on the appearance of bribes.

Grundwall said: "*The White Horse Inn* was always a favourite of mine. I took my dear wife to see it before the war." He hummed a few bars of one of the numbers. "That song in particular has special memories for us, doesn't it Gerta?"

His wife smiled. "Yes, but don't try and sing it now," she said. "We want to enjoy the coffee."

Grundwall shrugged. "Lisa, you sing it."

"No, please, don't embarrass me, Vater."

"Then, despite advance criticism, I shall." He sang one

stanza in a croaky voice before admitting defeat. "Well, something like that." The bit stanza he had sung translated as: "It would be wonderful indeed if you loved me as I love you."

"I don't sing that during the show," Lisa told me. "I only have a small role, not one of the leads." She seemed embarrassed at her father launching into song.

The pungent smell of coffee filled the room and sent them all into a sort of trance. "What a day this is," Grundwall said. "A cigarette, coffee, and of course the books you lent me. I have to pinch myself to believe I'm not dreaming." He cradled his cup in both hands and bent his head down, inhaling the aroma.

"The books are yours to keep," I said, " I've finished with them."

"Aren't we lucky, Mutti," Lisa said.

"We are, we are. Such kindness."

Given the paucity of my gifts their pleasure and gratitude seemed out of all proportion. It suddenly struck me that, for the first time since I had entered Germany, I was enjoying an ordinary conversation with an erstwhile enemy family. More importantly I felt myself instantly experiencing Charlie's *amour fou*: I could not see anybody but Lisa in the room.

"The fourteenth?" I asked. "I'll make sure I'm not on duty that night, and perhaps, I could take you for a meal after the show? With your parents permission naturally."

Lisa looked to them. "I don't see why not, do you, Gerta?" her father said.

"No, it is a kind invitation," his wife said, but there was a note of doubt in her voice.

"Although an actress, our daughter is not all that worldly," Grundwall added ambiguously.

"You needn't worry, I'll take good care of her," I said.

"We're sure you will."

The formality of their replies betrayed the fact that they

did have fears. I couldn't blame them, why wouldn't they? Soldiers were only out for one thing and my eagerness was too blatant. "Of course, only if Lisa wants to," I said. I smiled at her across the table. "Would you like to?"

Her response hung in the air for a few moments and again she looked to her parents. "Yes," she said. "Yes, I would."

"Wonderful." That agreed I was anxious not to overstay my welcome. I made my excuses shortly afterwards and left, praying nobody would have a change of heart.

EIGHT

In my euphoria about seeing Lisa again I kept thinking back to the moment when Charlie had revealed his feelings about Anna to me. I wanted to share my own emotions with somebody who would understand and not rib me, and Charlie, I felt, would be in my camp.

Detailed to escort a high-ranking SS prisoner to the dustbin in Celle, I requested Charlie as my driver, but when I went to the garage to pick up my vehicle I found he hadn't reported in for duty.

"Haven't seen him, CSM," the duty Corporal told me.

"See if he's still in the sack and, if he is, give him a bollocking and get him here double quick."

"No sign, sir," the Corporal said when he came back. "His bed hasn't been slept in. Think he's gone AWOL?"

"The stupid sod's going to be on a fizzer." I took another driver in his place, but when I returned later in the day, Charlie was still missing and there was a message for me to contact The Military Police. I discovered that he had been picked up the night before in the off-limits, red light district and held on several charges, the most serious being in possession of forged papers. I obtained permission to visit him in the cells.

Crestfallen, he greeted me with, "Boss, I let you down real bad."

"Never mind that, why on ever did you take such a chance?"

"No choice, boss."

"What d'you mean, no choice? You didn't need to go whoring."

"No whoring, boss. I had to see Anna."

"Anna? What's she got to do with it?"

"It's where she is, boss."

"In the red light district?"

"Yes, boss."

"You mean in a brothel?"

"Yes, boss, but she's not on the game, don't think that. Not my Anna. I thought it was the safest place, until I make other arrangements. I've visited her there before, just got unlucky this time. When she made her way to Hamburg I bribed one of the pimps to find her a safe room. Mine bloody godfathers, I always do right by him, paid him regular. What will happen to me boss?" he continued without drawing breath, the words tumbling out of him, all his old cockiness gone.

"Well, if it had just been a brothel visit and left to Colonel Machell to deal with, you'd have got off with a few days jankers and loss of pay, but this is dead serious, It's now the Provost Marshal's hands. You're in a fucking mess, Charlie, and I wouldn't like to predict the outcome. Why on earth did you have those fake papers on you?"

"Nowhere else safe to hide them," he said lamely.

"Do they know about Anna?"

"No way am I telling them about her. No way."

"You never listened to me, did you, Charlie? I warned you way back in Austria."

"I love her," he said simply. "She's my wife."

"Well, let's not open that can of peas. I'll do my best to help, but don't expect any miracles."

When his case came up I attended as a character witness and pleaded for his previous good record to be taken into account, citing his bravery during the Italian campaign, but the court was not persuaded to leniency. Possession of forged papers could not be ignored, especially when the accused was serving with Intelligence and therefore could come in contact with undesirables anxious to acquire counterfeit identities. Even though the marriage certificate had been found amongst his forged papers Charlie refused to betray Anna's whereabouts. He was sentenced to eighteen months in the glasshouse to be served in England, at the end of which he would be given a dishonourable discharge and deported back to Malta.

I managed to see him one last time before he was shipped across the Channel and he gave me the address where Anna was being hidden, together with a letter for her. The only way in which I could get this to her was by bribing one of our waiters to deliver it. I included some money with a note of my own breaking the news of Charlie's fate. They had become just two more pieces of human flotsam and the irony for Charlie's fate was that his cherished dream of getting to England had finally been realised.

On my next free day I paid another visit to Lisa's home, taking some more chocolates and soap, hoping that she would be there, but she was rehearsing and I found her father alone, his wife having gone out to queue for bread. "I'm sorry to disturb you like this," I said.

"No, please, I welcome the chance to stop work."

I offered him a cigarette and studied his narrow, bespectacled face as he allowed me to light it for him. One broken arm of his spectacles was held in place with an elastic band and there were flakes of dandruff on the shoulders of his shabby jacket. It was difficult for me to comprehend what life must been like during the Nazi years for a man of his obvious intelligence and intellect. The months I had spent interrogating had gone a long way to convince me that there was little honesty in post-war Germany. The majority of Germans were in denial. Yet here I was sitting down in the company of a man who seemed different from anybody I had previously come in contact with. There was a certain dignity about him.

"How are Lisa's rehearsals going?" I asked as he put his papers to one side.

"Well, I believe. The theatrical world is entirely foreign to me. But then it's true to say I find a much that is foreign these days. It must be odd for you, a long way from home, thrown into this chaos."

"Yes, it is, less so now that I've met you and your family. Your daughter is very beautiful."

"Thank you. I'm glad you think so. I think so, too." I saw that he was disconcerted by the remark. "Shall we have a cup of coffee? We have been rationing it, but there is still enough of our kind gift left."

"I must bring you some more."

"We would never want to abuse your friendship."

While he busied himself boiling the water he said: "Gerta and I were saying we're so relieved to be in the British zone. We expected draconian retribution, but we are being treated fairly. There are hardships, of course, and shortages of food, but that is to be expected. At least we did not exchange one police state for another." He brewed the coffee and poured two small cups.

"Are we what you expected? I am aware from your shoulder flashes that you are in a branch of intelligence, so you must have been brought into contact with members of the SS."

"Yes," I said.

"It was a terrible organisation. Not only for the enemy, but for us, too. Setting neighbour against neighbour, turning us into a nation of informers. Nobody was safe."

"So I gather. I guess the habit dies hard because informing still continues."

"How low we have descended." He was silent for a few

moments. "Can I ask you something, something that is seldom out of my thoughts?" He had lowered his voice though for he had been schooled to caution in the years when a loose word had meant denunciation.

"Please."

"I have to know the true facts about Belsen and such places."

"Belsen?"

"Please, say if you would prefer not to talk about such matters, but I have a great need to hear the truth from somebody like yourself. The photographs we were shown, were they authentic?"

"Oh, yes," I said. "Were you told otherwise?"

"There were some who chose to believe they were fakes, products of Jewish propaganda."

"They were wrong. There was no way you could fake horror on that scale."

"You saw for yourself, did you?"

"Yes. I was with the British contingent that liberated Belsen. We found thousands of unburied dead, hundreds of others dying of starvation in filthy huts. Typhus was rife, dysentery, spotted fever everywhere. Even after liberation the deaths continued, three hundred or more a day. We added to the death toll through kindness and ignorance."

"How was that?" He leant forward, listening intently.

"Being misguided good Samaritans, giving them our own rations, but they couldn't handle proper food. The medical teams arrived and stopped us, but by then it were too late, we had done the damage. A tragedy of good intentions."

As I described the remembered scene to him, one skeletal face out of so many hung before me, like Banquo's ghost.

Grundwall was silent for a while, then asked: "How could it be that we allowed such hideous places to come into being?"

"Did you never suspect they existed?"

"I would be lying if I denied I knew nothing of the policies being pursued. How could we not know? From the moment the Nazis took power the dream of Aryan purity became central to their ideal of a master race, all set down in Hitler's wretched, ill-written book we were required to read. His bible of hatred was mostly directed against those he held responsible for our defeat in the First World War, the Jews and Bolsheviks. Later, the net was extended to include the mentally ill, the sub-normal, homosexuals, cripples, anybody in fact deemed imperfect. By then nobody except the totally blind could have been unaware. It was happening all around us: Jewish shops smashed, Jewish books burned, synagogues destroyed, individual Jews humiliated, made to perform the most degrading tasks in public."

"Did you have Jewish colleagues in the university faculty?"

"Yes, several. One by one they disappeared. The story we were given, the story others and I allowed ourselves to believe, was they were leaving the homeland voluntarily to seek a new life abroad. I am ashamed now, ashamed of my passive acceptance, of permitting myself to swallow the official lies. I could not allow myself to accept that our government was carrying out a policy of sustained mass murder, that my country, the country that gave the world Goethe, Beethoven, Thomas Mann, could be capable of exterminating a whole race. It was.... It is, beyond comprehension.... And yet... and yet..." he trailed off.

"And now? Can you accept the world's verdict?"

"I must, and I will never forgive myself for my silence, my cowardice." He struck his head wIth a bony, white hand. "I should not say this of the land of my fathers, but it will take a hundred years to atone, and even then we should not be forgiven." He removed his ancient, spectacles and wiped his eyes.

His remorse seemed genuine and I wanted to believe him

– the admission of a man of conscience finally prepared to accept the unacceptable.

"Did you ever discuss these things with your wife and Lisa?"

"Gerta, yes, but not Lisa. I protected her, and in any case she was not living with us for most of the war. We sent her away to be safe from the bombing."

"But, presumably, she had to join the Bund Deutcher Madel? Weren't girls as young as ten compelled to belong?"

He thumped the table with his fist. "Ah! the Hitler Youth movement, another madness. Children sent to die in the streets when the war was already lost."

From long habit I slipped into interrogation mode. "And young girls like Lisa were required to read Der Sturmer, weren't they?"

"It was compulsory reading. Can you imagine the mentality of those responsible for poisoning the minds of mere children with such filth?" he said vehemently. "You can't.

I was still thinking of this extraordinary conversation when I went to the opening night of *The White Horse Inn*. and it was only the excitement of the curtain going up that drove it from my mind. Apart from one occasion when I had been treated to an amateur production of *The Pirates of Penzance* I had never before enjoyed a full-blown stage musical. Taking my seat in those front stalls reserved for Allied personnel, I felt how racy it was to actually know one of the actresses in the cast. As she had told me, Lisa only had a minor role and it took me a while to pick her out in the ensemble. Her heavy theatrical make-up masked her usual pallor, but she moved and danced with grace and I never took my eyes off her whenever she was on stage. The spectacle of a lyrical, peasant community singing the romantic tunes utterly seduced me and by the final curtain I was in love not only with Lisa but the whole world and joined in the standing ovation.

I waited outside the stage door for her. It was some twenty minutes before she came out, denuded now of greasepaint, the stage illusion gone, transformed back into the absurdly young girl I had first met and fallen for.

"You were so good," I said, "and you looked so pretty."

"A lot of things went wrong tonight."

"Really? Well, I didn't notice, because I only had eyes for you. I shall come again, probably more than once, every night if I could." I took her arm: so thin, so weightless. "Let's go and have that meal I promised."

The Nuffield Club was crowded as usual, the dance floor packed with Service personnel; the noisy throng of bodies made Lisa draw back on the threshold.

"I am allowed?" she asked.

"Of course."

I threaded our way through the crush and secured an empty table. "Now, what would you like to eat?"

"There is a choice?"

"Oh, sure."

"You choose for me, "she said. "I'm sure it's all wonderful."

"Would you like wine or beer with your food?"

"I don't drink," she said.

"How about a Coca Cola then?"

"Yes, I've heard it's nice."

I went to the service counter, light-headed and happier than I had been for months and ordered two mixed grills, not exactly gourmet fare on a first date, but I hoped eggs, sausage, chips and a rasher of bacon would prove a feast in her eyes. Taking the plates back to our table I found her being chatted up by a suave RAF type.

"This lady's with me," I said.

"Just testing, Sergeant Major." He gave a conspiratorial leer. "Get in, it's your birthday."

"Why did he say that?" Lisa queried. "Is it your birthday?"

"No, just a silly expression." I put her plate down in front of her. "I hope I've chosen something you'll like. Tell me if you don't and I'll change it."

"It looks wonderful."

"Well, here's to your performance." I clinked my beer glass against Cola. She took a tentative sip. "Okay?"

"Yes, thank you. I like sweet things. You're spoiling me."

"That's the idea."

It was touching to watch her savouring each mouthful of our taken-for-granted canteen food as though it was something extra special which would never again be put in front of her. I suppose it was special to her, just as being with her was special to me. Everything about her was delicate and vulnerable and I was filled with a desire to protect her. My emotions and anxiousness made me tongue-tied; I couldn't find the right words to express what I wanted to say. I didn't want to scare her by revealing too much, too soon, for on that first occasion I had no idea what she felt about me; perhaps she had only accepted my invitation out of deference to her parents wishes and there would be no future between us other than a casual, one-sided friendship. I had little or no experience of love other than the fumbled encounters of my pre-army adolescence, what I felt now was new and life enhancing. Every instinct willed me to reveal myself, but I held back, frightened of making the wrong move. Instead I made small talk. "Did you always want to be an actress?"

She shook her head. "Not really, there weren't any opportunities before."

"But now you enjoy it? You seemed to me to be a so at home up there on the stage. I'm sure they'll give you a bigger role next time. Are you in the next play they're doing?

"It hasn't been decided yet. I'm lucky to be in work."

"Do they pay well?"

"Not much, but everything helps, and we get a few luxuries."

"Such as?"

"A bar of soap every month, and the dressing rooms are heated."

"Do you think it's funny, sitting here with me?"

"Funny?"

"Well, not funny, but I wondered if you ever thought you'd be taken out to dinner by a British soldier. Did you?"

"No."

"Do any of the other girls in the cast get taken out?"

"Some of them," she said.

"And what do they think?"

"I don't know. Most of them are older than me."

"They probably resent us, I expect. It can't be easy to have your country occupied. Am we different from what you expected?" My probing seemed to embarrass her and I felt annoyed for embarking on this line of questioning, but I couldn't stop myself.

"I don't know what I expected," she said. "My parents think you are very kind. My father says he was so fortunate to meet you the way he did. He respects you."

"But what do you think?"

"I think you're very kind, too."

"Meeting your father was my lucky day, because I would never have met you otherwise. That was my real luck." I could not hold back any longer. "What would you think," I said slowly, "if I told you I've fallen in love with you?"

She looked down at her empty plate and put her knife and fork neatly together, but said nothing. "Do I have any hope that you could feel the same about me?" I waited.

"I like you very much," she said finally, but still didn't look at me.

"I'll settle for 'like' now," I said, "if it could ever become something more. Is there any chance of that? Give me some hope."

The noise of the band drowned out her reply.

"I didn't hear you."

"I said yes," she said, scarcely audible.

I reached across the table and took her hand. "That's all I wanted to hear. Now let's dance, but don't expect me to be Fred Astaire." She looked blank. "Have you ever seen him on films?"

" No, we only saw a few German films."

"Well, he's the greatest. Next time one of his films comes to our cinema, I'll take you." I led her onto the floor. The band was playing *Moonlight Serenade*. There was little room to move, and having her in my arms at last was like holding somebody weightless. The same RAF types passed us clinging to a pert little blond and gave me the thumbs up. Behind Lisa's back I responded in kind. We stayed on the floor for two more numbers. "I'd forgotten what it was like to be happy," Lisa said.

I kissed her ear. "You're always going to be happy from now on, I'll see to that. And now I'm going to take you home in case your parents get worried. I want them to trust me with you."

I had arranged for one of our drivers to have a car outside. We said little to each other on the journey as though neither of us wanted to break the spell, but when we parted she said: "When will I see you again?"

"I'm off duty on Sunday. Are you free on Sunday or are you rehearsing?"

"No."

"Then Sunday it is." I kissed her lightly.

"Thank you for giving me such a best time," she said. "You made me feel alive again."

And so it was that we began.

NINE

Now I no longer fretted about an early demob, happy to stay on in Germany for as long as the Army decreed. I saw Lisa whenever my work and her commitments at the theatre allowed and rather shamefully ingratiated myself with her parents, taking them regular gifts of food and cigarettes. With winter finally retreating and the longer hours of daylight there was a more hopeful atmosphere in the city. The *Trummerfrau*, or 'rubble women' worked to clear the remaining bombsites, spurred by an imaginative scheme devised by the British Town Major: for every half a dozen clean bricks the women brought in they were entitled to a bowl of soup; they and their families could return with more bricks as many times as they liked. By this method the worst of the streets became passable again and the number of night murders went down.

Lisa and I sometimes picnicked on the banks of the Alster in the Spring sunlight. An American friend took me to one of their PX stores and I bought Lisa her first bottle of French perfume and two pairs of nylon stockings – at that time the equivalent of gold dust. Because I saw to it that she ate regularly and well she gradually put on weight, colour returned to her cheeks and her slack breasts began to fill out. I was due for a furlough and instead of going home decided I would spend it with her. For my plan to succeed, my leave had to coincide with a period when she was not appearing in or rehearsing for a new play. I waited until her current play finished its run before I casually mentioned it.

Her face fell. "You mean you're going home to England?"

"I don' t have to, nor do I want to. I thought perhaps we could both have a holiday together in Austria."

"Austria? With me?"

"Yes. Good idea? Would your parents allow it?"

"I don' t know. I can ask them."

I never discovered how she squared it with them, if indeed she ever told them the truth – lies come easily for lovers.

I drove us back to Herr Walbrook's Gasthof at Krumpendorf, back to the same dining room where Charlie had introduced me to his doomed Anna and where, in the hallway, a candle still burned in front of the portrait of the Walbrook's dead son. It was there, in that same bedroom I had previously occupied alone, and where the tiled stove still burned at night, that we slept together for the first time. I've known a few men who boasted that taking a girl's virginity is the supreme male achievement, but now, so many years after when I relive that defining moment as, sleepless, I often do, it isn't a sordid triumph I remember, but a sort of wonder. Even now I can't ever catch the scent of pine without being transported back to that room and that moment.

That first night she asked me: 'will people know I'm different now? Will it show on my face?"

"You goose," I said, "what're you talking about?"

"I was told people always know when you've become a woman."

I pretended to study her closely. 'Yes, there's definitely a change everybody could see."

"What sort of change?"

"It's frightening," I teased. "A transformation. You've become even more beautiful."

"No, seriously."

"I am being serious. How come I was lucky to get you into my bed?"

66

" Our bed," she said. ""Our marriage bed."

The weather stayed fine and often we ate outside on a small terrace and three ponies would wander up through the orchard and stand quietly until we fed them with fallen apples. There was an old dog, blind and mangy, who lay on the stone steps of the terrace and remembered his croaky bark whenever the ponies came near. Some mornings, after making love, we took the path up into the hills, past the roofless church, the garish shrines, and the cider factory stinking of putrid apples. From the summit we could look down on Krumpendorf and try to pick out our room in the Gasthof, but the glare from the lake was too strong, blurring our vision. Descending, we skirted around the ruins of a castle that reminded me of Gibbs toothpaste advertisements, and stumbled across rutted field, the ground was lush and soggy underfoot with decaying pine needles. On our third evening there I persuaded Lisa to take a first taste of the local wine. She sipped it delicately, like a bird at a pool, but wouldn't try a cigarette. She didn't mind me smoking and said the smell reminded her of her father. There were no health warnings on the packets in those days: the only warning I heeded came from my heart, I was so anxious that nothing should harm what we felt for each other.

On our last night there we made love by moonlight, the shutters flung open. Afterwards I asked: "Did you ever think you'd fall in love with a British soldier, the dreaded ravagers of your country?"

"How about you? Did you ever think you'd fall in love with a German machen, the terrible enemy?"

"Maybe."

"Oh, I don't like 'maybe'," she pouted. "It means you must have been looking for somebody else."

"Well, if I was, I never found her."

"But you tried?"

"I admit nothing," I said. "And in any case the past is

unimportant now, nothing is going to come between us ever again. I want to marry you, if you'll have me."

She lifted her head from the pillow and stared at me. "Do you really mean that?"

"Shall I kneel by the side of the bed and make it formal?"

"No, you'd catch cold. Can we? Is it allowed by your Army?"

"It's allowed. What will you parents say when I ask them?"

"They'll be happy."

"You're sure?"

"Oh, yes. Otherwise I wouldn't be here, would I?" she said.

Awake when she slept, her nakedness touching my own, I thought, a new journey without maps begins. Some people have God as a guide. I didn't.

TEN

The moment we returned from Krumpendorf, I was ordered to take part in a new hunt for deserters. The target area was the dock area, a rabbit warren of derelict warehouses where many of those intent on trying to escape out of the country holed up. The task force consisted of a platoon of infantry supplemented by Military Police, with our Field Security as back up should we ferret out any ex-SS or Gestapo still on the run.

The entire area was sealed off just before dawn to achieve maximum surprise and the raid was a limited success, with some fifteen Allied deserters in the bag. We flushed out a solitary Waffen SS veteran who invited his own death by wounding a Military Policeman before being shot dead. We had come to recognise that the love of death was an integral part of the under-pattern of the Nazi character. Apart from this man there was nothing for us to deal with but, as we were leaving, the Provost Marshall handed me a battered leather pouch.

"This might interest your lot," he said. The pouch looked as though an attempt had been made to burn it, but a faded SS insignia was still discernible on the cover. I took it back to the office for closer examination. Inside were some scorched documents, typed on official SS headed notepaper. Grable made out the name Auschwitz-Birkenau on several of them and by piecing together the fragments we reconstructed two or three complete documents. They were dated early 1945, one signed by Himmler to the Commandant of the camp ordered him to eliminate as many of the remaining inmates he could before the Allies arrived. Machell had everything photographed and the originals sent to Group Intelligence to be crosschecked against the master files.

"Extraordinary," he remarked, " the Nazis compulsion to record their crimes. I mean, why write an incriminating order like that? Would you? If you look at the date, it was obvious the war was lost by then, so why not pass the order by phone instead of in writing? No, even at the eleventh hour in the final panic they continued to rubber stamp everything. What a mentality."

"They believed they had a god-given right to eliminate the Jews."

"Except they didn't believe in God," I said.

"Hitler was the Christ who had led them out of the wilderness. Accept that and everything else falls into place," Grable replied. "Who else could have persuaded children to fight Russian tanks with rifles in Berlin?"

This echoed what Grundwall had said to me. I had kept my affair with Lisa to myself, not wanting to invite the usual sexual ribaldry, but made sure we spent every snatched hour together. I had drawn out some back pay and rented a room in a small hotel. Whenever I was off-duty and Lisa was not rehearsing, we went there and made love, the element of furtiveness giving a fillip to the liaisons. Lisa never wanted to leave; I would have to plead, and threaten her. "Darling, we have to go," I'd say. "I'm on duty in an hour's time."

"Tell them you were taken sick."

"You're shameless."

"Yes."

"I'd much rather stay here, too, but I can't. Aren't your parents suspicious when you don't go home in the afternoons?"

"I pretend we have extra rehearsals, " she said, trying to draw me back down on the bed.

"Now, behave. You must get up, please. Lisa, please, be good for once. "

"I will get up, but only if you make love to me again."

"No, get up or I'll tip you onto the floor."

After one such session I returned to the office to find the others studying a new set of photographs sent by our American counterparts for checking against our own records. Although we were long since numbed to the horrors of such material, this latest batch chilled the blood. They depicted the hideous experiments carried out on Jewish children by Dr. Mengele and his team. It was evident that some of the operations had been performed without anaesthetics, for the small victims were strapped down on the operating table, eyes bulging in terror of what lay ahead. Included in the set were shots of body parts preserved in jars – human brains and hearts, even the severed head of a Mongoloid girl.

It was unlike Machell to show any emotion, but that day he could not conceal his anger. "What sort of man can bring himself to torture children? How do you function normally after that? Tell me." We said nothing. "Did he get up every morning, wash, shave, take a crap, and then think it nothing, just normal routine, to go to work on these tiny bodies? It defies belief," he said in a choked voice. " I thought I knew everything about evil but these acts are beyond my imagination."

The print that provoked this outburst showed three men in white coats dissecting a tiny corpse that looked more like a discarded rag doll than anything human.

Grable asked: "Where was this taken?"

Machell turned it over and read out what was written on the reverse: "Three members of the special SS unit known to have carried out experiments on children at Auschwitz-Birkenau under Mengele's supervision. Date of photograph unknown. Figure far left Identified as Karl Off, subsequently

71

committed suicide April 1945, Lunenburg Ref 2786-SS7A. The other two suspects currently unidentified. Further information urgently needed. Ongoing."

"If those other two are still at large, I want them found and I want to be there when they take the drop," Machell said.

I took the print from Grable and stared at it for a long time with a growing sense of foreboding before replacing it. I said nothing to the others but later that night I returned to the office, found the same print and took it to my room. I locked the door, poured myself a stiff whisky and scrutinised the print again, this time using a magnifying glass. Although it was creased the faces three faces were in the clear. From the moment I had first seen it I had prayed that my suspicion would be proved wrong, but it was not to be. I sat staring at it, refilling my whisky glass more than once, but the alcohol did nothing. I sat there, coldly sober, no longer in any doubt: the man in the centre of the group was Lisa's father.

My world, which a few hours before in the rented hotel room had seemed so perfect, now lay in ruins. I cursed myself for my stupidity, the blind, careless naivety that had allowed me to ignore rule one: never accept anything or anybody at face value.

The long months I had spent listening to lies and evasions had taught me that the death camps had been staffed by second-string SS, recruited from every section of German society – bank clerks, lawyers, waiters, nurses, bookkeepers, carpenters, locksmiths, petty customs officials, even restaurant owners – so indoctrinated by the ex-chicken farmer, Himmler, they could convince themselves they were carrying out a divine mission. To that corrupted band could now be added a university professor, the plausible family man and one-time poet.

I lay on the bed, fully clothed, my empty whisky glass dropping unheeded to the floor and behind my closed eyes the first of many nightmares swam in.

ELEVEN

Before going to the Mess for breakfast the next morning, I returned the print. Grable joined me with the greeting: "You look rough, Alex."

"Do I? Slept badly."

"Never have that problem myself. Sleep like a baby the moment my head hits the pillow. You must have a guilty conscience about something."

He babbled on with his usual small talk until I could have hit him. All my own thoughts were centered on what I should do next.

A line had been drawn in the sand between my love for Lisa and my duty. I had to believe that she was innocent, that I had not been taken in by her in the same way that her father had taken me in. Or did she wear a mask like him? I could not keep the discovery to myself, sooner or later I had to share it whatever the consequences.

I left Grable and on an impulse drove to the university campus to verify that aspect of her father's story.

"Oh, yes, sir," the female Registrar confirmed. "Professor Grundwall is an active member of the faculty." A grey-haired woman of indeterminate age, she immediately assumed a servile manner. "He's lecturing at the moment, but I can interrupt him if it's urgent."

"No, that isn't necessary. Can you tell me how long has he been a member of the staff?"

"Let me consult his file to make sure, sir." She went to a steel cabinet and took out a folder. "Here are the details.

Herr Grundwall resumed his duties in March 1945, sir."

"Were you here at that time?"

"Yes, sir. Although the university was closed after the great fire raids, we maintained a skeleton staff, of which I was one. Naturally, during the war the faculty was greatly reduced.

"Does the professor's file detail his war service?"

"Yes, indeed, sir. Like others he was required to play his part. He was in the Wehrmacht holding the rank of Haupsturmfuhrer."

"And where did he serve?"

"I have been given to understand that he was on attachment to the Ministry of Communications. As a translator," she added, suddenly anxious. "There's nothing wrong, is there, sir? He was given clearance by your Tribunal before being allowed to resume his academic duties."

"No, this is just a routine enquiry we carry out. It's just that our own records don't always tally, and we like to be accurate. We've come across an entry from another source that somebody of the same name was a member of the SS."

She was visibly shaken by this. "Oh, no, sir, I'm sure that must be a mistake. Not the Professor."

"Can I take a look at his file, please."

She handed it to me. It stated that Grundwall had appeared before a de-Nazification Tribunal after the unconditional surrender, and had been cleared to return to his peacetime occupation. Details of his war service were as she had stated. It gave his age, marital status and his CV. I noted that in addition to his academic degrees at the start of his career he had been to a medical school and qualified as a doctor in general practice.

"Yes, well it all seems be in order," I said, "If I may borrow this, I'll see to it that our faulty records are corrected.

"Of course, sir."

"I'm sure you agree that for the University's sake, it's

important to ensure everything is accurate."

"Yes, I understand, sir."

"Thank you for your help."

I left the campus knowing that I could not forever delay sharing my belief in Grundwall's guilt, for I was convinced there was a case to answer. The fact that he had been cleared was not a guarantee of innocence. Records could be forged, or lost in the general chaos that followed the end of hostilities. In the immediate aftermath all four victorious powers made their own agendas, imperfect as they proved to be. The whole of Germany had been thrown into the melting pot with two million people on the move. Nobody on our side had worked by the book because there was no book, we wrote it as we went along and hoped for the best. Until some semblance of law and order was patchily established, it was inevitable that many of those we needed to apprehend slipped through the net. Some, like Grundwall, had been clever, skilfully covering their tracks. Had that photograph not survived, the chances were he would have been secure, for the university was an unlikely place in which to look for war criminals.

I had arranged to meet Lisa later that afternoon after she finished rehearsals and although I knew what course I now had to take, I still stayed my hand and collected her at the stage door, determined to quell one last doubt. I loved her and I owed her that.

We walked the short distance to the Salvation Army Canteen and I made an effort to act normally. Lisa immediately spotted something different about me and reached for my hand across the table.

"You look so worried," she said. "Has anything happened?"

"It's been a pig of a day. How's yours been?"

"Oh, so so. I couldn't remember my lines."

"Have you got a lot to learn in this one?"

"Enough. I knew them perfectly last night, but when I got on stage I had a complete blank."

I knew I was acting oddly, but I couldn't stop myself. Looking at her sweet, trusting face I willed myself to believe that she knew nothing of her father's past.

Oblivious of my thoughts, she said: "I've got Friday afternoon off while the new set is put up, so we could go to our room and make love."

"Friday? Let me think. I'll have to check. This is a heavy week for me, we've got to prepare for an inspection."

"Try," she said.

"Of course, darling, of course I'll try and make it. If Friday's not possible, then sometime soon."

"Very soon," she said. "I miss you so much."

"How are things at home?"

"Good. They're so grateful for everything you bring us. My mother has put on weight. The only thing is she says that because you supply my father with cigarettes, he smokes too much."

"There are worse things," I said. "I smoke too much. Does he ever talk about the war, what he did in the war?"

She shook her head. "No, he wants to forget all about it. I'm so happy he didn't have to fight."

"Yes, he told me he had a desk job. Translating our broadcasts, isn't that right? Don't suppose you saw much of him, or your mother."

"Mother visited me in the country when she could, but you had to get special permission to travel."

"And you didn't ever see your father?"

"Not until it was all over and I came home. He had changed so much."

"The war did that to people," I said.

I hadn't the heart to probe her further and did my best to keep up a conversation until we parted, wondering whether, when next we met, her happiness would be shattered, the father she adored proved a monster.

After agonising for a second night, I awoke the next morning knowing I had to act now or never. I went straight to Machell, but before I could put my suspicions to him, he pre-empted me.

"D'you want the good news first, or the bad?" he said cheerfully.

Taken off guard, I said, "Give me the bad."

"Your demob has been delayed again. Don't ask me why, but somebody must think your services are too valuable to lose. The good news, but sad for me, is you're being transferred to MI6."

"What does that mean?"

"It means you're being transferred."

"But beyond that?"

"God knows, dear boy. We are but pawns, to be dismissed or advanced at a whim. However, and I've saved this until last, there's a sweetener – three weeks home leave, a posting to Berlin on your return and an immediate commission. You can put up three pips. Official confirmation will follow you home. Congratulations, Captain Seaton."

"Did you fix that? "

"Good God, no. Beyond my limited influence."

"I can't take it in."

He waved my furlough documents. "Your Blighty boat sails in a four hours, so get your skates on."

"Sir, before you sprang all that on me, I came to discuss something very important." I produced Grundwall's file. "That print of the three men at Auschwitz we examined."

"What about it?"

" I believe I've identified one of them. Is it still with you?"

"Yes," he said. He extracted it from the pile on his desk. I pointed to Grundwall. "That one. I'm pretty sure I interrogated him when we first set up shop here," I lied. "He was cleared at the time and requested permission to resume his pre-war post as a member of the University faculty, which was granted. Before coming to you with my suspicions I felt I ought to check on that. So yesterday I went to the campus to make sure he was still there and examine his file. I gave the Registrar some excuse about a routine administrative query."

"Did you see him?"

"No, I didn't want to risk alerting him. He is on the faculty as a Professor of Philosophy, but as you'll see from his CV he once trained as a doctor, which is material."

"How sure are you that he's one and the same?"

"Enough to think we should take it further. I'd handle it myself, but in view of my imminent departure, can I leave it with you?"

Machell considered for a moment. "Yes, okay, I'll see he's brought in and given another going over, confront him with the photograph and pass all the information to the Jewish War Crimes Commission. They have survivors they can tap for positive identification, make it watertight. "

I returned to my room, packed and hastily penned a note to Lisa telling her why I wouldn't be around for a bit but would write more fully as soon as I got home. After handing in the letter at the Post Room I caught a train to the port. A couple of hours later I was standing on the dock waiting to embark when somebody called my name. I swung around to find Chivers behind me. He now sported a moustache and a swagger stick.

"CSM Seaton," he repeated. "How about that? I never forget a face or a name. You off home for good?"

"No, just a spot of leave. Are you catching this boat too?"

"Lord, no. Too much to do over here. Enormous job, but I think I'm getting on top of it."

His attitude was as insufferable as ever, behaving as

though he was responsible for the whole burden of putting Germany back on its feet single-handed.

"A bit of luck bumping into you like this, because I'm just here on a flying visit. I was hoping to find someone to run an errand for me and you'll do nicely. I've got a letter that urgently needs to get to my London bank and the Army mail is so bloody unreliable." He opened his briefcase and took out an envelope. "This is hot stuff. Between you, me and the gatepost, I was given a nod and a wink the other night dining with some City heavy hitters who were over here sussing out business opportunities. I did them a few favours and quid pro quo, they told me about the killing waiting to be made back home." He looked over his shoulder. "Property."

"Property?"

"Yes. All those empty bombsites sitting there."

Seeing my blank expression, he elaborated. "I'm reliably told they can be had dirt cheap. Vacant land is prime building material, sport. Atlee's proletariat are going to need real houses, lots of houses, not those bloody pre-fabs. The characters I met said they're picking up freeholds all over London for five thousand a go. Copper-bottomed investments. There's nothing like getting in on the ground floor. He who hesitates etcetera." He tapped the envelope. "I want to get my money down double quick, so, if you could post this the moment you land, you'll forever be on my Christmas card list."

I accepted the letter with nil enthusiasm.

"My address is on the back of the envelope. Make a note of it because we must keep in touch. Never know, I might be able to row you in one day. I'd row you in on this, but I was sworn to secrecy. They don't want too many punters getting their noses in the trough. Really good to see you again, sport. Have a good leave."

He turned and walked away, as though, having dealt

wIth the messenger boy, no further dialogue was necessary. I wanted to shout after him, "Say, thank you," but he was already lost in the crowd.

On the sea voyage thoughts of the unfinished business I was leaving behind never left me. I wanted to believe that on my return nothing would have changed, that Lisa and I would be as before, but doubt blurred my vision as I stared towards the approaching English coast. What lay ahead was as impenetrable as a dark forest.

TWELVE

When the boat docked, I telephoned my parents to tell them of my unexpected arrival, and then caught a slow train to Lincolnshire. My father farmed fifty leased acres of fenland near Tattershall. Most of the acreage was given over to potatoes and sugar beet, with some pasture for grazing a few cows to provide milk and butter for the house. The area around had been dotted with operational airfields during the war, our Lancaster's, Wellingtons and Halifax bombers darkening the evening skies like slow-flying geese as they lumbered off for Germany. Although during 1941 their Lufwaffe counterparts flew over the Fens on their way to flatten the Midland cities, apart from the occasional Dornier jettisoning its bomb load by chance, most of our part of the world had escaped relatively unscathed. The Fens have a stark, rather than picturesque, quality that some find dull but, as a child knowing nothing different, I had always seen them as mysterious and enchanted.

As the train got closer to home I began to pick out familiar landmarks and my heart quickened. Journey's end was Woodall Spa, a small halt rather than a full-blown station. In pre-war days it had won prizes for its flowerbeds; the Stationmaster, dressed in a frock coat and peaked cap, would always hold up a train if he saw a pony and trap approaching along the road from nearby Walcott Dales – travel was more civilised in those days. There would be a coal fire burning in the waiting room during cold spells and a porter willing to help with luggage.

After being hugged and greeted by my father, he drove me home in his battered Woolsey that stank of cattle feed. It wasn't until our farm came into view around the last bend of the single-track road that ran on top of the bank, parallel to a sluggish River Witham, that the realisation I had come through the war finally struck me; the day I had left to join the Army I had been convinced I would never see my home again.

As the Woolsey bumped its way down the rutted drive we passed two men blue uniforms heaping straw on a potato grave.

"Who are they?" I enquired.

"My German POWs," my father replied. "I had three at one time."

"How d'you get on with them?"

"Oh, with a bit of give and take. Can't complain, grateful for the help. They put in a fair day's work. We fixed up one of the outhouses for them to sleep in. Nothing much, but I guess it's better than being behind barbed wire."

When I got out of the car I looked back at them. They had stopped working and were staring in our direction, concerned perhaps at the arrival of somebody in uniform.

My mother had cooked up a storm for the homecoming, the kitchen table laden with dishes I had all but forgotten: a whole ham, cold chicken, home-made bread, salad, a brick of butter, baked apples stuffed wIth raisins and a bowl of custard. "I thought you were still rationed," I said.

"So we are, but not today," mother said. "They say rationing will be with us for years, would you believe? Course we're luckier than people in the towns, because we grow our own."

"It's all due to old Sir Stafford Craps," my father chimed in, deliberately using the rude name people used for Sir Stafford Cripps, the vegetarian Labour Chancellor noted for his austerity measures.

"You shouldn't use that word, Tom," my mother admonished. "Not on the boy's first day home."

"All right, all right, just a bit of fun. It's no wonder old Sir Stafford looks like a scarecrow, he don't eat good red meat. They say he lives off watercress grown on blotting paper, silly old fool."

"Now that's enough! I don't like you talking disrespectable like that."

As I studied them both more closely I saw how much my father had aged, how stooped he had become. He had worked hard all his life and farming was far removed from the popular conception of a healthy open-air idyll – all the women rosy-cheeked and the men ruddy and strong. Although he owned a Fordson tractor, much of the day-to-day grind was still done with the help of two massive Shire horses. Always up before dawn, mucking out, feeding and watering the livestock, humping bales of fodder in winter, a Woodbine too often burning down to the last half inch and browning his upper lip, his life was an endless round. As he cut thick slices of ham, I saw his hands were callused and ingrained with soil. Although he had put on his best suit for the occasion, it seemed foreign to him – he was still unmistakeably a labourer, his neck russet red. I was well aware that, during the war, he had needed the help a son would have given, but he had somehow managed to keep everything together. My mother's role had always been to look after the score of Rhode Island hens that scratched around the house, milk the cows, churn the butter, skin the shot rabbits, boil the washing in soft rainwater from the butts and put it through a wooden mangle. It was a list of chores that would have defeated most, but I had never heard her complain. She, too, looked worn, though to greet me she had powdered her cheeks and put a smudge of lipstick on her mouth.

"How d'you get on with your Germans, Mum?"

"Don't have over much to do with them. Don't want to. In any case, we're told not to fraternalise."

"'Fraternise', mother," my father corrected gently.

"Well, whatever they call it. I've heard some local girls walk out with them." She lowered her voice. "A girl over at Coningsby had a child by one of them, so they say."

"They're allowed out then?"

"Within limits."

"I imagined they'd have been returned home by now,"

"Old Atlee decided they must stay and help repair the damage they caused. Quite right, too. Make the buggers pay something back."

"Now, don't use that language," my mother said. "I've told you before."

"Do they resent having to work for you?"

"The first couple they sent me were stroppy, so I got shut of them. The two we've got now are as good as you can expect."

After the meal I wandered around, re-familiarising myself with the rest of the house. Nothing had changed; it was just that all the furnishings looked fusty. The downstairs rooms were still lit with oil lamps, the bedrooms with candles and although there was a bathroom, everybody had to use the outside privy, where cut squares of newspaper hung on a nail. I went upstairs to my old bedroom. The last time I had looked at myself in the mirror over the chest of drawers, I had been nearly four years younger. The mirror had patches of brown on it where the silver backing had peeled away, reminding me of the age spots on my mother's hands. The face that stared back at me four years later was thinner, scaled down from the boy who had last slept in the room. I lifted the mirror from its hook and turned it over. Pasted on the reverse was a faded photograph of a nude cut from a magazine. I remembered using it as a spur to masturbation. There was a row of Penguin paperbacks stacked on the windowsill, most of them foxed; the jacket of *A Farewell to Arms* came apart as I picked it up. From the window I could see the perfect Norman Keep of nearby Tattershall Castle which, although a landmark, mercifully had escaped the attention of German bombers. Testing the springs on my old bed, I thought of nights I had lain there listening to small animals scurrying about in the eaves. I caught the familiar smell of the lavender polish my mother always used. It was all the same, yet strangely alien, as though I had never before been there.

Downstairs, the window in the 'Best Room', as my mother called it, remained boarded up. Pre-war it had only been used for special occasions, christenings and funerals, for the patterned lino on the floor had been considered an expensive luxury when first laid. The single sash window still had a blanket nailed to the frame and outside it was blocked up with rotting sandbags, the result of following government guidelines at the time of Munich urging everybody to make one room safe against gas attacks. Standing there, I thought how tragically ineffective such measures would have proved in the event. Now the room reeked of damp, preserved like a museum exhibit.

With the light fading I went outside and walked along the riverbank. As a child I had often earned six pence pocket money making cans of tea for the weekend fishermen who came to spin for pike. One Christmas the river had frozen over, the ice thick enough for skating, but I had been too scared to test it, just as I had been frightened to go near the Shire horses. But now when I went to their stable the current pair stopped chomping sweet hay and turned to regard me. They still looked enormous, but their noses were velvet soft when I stroked them and I no longer felt menaced. The stable was warmed by a stove where, on frosty mornings, their bran mash was heated and I roasted chestnuts on the red-hot lid. Next, I visited the chaff house, where huge Bramley apples were buried like sawdust-hidden prizes in a circus lucky dip. Rats jumped and scurried away as I opened the door.

As I retraced my steps to the house, I came face to face with the two Germans washing themselves under a pump. They instinctively stiffened.

"Relax," I said in German, "The war's over for all of us. Are you happy working for my father?"

The younger-looking of the two answered: "It is okay."

"Does he treat you well?"

"Ya."

"Where were you taken prisoner?"

This time the other man answered me in English. "At Falaise."

"And have you been in England ever since?"

"No. Before, we are sent to America."

"You speak good English."

"You speak good German." he replied with a certain arrogance.

"What were you in?"

"12 S.S. Panzer Division. And you?"

"Intelligence."

He shrugged, implying I was not an equal combatant.

"Why are we not treated as prisoners of war?"

"Aren't you?"

"No. We are forced labourers, this is contrary to the Geneva Convention."

Sod you, I thought. "Didn't you invent forced labour, or am I wrong? Wasn't your great Atlantic Wall built with it? You also gave the world Dachau." I reverted to German again. "Listen, I'm not looking to start an argument. I'm sure my father treats you decently. I'm sorry you're here and not at home, but don't blame it on us, blame that asshole with the stupid moustache." I walked away, angry with myself for losing my temper.

That evening after my mother had gone to bed, my father

produced a full bottle of Black Label and a box of cigars. "I saved these," he said. "Kept them moist with lettuce leaves, so I hope they're alright."

"They're fine." He lit two from the same match.

"Your letters didn't tell us overmuch. What's it really like over there?"

He had never travelled out of England, his most ambitious trips being visits to the seaside at Skegness and once to London for the Smithfield Cattle Show, so my descriptions of Germany and Austria amazed him. "How about the women?" he said giving me a sly look. "Anything you want to tell me now we're on our own? They're all blonds, aren't they?"

"Not all. Some."

"And?" He gave me the wink. "Have a good time, did you?"

"When we first got there we were forbidden to fraternise, but nobody took much notice and eventually the rules were relaxed. Yes, I did have a friendship with a German girl, the daughter of a Professor."

"A professor, eh? Educated girl I take it?" he said, as though anxious to assure himself that this somehow mitigated against her nationality.

"Actually, she's an actress."

"An actress?" His voice took on a new note of concern.

"I got to know her after seeing her in a musical play," I said.

"Sow your oats while you can. Long as you don't marry her. Now what? You'll be home for good soon."

"Not as soon as I'd hoped."

"No? Why's that then?"

"They need certain people like me to stay on. I should have told you before. I've been promoted again and have to take up a new job in Berlin when I get back."

"Promoted?"

"Yes, you've got an officer in the family."

"Well, well, that calls for another drink." He refilled our glasses. "What are you now then?"

"Captain."

"Isn't that something? Wait 'til I tell your mother. And Berlin, eh? Be funny to think of you there. Well, looks like what I've been planning will have to wait a while, but I'll show you anyway." He got up and went to the dresser and took some papers out of a drawer. "Take a look at these." They were bank statements. "I've managed to salt away a bit. Two and a half thousand and nothing owing."

"Wonderful, Dad."

"It's all yours when you finally hang up your uniform."

"Mine?"

He grinned. "Yes. My gift to you."

"I couldn't take it."

"Course you could. I've been putting it aside for you from the moment you left. What's more there's a farm going nearby. You remember old Leggatt, don't you? Well, he died a few months back and his widow can't afford to keep it going. Not as big as this, only forty acres, but decent soil. The house isn't up to much, but you can live here until you get it fixed."

His face as he outlined his plan was bright with expectation. "Sounds a very good buy," I said.

"I thought you'd go for it." He stubbed out his ragged cigar and downed the last of his whisky. "That's settled then."

That night, lying awake in the bed that should have been familiar but wasn't, I tried to think of ways to refuse his offer without hurting his feelings. The prospect of coming back to wrest a living from the earth as he had done chilled me, but during the following week I went through the motions of being keen, and spent a morning going over the Leggatt property. It was a depressing holding, the farmhouse in urgent need of renovation like the accompanying cluster of outbuildings. I kept up the pretence of being interested by seeing the solicitor handling the sale and was relieved to find there was another prospective purchaser prepared to pay over the asking price. I relayed this to my father.

"Well, we'll match him, top him if necessary. The bank manager owes me. I kept him in chickens and eggs during the war."

"No, I couldn't let you do that, you're being generous enough as it is. The truth is, Dad," I began tentatively, "when I do get back, I want to think carefully before making up my mind. I might try my hand at something other than farming."

He stopped what he was doing and straightened up. "Are you saying you don't want the Leggatt farm?"

"It's just that everything's happening too quickly for me."

"You have to act quick sometimes otherwise you lose the chance."

"You're right, but I need to think about it more if you'll let me. I'm sorry, especially because you've been so generous."

"I'm sorry, too. It's an opportunity that won't come again in a hurry."

He walked away from me, reached for a Woodbine and stood staring across the fields. "There it is then," he said. "I thought you'd want to get back to normal."

"Dad, I don't know what's normal any more. I don't want to sound ungrateful."

"No, better you should say what's on your mind. Have you mentioned anything to your mother?"

"Not yet."

"Let me tell her. She was living for the day when you'd back for good."

During the remainder of my leave I spent time tidying up the 'best room', removing the decayed sandbags and giving all the woodwork a coat of paint. I also made the social rounds, catching up with relatives and friends, and was saddened to learn Bennet, my old headmaster, to whom I owed so much, had been killed in a road accident during the blackout. My mother proudly sewed three pips on my uniform and out of curiosity more than anticipated pleasure I went to the village hop one evening and was greeted as a war hero. Dancing to music by an amateur four-piece band, I felt ever more alienated, remembering the first time I had danced with Lisa. I partnered a girl I had once been sweet on, but her early lushness had faded and I had to carefully resist her efforts to rekindle the flame. All too clearly I saw the constricting sameness of village life, the cycle of birth, marriage and death taking place within narrow boundaries. The encounter intensified my longing to see Lisa again. I had written her regularly since arriving home, but had received no word back. Suddenly seized by the need to hear her voice, I took my father's car and drove to Woodhall Spa. There I spent a fruitless hour using the one public call box trying to get through to the theatre stage door, but making a connection to Hamburg proved impossible.

My leave finally over, it wasn't until I was packing that I came across the envelope Chivers had entrusted me with and which I had completely forgotten. My first thought was to destroy it but in the end, I bowed to conscience and wrote him a mea culpa letter full of remorse.

THIRTEEN

The moment I arrived back in Hamburg I went straight to the theatre. Posters for the next production were displayed outside, featuring Lisa's name for the first time. The foyer doors were open and I went through into the darkened auditorium to find a rehearsal in progress on stage. After my eyes had adjusted to the gloom, I spotted Lisa sitting in the front row stalls. I took a seat in the row behind her and kissed the nape of her neck. She wheeled around, startled, and clapped a hand to her mouth when she saw it was me.

"When do you break?" I whispered.

"Soon," she whispered back. "But we only get half an hour for lunch."

The Director, an obvious queen, flapped a limp wrist at Lisa and shouted, "Would it be too much to ask if we all concentrate? Lisa, you missed your cue!"

She got up quickly and mounted the steps to the stage. The queen glared at me. "We don't allow strangers at rehearsals, so would you mind leaving? Thank you."

I waited outside the stage door. When Lisa appeared, I saw she was crying.

"Darling," I said, "That was my fault, I shouldn't have barged in like that, I'm so sorry. Did he take it out on you?"

"It's not him,"she said. "I'm not upset about him."

"What then? Tell me."

"Don't you know?"

"Know what, darling?"

She looked over her shoulder before answering in

91

German, something she seldom did now." My father was arrested and taken away. Your people came for him."

I took her arm and hurried her into a nearby café. Once I had ordered sandwiches and coffee, I pretended ignorance and said: "Now, come on, don't cry any more, tell me exactly what happened. Why would they arrest him?"

"I don't know. A week ago when I got home after rehearsal there were soldiers outside the door. Papa had already been taken away and they were searching the apartment."

"Searching it for what?"

"I don't know," she said again. "They wouldn't tell us."

"What about your mother? Did they arrest her as well?"

"No. She went to stay with relatives. I had to find somewhere else in Hamburg, so I am sharing a room with a friend."

"They must have told you or your mother something, given some reason."

"No."

"What about the university, does anybody there know why?"

She shook her head. "I went there, but they couldn't tell me anything."

"It must be a mistake," I said, "We make mistakes like everyone else."

"Do you? Tell me you do," she said clutching at straws.

"They've probably mixed up his file with somebody else. It happens," I told her with a false glibness.

She withdrew her hand from my grip and wiped her wet cheeks. "Will you find out?"

"Yes, darling, of course."

"When? When will you do it?"

"As soon as I can," I said. "Just try not to distress yourself. Drink your coffee and eat something, please."

"I can't eat. It could be a mistake, couldn't it, like you said?"

"Yes." Her trust in me to solve everything made me ashamed. "I'll find out whatever I can before I leave for Berlin tonight."

"Oh, that's right," she said. "You told me in one of your letters you were being sent there."

I pushed a notepad and pencil to her. "Write down your new address for me. Have you got money?"

"Yes," she said, but I persuaded her to accept some more. On the way back to the theatre she kept saying, "Promise you'll do something, make them see it's all a mistake."

"I promise. I love you," I said, as though love alone could end her nightmare.

After leaving her I straightaway rushed to find Machell. He greeted me with, "Alex, dear boy, you're meant to be in Berlin saving democracy from the KGB. Can I offer you a mahogany?"

"No thanks, thanks all the same. I'm on my way there, but first I have to find out what happened to that man I picked out from the photograph. You said you'd deal with him."

"Well, we did. Grundwall, isn't that his name? Very plausible on the surface, but Grable broke him down over three sessions. Your hunch was right, he was one of the men in the photograph, subsequently confirmed by two survivors of the camp who picked him out on an identity parade without hesitation."

"They did? Oh, God," I blurted, unable to help myself.

"Why, 'oh, God'? I thought you'd be chuffed."

"I am, I am. So where is he now?"

"Banged up in Nuremburg awaiting trial."

I hesitated. "Look, there is something more I should have told you, but I held back in case my hunch was wrong... . Something that complicates matters... . I hadn't interrogated him before, that was a lie. I recognised him because I knew him. I've been having an affair with his daughter."

"Ah," Machell said. "Definitely a complication. How much did she know about her father's past?"

"Nothing," I said too quickly.

"You're sure of that?" What if she took you in? Maybe she knew and protected him?"

"I'd stake my life that she knew nothing. Should I reveal my relationship with her?"

"Well, you'll almost certainly be called as a witness at his trial, so my advice would be confess it now, rather than have somebody pull it out of you. Then walk away, end it. Don't see her again."

"I'm not sure I could do that," I said slowly. "I love her."

"Don't give yourself grief because you allowed yourself to be pussy-whipped by a piece of German totty. You can't change anything now, the due processes have taken over and if he's proved guilty, then fuck him, he deserves whatever's coming."

"But I started it."

"No, you didn't. It started before you ever wore that unIform. You just did your job."

"It's her father, for Christ'sake. That's the difference."

"It's always somebody's father. Even Himmler had one," Machell said.

Ignoring his good advice, I commandeered a Jeep from Transport pool and set out for the address Lisa had given me, armed with a bottle of wine. The journey ended outside a large tenement building in a working class suburb, bomb-scarred like most. Climbing concrete stairs to the third floor I located the number of her apartment. Another young girl opened the door. Fear jumped into her face immediately she saw my uniform.

"I've come to see Lisa," I said in German.

The girl did not answer and we stood facing each other until Lisa appeared behind her.

"It's alright Greta," she said in a flat voice. It was

obvious she had been crying again

Greta pushed past me and left as I went inside. The room I found myself in was clean but sparsely furnished with odd, ill-matched pieces. There was a sepia photograph of Lisa's parents on the mantelpiece and some clothes hanging on a rope in one corner. It was a room made for bad news.

"I didn't expect to see you again so soon," she said.

"Well, I couldn't go and leave you in that state. Have you got a corkscrew?"

She found a corkscrew and I opened the wine and filled two tumblers, all the time trying to think of the right words with which to pacify her. "As promised, I found out where they've sent your father. Here, it'll do you good." I handed her a tumbler. "He's in a holding prison."

"Where?"

"Nuremburg," I said as casually as I could.

She was about to drink but stopped. "Nuremburg?

"That's where they hold the trials."

"Why would they try him? What for?"

"Darling, they're saying that he didn't work as a translator as we both believed, but was an officer in one of the death camps."

Her face was becoming blotchy and she shook her head from side to side in disbelief. "That's not possible."

"Witnesses, survivors from the camp, have identified him as one of the SS."

"But he wasn't."

"Darling, photographs exist."

"Then they're fakes," she said.

"No, I've seen one of them. Taken at Auschwitz." I finally named the camp.

Her body started to shake violently and she gave a cry like some trapped animal. "No, no, no, don't say that, it's not true, not Vater, not him." She fell to the floor, knocking over her wine over as she collapsed. I cradled her, attempting to stop the tremors wracking her body, but she pushed me away. "Not Vater," she kept repeating," not Vater, please no."

"I never wanted to be the one tell you all this," I said, but she was beyond comfort, her misery was absolute. When I finally managed to quieten her I carried her into the tiny bedroom she shared with Greta and laid her on the double bed. She still continued to whisper the same mantra again and again.

"Don't," I said. "Please don't, darling," my face close to hers until, finally exhausted, she fell silent and seemed to sleep. With my arm cramping beneath her, I lay without moving for a long time as the room gradually darkened. Then she turned into me, pressing her body against mine, seeking my mouth, kissing me with hungry desperation as if we were about to part forever. I allowed the kiss to obliterate all reason, all common sense, my sexual hunger matching hers. We tore each other's clothes off, she crying for me to take her quickly, willing me to a sort of rape as though only such a violation could obliterate her misery. She became in those moments somebody I did not recognise, somebody possessed. As I entered her, I realised all too late that I was not wearing a condom, but by then I could not have stopped. When the moment came it was so intense that it bordered on pain. Spent, I lay with my head nestled into her damp neck as our bodies slowly relinquished each other and our hearts gradually slowed.

Long afterwards Lisa said: "Will I ever see you again now?"

"Of course you will," I said. "I love you, nothing will change that. I won't be able to see you as often as before, but I'll come back here whenever I can and I'll write often." At that moment I believed I could honour such promises.

"He must have been forced to it," she said suddenly. "That's what must have happened."

"Yes, I'm sure you're right. Listen, darling, I must go now and catch my plane to Berlin. Have you got enough money?"

"I can't take any more money from you."

I got out of the bed and started to dress, then took my wallet from my uniform jacket. She had never noticed that I was now an officer, nor had I mentioned it. "Here, treat yourself, take Greta for a meal somewhere. I want you to promise you'll eat properly and take care of yourself."

"Come back soon," she said.

"I promise." I kissed her twice and then left quickly before she cried again.

FOURTEEN

At that time the British zone in Berlin was a curious outpost. The division of spoils had resulted in the city being isolated within Soviet East Germany, chopped like a cake into four sectors. The Russians closed off their sector from the other three, renamed the streets and set about imposing communist rule in place of Hitler's brand of National Socialism. At night, as well as the concrete barriers, a frontier of darkness separated the Soviet zone from the brightly illuminated Western sectors. Officially, we were all still buddies, but that wasn't the reality. The reality was obstruction, tension and endless bureaucratic obstruction.

My scant knowledge of pre-war Berlin had been gleaned from Isherwood's novels, but Sally Bowles' world was a far cry from the city in which I now found myself. On arrival, I was billeted in a tumbledown hotel reputed to have been a luxury brothel catering for every taste. My room was lined with shabby red plush wallpaper; a broken chandelier hung from the bullet-pitted ceiling giving it an air of seedy decadence.

After stowing my gear I reported to the SIS station housed close to old Olympic Stadium which, by some quirk of fortune, had escaped major damage. The SIS operated from undercover as part of the Control Commission's Political Division.

My Head of Station was a career diplomat called Graham Green. Middle aged, grey faced, heavy pouches under spaniel eyes, wearing a well-cut pinstripe suit, blue shirt and faded

Garrick tie, he unnervingly, barked staccato non-sequetors at me the moment we met.

"No connection, by-the-way. Different spelling."

"Sir?"

"That Catholic writer chap of the same name. Most people ask. Wrote that book about the Brighton race gangs. One of us during the war, somewhere in Africa. Freetown. That's a misnomer. Bloody awful place Africa. Flies, dysentery and the clap." He looked me up and down as though I might possibly be a carrier. " Lethal combination. So have you?"

"Sir?"

"Read him? My namesake?"

"I've read Stamboul Train, sir, a thriller about the Orient Express."

"Prefer Wodehouse myself. More cheerful. He's persona non grata now, blotted his copybook broadcasting for the Boche, stupid sod." His dialogue hopped from subject to subject at bewildering speed, "Took that train once pre-war. With the wife. First wife that is. She hated it. Last holiday we had together. She fell off the perch a few months later. You religious?"

"No, sir."

"Glad to hear it. Steer clear of the Bible punchers, especially the holy Romans. He was a convert, you know."

"Who, sir?"

"The writer chap. Funny, the more intelligent they are, the more they buy all that mumbo jumbo. I was cured early on, in prep school. Chaplain made a pass at me. How about clubs?"

"Clubs, sir?"

"Yes. Belong to any?"

"No, I don't."

"White's and Garrick, myself. By the way do feel free to wear a suit and tie. Less conspicuous."

"I don't possess a suit, sir."

"Don't keep calling me 'sir'. First names here. What else have you read? Lawrence, The one who dressed as an Arab?"

"No, I haven't." I was completely lost now.

"Arabia. That's another place to avoid. First posting I had. What's your first name?

"Alex."

"You a Cambridge man, Alex?"

"No, Horncastle Grammar."

"Really?" For the first time he seemed stymied. "Better advance you some pay, then point you in the right direction to get a suit made. Very reasonable, because they're desperate for work. At one time we were paid in sovereigns, did you know that?"

"I didn't no."

"Oh, yes. No questions asked in the House. Well, good to have you on board, Alex. When you've settled in, you'd better take a course in codes and ciphers with our man in Vienna. Been there, have you?"

"No, I never got further than Graz."

"Old Hugh will show you around. Hugh Dempster-Miller. Bit of a mouthful, but you'll like him, he makes a mean bowl of flaker." When I looked blank, he explained: "black coffee with a tot of rum in it. In Hugh's case, two tots. By the way, never ask for *eine Tasse Kaffee* in Vienna, shows you're a stranger. It's a 'bowl' of coffee always – *eine Schale*. Old hand, Hugh. Seen it all." He broke off and stared at me as though weighing me up for a difficult decision. "What're are you doing for tiffin tonight?"

"Nothing, I haven't made any plans."

"Good, I'll take you to my favourite watering hole in the French zone. Don't get many things right, the French, but at least they know what to put on your plate. Strange bird, de Gaulle. Met him once. Thinks he can walk on water. Probably can, wouldn't put it past him." He moved away from his desk and stared out of the window. I waited, uncertain as to whether the interview was over. "We've got to watch our backs, Alex," he said finally. "This bloody place is the Last Chance saloon. We bitch this one and it's curtains. I'll fill you in over dinner. Seven o'clock. Collect you at your hotel."

I took this as a dismissal but, as I moved to the door, Green fired a parting shot.

"I don't know what you were told about me in advance, Alex. But whatever it was, ignore it. I only have one thing in my favour, I look after my own."

I was waiting outside the hotel well before seven, still wondering what was in store for me from this odd character who was now my boss, when a car drew up and Green, leaned across and opened the passenger door for me. "Let's go," he said. The moment I was inside he gunned the engine and drove off at speed, gripping the steering wheel in the orthodox ten to two position and changing gear frequently with professional skill.

"I spoke too soon," he said after when we had gone a mile or so. "Tempted fate. Should have known better. Never take anything for granted in this town, Alex. Arrivals and departures. You arrive and another departs," he added cryptically. After that he was silent and we drove for half an hour before he pulled up outside large nondescript apartment block where a few lights were burning in the windows. Killing the engine, he reached inside the glove compartment and took out a Mauser and clicked a full magazine into place.

"You've got your own pea shooter, I take it?"

"Yes."

"Have it handy. Rawnsley said it was all clear, but one never knows."

"Rawnsley?"

"One of us."

We went into the building and climbed a dirty stairway all the way to the top floor. Bare bulbs burned on each landing. A smell of damp and rancid cooking oil filled the stairwell. I followed him with my Walther cocked. When we reached the last landing we were faced with a long corridor with identical doors at intervals on either side, all painted a drab battleship grey. Cold air blew in from a broken window at the far end as Green led the way to door which was ajar. He gestured caution before pushing it wide open with his foot. We edged into a room which reeked of stale cigarette smoke.

Green called: "David?" and immediately a young man appeared, a Smith and Wesson in his hand. He stared at me.

"This is Alex," Green said. "Where is she?"

"Through here." Rawnsley led the way into a bedroom. At first glance nothing seemed untoward. The only illumination was provided by a lamp on the bedside table. There was a large pink Teddy bear propped against the pillows on the neatly made bed and it wasn't until Rawnsley tilted the lamp to shine on the space between the bed and the wall that I saw the girl. She was fully clothed and very dead. Even so Green knelt down beside her and went through the motion of feeling the side of her neck. She was pretty, or had been, her Slavic features now relaxed in death, the eyes open. Green passed a hand over them to close the lids.

"She was still warm when I got here," Rawnsley said.

"How long ago?"

"Half an hour. I'd arranged to collect her at six. I was on time," he added.

I said, "Can I ask who she was?"

"Somebody who ran errands for us," Green replied.

"German?"

"Yes." He got to his feet. "Have you called the garbage collectors?"

"On their way," Rawnsley said.

"I want a post mortem before disposal." Green looked

around the room. "Did you find anything?"

"These." Rawnsley produced a gold-tipped cigarette butt and a spent hypodermic syringe.

"Not like them to be that careless," Green said.

"Must have been in a hurry."

"When you said you'd collect her, did you telephone ahead?"

"Yes."

"That, too, was careless. Who else knew?"

"Nobody."

When he turned away from the scene, Green's face had sagged. "Lock the door when everybody's finished, David, then throw away the key. We won't be using this again." To me he said brusquely: "Right. We're out of here."

Once we were at ground level again, I asked: "D'you still want to have dinner? I'd quite understand if you don't."

"No, I'm looking forward to it."

He drove in silence to a small bistro in the French sector where the clientele was exclusively French officers and their girl friends. A group of them nearest the door looked vaguely disgruntled at our arrival. We were shown to the only vacant table and Green ordered a carafe of the house red as soon as we sat down. There was a marked change in him from earlier in the day, the pouches under his eyes had become darker, the voice was softer and he no longer used the machinegun delivery that had thrown me at our first meeting. "Best kept secret in Berlin, this place, and long may it remain so. I don't go a bundle on German cuisine. Too much bloody pork."

A waitress in a tight sweater arrived with the carafe and poured some for Green to taste. He sampled it and pronounced it acceptable in impeccable French. When she had filled both our glasses and withdrawn Graham drank a full glass and then gave himself a refill. "I'm sorry our first meal had to start on such a down note." He stared into his glass. "Not what I intended."

He picked up his menu and studied it. I did the same, but the dead girl's face swam before me, obscuring the menu text.

"I can recommend the veal," Graham said. "If you like veal, that is. Some people don't. My first wife didn't, had a thing about eating young animals. Or try the *coq au vin*, usually excellent."

"Fine. Sounds good."

He beckoned for a waiter and ordered for both of us plus another carafe of wine.

"You said the murdered girl used to run errands for you. What did that mean exactly?"

"Dead letter drops and pick ups."

"You'll have to forgive me, I'm not familiar with the jargon."

"You'll learn soon enough. She was permitted to visit her mother in the Soviet sector once a month. The old woman elected to stay there when they closed it off, and the girl acted as our postman, a job she volunteered for." He fiddled with his knife and fork, straightening them by the side of his plate.

"Do you use many like her?"

"We use who we can, Alex, those we can trust, which is a very inaccurate science." He poured the remains of the first carafe into our glasses. "A dangerous game for all concerned, but one, unfortunately, we have had to resume from necessity."

"So soon?"

"That surprises you?"

"Yes," I said.

"Get used to surprises, Alex, they come thick and fast here. Just when we thought we could sit back and enjoy the fruits of victory, the rules changed again." He stopped arranging the cutlery and looked up at me. "This is where it might all go pear-shaped one day.

While I tucked into my meal I noticed he only played with his food while drinking steadily and it was some time before he spoke again. "At least they killed her by injection, which is a sort of comfort."

"How long had she been working for you?"

"Too long it now appears. I blame myself." Then he surprised me. "Before somebody gets to you with the wrong version, I should tell you she was my mistress."

"I see," I said lamely, at a loss to find the appropriate response.

He was silent again and pushed his plate to one side. The headwaiter came up to enquire whether anything was wrong.

"No," Graham replied in French. "It's excellent as ever. Just that I've lost my appetite."

"You wish me to get you something else, monsieur?"

"Thank you, no. You can remove my plate."

When we were alone again, he said, "Funny thing, falling in love at my age. Once passed the big five O one should have more sense." Flushed of face, his features crumpled. "I should never have used her in the way I did." He filled his glass, and then remembered me. "Sorry. Have some. I apologise for being such lousy company."

"You're not. I understand completely."

"I doubt that. The hardest thing, you see, is the thought of somebody you've made love to being cut open."

"Who d'you suspect killed her?" I said, anxious to show sympathy.

"Oh, it was a KGB job. Bears all the hallmarks. When the shooting match stopped, Moscow Central went straight back to business as usual. They never thought of us as an ally, those wartime get-togethers of the big three were charades. Roosevelt trusted Uncle Joe Stalin. Big mistake. Churchill was pragmatic because the Russians bought us time before D Day and, let's face it, they had the worst war, even though they brought it on themselves. We tipped them off you know, told them the exact day, the exact place and hour that Germany would Invade. Stalin ignored our warning, he was too busy killing most of his best generals."

"How did we know the date?"

"The Bletchley boffins had broken the German Enigma code."

I put my glass down. "Bletchley," I repeated. I met somebody in Hamburg who said he'd worked there, but I didn't know the significance."

"Who told you he worked there?" There was an edge to Green's voice."

"A Control Commission Major called Chivers. Dodgy sort of character, I thought."

Graham frowned. "Very dodgy if he volunteered that information. Bletchley's still top secret, nobody's allowed to mention it."

Over coffee and Armagnac he returned to the subject of his dead mistress. "The last thing that ever entered my mind was I'd would fall for a German girl."

"Same here," I said, " that's my situation too." If I thought this would show solidarity, I was wrong.

"Is it?" He betrayed no interest. "I wasn't a good adulterer. Some characters can carry it off. Not me. I could rationalise it to myself – away from home, the end of a long war, every man needs to get his oats, middle-age crisis, etcetera, but guilt was always there. Are you married?"

"No."

"Ah! There's the rub. My wife, my second wife that is, is a good woman, true blue, deserves more."

I had the sense he might weep, but then a safety switch was pulled, and he downed his Armagnac, pushed his chair back and signalled for the bill. "Let's go."

He drove erratically on the way back, twice narrowly missing pedestrians. His goodnight was perfunctory, more a dismissal than a social convention, as though, even full of alcohol, he was aware he had revealed too much: confidences stored up problems.

FIFTEEN

That night, my brain racing from too much Armagnac, I began several letters to Lisa, but binned all of them, unable to find the right words of comfort, unwilling to lie to her.

Green made no further mention of his murdered mistress when next we met, but honoured his promise to advance me some pay together with the details of a local tailor. "Sweeten him with a packet of cigarettes and he'll kit you out in a week. I've got a bit of a chore for you before your trip to Vienna, which is going to be delayed anyway. The Yanks have asked whether we have anybody who could escort one of their star war correspondents around our sector. Bit of a strange request to dump on us, but one likes to oblige if one can. Might also help you to get acclimatised."

"What's his name?"

"Her." He searched amongst the papers on his desk. "A Beth Eriksson. Ever heard of her?"

"No. You say Vienna's delayed."

"Yes. Old Hugh, has gone on leave for a couple of weeks. Never know, you might enjoy taking this Yank floozy around."

The Yank 'floozy' turned out to be an attractive woman in her early thirties with close-cropped blond hair framing a tanned face devoid of make-up. She greeted me wearing faded US battledress, the trousers tucked into paratrooper boots. "Hi, I'm Beth. This is so nice of you, Captain. Hope it isn't a bore."

"Not at all. And please call me Alex. I won't be the greatest guide, because I'd better confess I'm a recent arrival myself."

"No sweat, we'll explore together. I thought I should at least set foot in the Tiergarten before heading home."

I had never met anybody else like her before. She was good company, her conversation a cocktail of gossip, expletives and raunchy American colloquialisms that had to be explained to me. None of the women of my acquaintance used the f-word so openly, but it was curiously inoffensive coming from her. During our tour she occasionally used her battered Leica to take a shot of a particular ruin, handling it casually, no fiddling with focus or stops but with the expertise of a professional. At one point she said: "We sure fucked up here, didn't we?"

"You think so?"

"Yeah. In spades. Either Bradley or Montgomery could have got to Berlin first if Ike hadn't succumbed to political pressure. Would have saved us the crazy half-assed solution we're living with. Ike never rated Montgomery, they were too far apart in personality. Ike is basically a fucking lucky West Point desk job, Cary Grant with four stars who knows how to pass the cocktails around. A cold martinet like Monty, with no apparent vices, would have fazed him. For one thing Monty doesn't smoke and Ike smokes like a chimney. Plus he was humping his Wac driver throughout the war. Adultery wouldn't have sat well with Monty." Seeing my blank look, she said: "Didn't you know that?"

"No."

"The Press corps were onto it, but kept it under wraps. They even put it around that Monty liked to be surrounded with good looking fags at his command post."

"You are an extraordinary character," I said. "How d'you know so much?"

"Didn't you ever learn that the first casualty of war is

truth? Like, FDR was crippled by polio, wore steel braces on his legs and had to be supported in public, but that, too, was kept under wraps. We couldn't have a great war leader who couldn't walk. I guess we'll have to wait for the memoirs to be published before the whole story comes out. Bet your bottom dollar they'll all claim the credit and none of the blame."

She told me she had been attached to Patton's army for most of her war. "My personal contribution to morale was to distribute my favours, such as they were. The only one that meant anything was this kid," producing a photo of a young pilot: it was the face of a boy who didn't look old enough to drive a car let alone take to the skies in a Mustang. "He was shot down over Holland. The last time we slept together I knew his luck had run out. I could always tell, it was there in their faces. It sometimes seemed I only fucked young men destined to die. Still, better to burn out like a rocket, than to fade slowly."

I found myself becoming captivated by her; she was so alive, so emancipated compared any other woman I had known, which admittedly was limited. I also discovered that her gung ho attitude was only surface deep; despite her surface toughness she had been scarred by the horrors she had photographed. She showed me some of the prints she kept in her camera bag. "Taken at Dachau," she said. It was a shot I had seen reproduced in a newspaper – a little boy with the face of an old man lying naked beside corpses piled like some monstrous avant garde sculpture.

"How do you take shots like that?" I asked.

"You don't think about it, if you did you'd never press the button. All war photographers will tell you the same. Just aim and hope you've got the exposure and stop right. Mind you, I threw up afterwards."

She showed me other examples of her work: a garrotted concentration camp guard, his face knocked out of shape, the eyes open but frozen in a last expression of terror as he met the fate he had meted out to so many others. "God left early in Dachau, if He was ever there." Beth said.

"Why did you stay on? Surely you could have gone home the moment it all ended?"

"Yeah, I could have, but I didn't. I'd never set foot outside the States before and over here I was treated like an equal. In any case, I don't have anything to go back to. War correspondents need a war."

"No family?"

"Put it this way, nobody's missing me."

We had dinner together in her hotel in the American zone and she was amused when I remarked on the size of my steak. "Everything we Yanks do is larger than life, honey. The reason the rest of the world loves us rIght now and will eventually hate us, is we're so fucking full of ourselves. We have too much of everything. That's the way America works. Don't fuck with the dollar, baby."

When I pressed her to tell me more she painted an intriguing picture of life in small town America where she had grown up; she described a closed community where everybody knew everybody and nothing ever changed.

"I'd love to get to America one day," I said. "All I know about it is from films."

"Well, if you ever make it across the water, look me up."

She chain-smoked throughout the meal and downed several neat shots of Jack Daniels. Although I couldn't match her, I drank too much.

"So, how can I thank you," she said. "Want to fuck?"

Not knowing how to reply, I tried to make a joke of it. "Am I young enough for you?"

"I can make an exception."

"Are you serious?" I said.

"I wouldn't have asked if I wasn't."

"Well, I'm flattered, but I've got a girl friend."

"I'm not looking for marriage, honey. We're just two ships that shortly will pass in the night, but its no big sweat if the idea doesn't grab you. I won't take it personally, I'll just put it down to your famed British reserve."

The friendly jibe struck home. Why was I hesitating? I had felt attracted to her from the moment we had met, but the idea of taking it further had never occurred to me. Now I felt myself being pulled towards that deciding point when desire extinguishes conscience. An inner voice said Lisa won't find out – that age-old justification for betrayal. In any case, I told myself, Lisa was already lost to me. I loved her, but my actions had ensured I would eventually lose her. So why not burn, as Beth had said?

"Yes," I said, before my silence became rudeness. "Let's go up to your room."

It proved to be the room of somebody of no fixed abode as they say, the temporary occupant always in transit. Beth slung clothes, camera bags and newspapers off the unmade bed. "The powder room's through that door," she said and there I found the same state of disarray – wet towels littering the floor, a full ashtray on the edge of the bath, underwear strung on a string, an empty bottle of Jack Daniels by the toilet. I undressed and took a condom from my wallet before going back to the bedroom. Her shapeless battledress had concealed her true shape and I stood transfixed by her nakedness.

"What are you staring at?" she said.

"You. Your body."

"Haven't you seen one before?"

"Not one like yours. How lovely you are."

"Well, it ain't going to last, honey, it's just on loan, so enjoy it while you have the chance." After we had kissed she saw the condom in my hand. "What's that for?"

"Shouldn't I wear one?"

"Hell no."

"What about the risk?"

"Risk of what? You aren't about to give me a dose, are you?"

"No, of course not. I meant risk of a baby."

"If I have a baby it'll be a medical first. I had a hysterectomy when I was twenty. I never wanted children anyway. Who would want to bring them into this world?" She pulled me down on top of her and with a practiced hand guided my penis inside her. "This is the only thing God got right, don't you agree?" she said. Her lovemaking had an uninhibited urgency, difficult to describe without resorting to the clichés of shop girl fiction. Her speech became louder and more incoherent as we thrashed about and I was scared that somebody would bang on the door and tell us to be quiet. Several times she cried out the name 'Steve', perhaps the name of the doomed pilot she had once loved. There was nothing fake about her orgasm when she came and my own was more intense than I had ever experienced before. Afterwards, I wish I could admit to having had remorse about Lisa but, with my racing heart slowing to normal, there was only a sensation of feeling wasted, as though I had run a long race.

When Beth also rejoined the land of the living, she padded into the bathroom, returning with two tumblers and a full bottle of Jack Daniels. "Pour some, honey, and let's have a Philip Morris post-coitus moment."

She lit two cigarettes and put one in my mouth. "You needed a fuck as much as me, didn't you?"

"Yes. Yes, I did." I ran my hand through her thick, cropped hair, then traced with a finger traced circles around her nipples. "Just like Miss Blandish," I said.

"Who's Blandish, your girlfriend?"

"No, a character in a book we weren't supposed to read as kids. The author described her as having tits with nipples like bing cherries. I thought that was the most erotic thing ever. Never knew what it meant until now."

"Well I'm glad I solved that for you before I leave tomorrow."

"Why tomorrow? Why can't you stay a bit longer."

"If I stay I might get serious about you and that wouldn't be good for either of us, believe me."

"Perhaps I'd like you to get serious."

"There's no future in me," she said. "Always quit while you're ahead, honey. We had a good time in the sack, don't spoil it."

I went to Templehof next morning and watched the Douglas DC3 lift off and climb into the sullen sky, staying there until it vanished into the clouds. Some weeks later I got a letter from her enclosing a print of her saltbox house in Maine with 'Will provide rocking chair and condoms if you ever make the trip,' written on the back. I replied, but that was the last I ever heard. Years later I picked up a copy of TIME in a dentist's waiting room which featured an obituary saying that, after a distinguished career as a war correspondent she had died of an embolism aged thirty-eight. A collection of her photographs was published posthumously with the shot of the child at Dachau on the cover. It received considerable critical acclaim.

SIXTEEN

I acted on Machell's advice, admitted my association with Lisa to the investigation team in Nuremburg and gave a written statement. From them I learned that other eyewitnesses had been found to identify Grundwall and that a damming case against him was being prepared. When next I wrote to Lisa I chose my words with extra care so as not to raise her hopes, but reading my letters before posting them they appeared so trite; I thought of CharlIe Boag who, despite his fractured, inarticulate English had still managed to convey genuine love, whereas my own efforts had a falseness about them, as well they might, for guilt about my night with Beth nagged at me like a bad tooth.

I carried that guilt with me when I took the train to Vienna. On arrival Dempster-Miller immediately gave me a tour. "It's important to get the feel of this place," he said, "and don't be fooled by the surface atmosphere. Those with short memories still believe they can detect distant strains of Straus and Ravel, poor souls. They can't see behind the facade. This place may once have danced to the music of Time, but to me it's a sinister enclave. The Austrians have always played a double game, bending like reeds to whichever wind blows their way."

Miller was in his late fifties, a short, hyperactive man with a round, Pickwickian face; small, deep set, but bright eyes, an engaging smile, which descended to his double chin. There were flakes of dandruff on his shoulders, frayed cuffs to his double-breasted suit, a general crumpled look, as though he slept in his clothes. Like Beth, he chain-smoked, letting the ash fall where it may, and was never without a tin of Capstans bulging a side pocket of his jacket. Although many of his opinions mirrored Green's, he had a more pragmatic approach to the problems now facing us, unlike the disillusionment that Green exuded like stale body odour. As a teacher he was thorough, taking me through the intricacies of the cipher codebooks with infinite patience. "An old-fashioned trade ours, Alex," he said. "Despicable probably . . . no, correction, definitely despicable. . .but deemed necessary. We've always been amateurs at it. It's the British character to rather despise professionals. We prefer the Gentlemen versus the Players approach, as in cricket. Let the enemy bat first, then try and bowl them out with spin on a crumbling wicket. The station here is understaffed and under funded, consequently we're always at a disadvantage, but try getting London to do something about it." He gave a sudden chuckle and lit another cigarette from the one still smouldering. "Not that I'm bothered any longer, if they don't want to listen that's their problem and I won't be here to worry about it."

"You're near the end of your tour, are you?"

"What a nice way of putting it. No, but I'm living on borrowed time. Piss all night. Prostrate. Could do something about it, I suppose, but I'm not keen to go under the knife, prefer to bite on this handy little comforter when it becomes too much to handle." He fished in a coin purse and produced a small capsule. "Cyanide. Took it off a SS prisoner."

"Maybe it won't come to that," I said, at a loss to know exactly how to react to such intimate details of a stranger's life. I was swiftly coming to the realisation that I had joined a band of eccentrics – first Green and now Miller. Neither had waited long before confiding their Achilles heels to me.

"What exactly is our job now? Be helpful if you could tell me."

He looked nonplussed. "It's flattering of you to think I know. There's a manual for codes, but no Boy Scout instruction book for the rest of our job. We've always had to work things out for ourselves as we go along. Trial and error, mostly error. Take me, for instance. Guess where I started."

"Foreign Office?"

"Good God no. In prison. Wormwood Scrubs. I was recruited by one of my old tutors at Charterhouse. Immediately drafted into an outfit called Radio Security Service, a real Heath Robinson affair, one of the department's curiosities that sprang into existence at the beginning of the war. Nobody knew what we were supposed to do but, after commandeering the Scrubs, we kicked out all the inmates and used their vacated cells as offices. I don't think anybody knew we existed. Our C.O. was a dotty old cove, ex-actor, who had once played the lead in The Desert Song, hardly the best foundation for a career in espionage. When the phoney war ended we were all scattered into more worthwhile causes. I wangled my way into MI6, at that time pretty much a shambles, because the moment France collapsed our European network went up the spout. After Churchill took over we slowly got our act together, but there was always too much rivalry between us and MI5. Still is. So what did you ask me, Alex? Oh, yes, I remember. What's our job now? Same as ever. To watch our backs. It often seems the enemy within is the one to fear."

"That's a fairly gloomy prognosis," I said.

"I'm a fairly gloomy character, always had a sick sense of humour. Probably because I've spent too long practising the black arts," he said, breaking into a smile. He lit a fresh cigarette while the old one still smouldered in his coffee cup saucer and a glob of ash fell onto his flies unnoticed.

I enjoyed my short stay with him and although he liked to give the impression that he had perfected the casual approach to any problem, there was a steely purpose to him.

Like Green, he was convinced that the Soviets had never had any good intentions towards us. If he knew of Green's mistress, he didn't let on and I thought it politic to say nothing. He struck me as a solitary remnant of a dying breed.

While in Vienna I kept in touch with the Nuremburg legal team, but no date had been set for Grundwall's trial. Lisa lacked a phone in the flat she shared with Greta, and although I rang the stage door number several times I failed to get her. Because of the uncertainty my life had an emptiness; nobody had trained me how to heal another's unhappiness, only to cause it.

SEVENTEEN

On my return to Berlin I could not rid myself of the feeling that I had made all the wrong choices. I missed the comradeship and comforts of my old unit, I even mourned the bleak familiarity of my bedroom in the hotel Kronprinzen, for the red wallpaper of my new billet only served to remind me of the copy of The Scarlet Letter I had bought the day I first encountered Grundwall. Sometimes I awoke expecting to find Lisa's face on the pillow beside me.

The first day back Rawnsley buttonholed me on my way to report to Graham. "In case you were thinking of raising the subject, don't," he said.

"What subject?"

"His girl," he said with a trace of irritation as though I should have been automatically tuned to his wavelength. "They killed her with a nerve gas, a type developed for the SS, which no doubt the KGB now use. Attacks the respiratory system, causes death in a matter of minutes."

"I suppose that's some small comfort. How did Graham receive that news?"

"No idea. He doesn't discuss it, nor do I wish to enquire."

His note of disapproval warned me that if he ever learned of my involvement with the Grundwall family, he would bracket me with Graham as another who only had himself to blame for getting involved with foreigners.

"Has anything been heard from the girl's contact since?"

"No, nothing."

"Who is he?"

"More likely who was he? A Pole. Hugh Miller put him in place originally and passed him to us to run. He was supposed to come in from the cold if the girl failed to make two consecutive drops."

"Miller believes our operation over here has been infiltrated."

"Yes, well, he's always pushed his 'there's a red-under-every-bed' theory. Convinced that London has more moles than the average lawn. And he could be right. I'm never certain who we're fucking or whether we're being fucked."

This dialogue continued later that same day when we were parked in a nondescript Volkswagen two hundred yards from Checkpoint Charlie, keeping observation on the East German border guards as they stopped and searched the human traffic entering and exiting our zone.

"One thing I've been wanting to ask you," I said. "How did Graham's girl bring out the information?"

"Micro film concealed in her sanitary towel."

"Original."

"You can say that. Prefer not to go there, but she got away with it." He dropped his field glasses into his lap and fished for a cigarette. "What did you make of old Hugh?"

"Cheerful old sod, I thought, despite the fact he believes his days are numbered."

"Really? Why is that?"

"He told me his prostate is dodgy. Never been quite sure what the prostate is or what it does."

"One of the Almighty's nastier tricks on us men," Rawnsley replied. "Only the size of a walnut apparently, but can be a killer. Poor old Miller. Always thought him a thundering bore, but wouldn't wish that on anybody."

As we watched, the Vopos dragged a young man out of a battered truck and spread-eagled him across the bonnet. An officer appeared from the blockhouse as a third Vopo trundled a wheeled mirror under the vehicle. Adjusting focus on my binoculars, I got a closer look at the man before he was frog-marched away.

"Why are they so bloody determined to stop their people getting to the West?" I said.

"I imagine they know that if they once relaxed there'd be a mass exodus." Rawnsley roamed the scene through his own glasses. "I'll tell you what's wrong with the Russians. They don't play cricket. There's something fundamentally missing in a race that doesn't play cricket."

"What a sage you are, Rawnsley," I said, for once daring to mock him.

"I just echo our fearless leader."

"How d'you read Graham?"

"He fancies himself as Polonius."

"Did you ever meet the girl?"

"Once. Briefly. I bumped into them both at the cinema. Can't say I thought she was worth risking a career for, but then it takes all sorts."

I plunged at that point, the need to confide in somebody, even Rawnsley, overcoming discretion. "I've got a girl in Hamburg. An actress."

If I thought this would provoke one of his sardonic comments, I was mistaken. He surprised me by merely commenting: "Is that so? My wife was an actress. She was in a play called Quiet Weekend when I met her. Ever see it?"

"No. I was taken to a pantomime once."

Rawnsley groaned. "Ghastly English convention, pantomimes. Likewise Peter Pan. I always prayed for Tinker Bell to die. Didn't you?"

"Who's Tinker Bell?"

"You're not serious? Didn't your Nanny read the bloody book to you?"

"I didn't have a nanny."

My answer threw him. "Good God. Really? How

extraordinary." He was silent for a few moments, hesitating, I imagined, between feeling sorry for me and being genuinely at a loss to understand how I had got this far without a normal upbringing.

"Is your wife in a play now?"

"Oh, no. I made her give it up when we got married and concentrate on being a proper mother."

"Did she mind that?"

"Well, if she did, she had to lump it. You can't mix these things," he said obliquely.

"D'you have children?"

"Yes."

"How many?"

"Three. Needed three attempts before I produced the son and heir. Put him down for Eton the moment he was born. That's why I've got my sights fixed on the Washington desk."

"That's a good posting, is it?"

"La crème. You're not Oxbridge, are you?"

"No," I said.

"Oh, that's right, I read your file. Strange the way we recruit these days. This used to be an occupation for gentlemen, like publishing." He seemed unaware of the offensiveness of the remark.

We resumed our watch. Two cyclists, a young boy and a girl, came into view and were flagged down by the Vopos. Instead of stopping they started to peddle furiously. Shots were fired and the boy careened around in erratic circles before crashing into one of the barriers and falling. A moment later the girl was brought down. Through our glasses we could see no signs of life from either of them. The whole incident had been like something in a silent film. Neither of us said much after that. There wasn't much to say.

EIGHTEEN

It was a time of waiting, a feeling of not knowing which way the pendulum would swing.

In the seven weeks since we had parted in Hamburg; Lisa had only written once, a sad little letter, such as a schoolgirl might pen to a first crush: 'The rehearsals are going well but Herr Director is still picking on me and we have had foul weather the past few days which means I get drenched walking to the theatre. Greta and I have eaten out twice on the money you gave me, really good food for a change and I think some of the other members of the cast are envious that I have you. I still feel badly about taking your money but perhaps one day I will earn enough myself to treat you. Your love is everything to me and I miss you very much, especially now, so don't forget me and write very often and give me any news about Vater. I think of little else with every day that passes. I will always love you.'

I attempted to write back something that would keep her hopes alive, though in my heart I knew that the eventual outcome could only bring grief. For separate reasons I felt unable to confide either in Graham or Rawnsley as I once had with Machell.

Hoping to push the situation to the back of my mind for a few hours, I put on my new suit and went to sample one of the new nightclubs that had been permitted to open. Graham had told me that they were making an effort to recapture something of the gaiety and decadence that had characterised pre-Nazi Berlin, but there was something ersatz about the

Blue Cockatoo, my random choice. It welcomed customers in the refurbished basement of a bombed building and had made an attempt to rekindle the atmosphere of Brecht's Mack The Knife, dim lighting throwing shadows on walls decorated with suggestive murals, red plush banquettes circling a small dance floor. These could be curtained off for clients wanting something more than the over-priced drinks.

A few couples were dancing to canned music in desultory fashion when I entered and was conducted to one of the banquettes past half a dozen flashily-dressed girls waiting expectantly at the bar. The moment I sat down a hand came around the curtains from the adjoining banquette to tug at my sleeve and a voice said: "Small world, eh, sport?"

I turned and found myself confronted by the unwelcome, grinning face of Chivers. He was with a girl young enough to be his daughter with a thin, lamb-to-the-slaughter expression.

"Why d'you think it is our paths cross so often?" he said.

"Sheer bad luck, I suppose."

"Oh, full marks, I like that. You always did have a droll sense of humour. Don't sit on your own, come and join us. This is Inga. Move over, darling girl and make room for my friend."

Accepting the invitation with reluctance, I eased myself in beside Inga. I caught a whiff of Chivers' overpowering after-shave.

"Let me buy you a drink. I see you're back in civvy street."

"No, just happen to be out of uniform tonight. Like you," I said pointedly.

"Still a Sergeant Major?"

"No, I was promoted.

"What are you now?"

"Captain."

"Well, congrats, sport. I should be in line for a leg up

shortly. So, what's your fancy Captain?" he asked as a waiter hovered. "We're on champagne."

"I'll have a Scotch."

"Bring a Scotch and another bottle of champers," Chivers said. He had his arm around Inga's neck and was fingering the lobe of her ear.

"Do you ever see First Officer Babs these days?" I asked.

"Who?"

"The Wren you were with the first time we met."

"Oh, her. No. Gone the way of all flesh, sport. I've transferred my unlimited charm to the natives, like little Inga here."

"What brings you to Berlin? Apart from the nookie that is."

"Nookie. What a lovely word. Haven't heard that in ages. Just flew in to check out a new business proposition. And by-the-way, I owe you a big thank you."

"You do? How's that?"

"Remember that letter I asked you to post way back?"

I arranged my face to express uncertainty. "Remind me."

"We bumped into each other at the docks and I entrusted you with an urgent letter."

"Oh, yes now I remember. And I stupidly forgot to post it."

"Happily it's not important now. You did me a favour as it happens. Had it not been for your fortuitous loss of memory, it would have been delivered and landed me in Queer Street. The scheme I was about to join turned out to be a con, but because of you I missed the deadline and my money never went in. If it had, I'd have lost the lot."

The drinks arrived at that moment and we clinked glasses. "Well, thank God, I had a lapse. And now you're onto to something new, are you?"

Chivers looked around before answering, but nobody was paying us any attention. A few couples still drifted aimlessly on the dance floor. "Strictly entre nous," he said confidentially, "cameras."

"Cameras?"

"Yes. Leitz, who made Leica's, ended up in the Soviet zone but the patents are no longer valid, so there's nothing to stop them being copied. The Yank I met here says he can cut me in and produce the things in Canada. People back home haven't been able to buy a decent camera for seven years. As you know, Leica's are the crème de la crème for the shutterbugs, sport, so one could clean up."

"Until the Russians catch on presumably."

"By then I'll have made a killing."

Like the previous get-rich-quick scheme I had saved him from, this sounded highly dubious. I was conscious that Inga was being totally ignored. "Are you a Berliner?" I asked her in German.

"Yes," she answered.

"How are you finding things now?"

She shrugged. "We have good days and bad."

"What sort of day is this?"

With a knowing smile she said: "It's too early to say."

"You're not muscling in on my date, are you, sport?" Chivers said.

"Wouldn't dream of it. How's life in Hamburg these days?"

"I'm getting it sorted. And you, are you enjoying the change of scenery? This must be a strange place. I want to take a look at the Russian zone before I head back."

I finished my whisky and stood up. "Well, thanks for the drink."

"Not going to make a night of it, sport? We could make it a foursome and have a good time."

"Not tonight." The idea of sharing his idea of a good time repelled me. "Good luck." My farewell was for Inga rather than Chivers.

As I climbed the stairs to the street a sudden gust of wind twisted dust and litter into a spiral that danced along the pavement ahead of me. The lights of the Western sectors bounced back off low clouds emphasising the blackness beyond. I felt my life was like that, sliced in two, darkness and light, like everybody I knew scarred by a secret history: Machell dreaming of his lost love child, Graham mourning his murdered mistress, Beth finding a sort of fulfilment in casual sex.

Lost in such thoughts I suddenly felt something sharp being jabbed into my back. I wheeled around to find myself confronted by a ragged man of my own age.

"Give me your money," he said in German. "Quick!" He again prodded me with the knife. "Give it to me or I'll kill you."

Keeping my movements deliberate and slow, I put a hand inside my jacket as though reaching for my wallet but, instead, feeling for my Walther in its shoulder holster and releasing the safety catch. As he menaced me again I whipped the gun out and pointed it straight at his forehead.

"Drop the knife and back off otherwise I'll blow your fucking head off," I shouted in German.

"Nein, bitte, entschuldige`n bitte," he said in a pleading whine, all aggression gone at sight of the gun. "Itch habe ein frau und kinde."

"Against the wall," I shouted. "Hands on your head."

The knife clattered to the pavement. With my free hand, I frisked him for any other weapons, but he had none. I looked both ways up the street, but there was no sign of a Military Police patrol. Now that my adrenalin level dropped, it wasn't anger I felt at him, just a sense of resignation.

"Absteigen," I said.

He turned around, unable to believe his luck.

"Absteigen," I repeated, "Raus! Schnell! " Then I reverted to shouting in English: "Go, you stupid berk, before I change my mind!"

126

"Danke, danke, "he said. As he moved off his legs buckled and he stumbled, nearly falling before breaking into a run. I watched until he disappeared from sight before putting my gun away.

That night I had a confused dream in which Lisa was together with Chivers, laughing, sharing confidences I was not party to. I stood apart, a passive spectator. The images stayed with me while I shaved the next morning and I twice nicked myself. As soon as I could I rang the theatre desperate to hear Lisa's voice again, but although I got through she was not available to take the call. A telex came in from Nuremberg stating that Grundwall's trial had been set to begin in three days time and that I was subpoenaed to attend as a prosecution witness.

"Bloody inconvenient," Graham said. "Who is this character?"

"A man I identified as an SS officer. He proved to be wanted for crimes at Auschwitz."

"How long will they keep you there?"

"As long as it takes, I imagine."

I packed and caught the daily courier flight to Nuremberg. It was dark when it touched down. A member of the British prosecution team met me and took me to the Grand Hotel, where most of the lawyers were housed. After I had checked in he gave me a thorough briefing on the procedures I had to follow together with a file outlining the prosecution's case plus photographs of some of the experiments carried out by Mengele and his associates. After a quick supper I retired early and studied everything I had been given. It was then the realisation struck me that I was a prisoner of Fate as surely as Grundwall.

NINETEEN

Ironically, the nineteenth century prison at Nuremberg, attached to the Palace of Justice, had escaped major damage from our air attacks. The accused were housed on two floors of one wing, and kept under twenty four-hour suicide watch.

I was not allowed any contact with Grundwall, but I was granted permission to visit the cellblock and observe him through the small observation slit in the door. His cell was illuminated by a bare bulb hanging out of reach high up on the ceiling and kept burning night and day. It was sparsely furnished with an iron bedstead, a straw mattress, washbasin, slop pail, small table and wooden chair. Peering through the slit I saw somebody who bore scant resemblance to the man I had first encountered in that Hamburg bookshop. Grundwall lay on the bed in the foetal position, legs drawn up to his chest. He seemed diminished in size.

"Does he give you any trouble?" I asked the burly young GI Guard.

"No. Never talks. Just takes his chow without a word. Spends most of his time writing. The sooner they're tried and I'm outta here the happier I'll be. Can't wait to get State side again."

"Where's your home?"

"Austin, Texas. Know it?"

"No, I don't. I've never been to America."

"Great country. Sure beats this shit hole."

Grundwall's trial was scheduled to begin the following day, but the young guard told me that, during the night, despite tight surveillance, a recently convicted prisoner had managed to commit suicide, hanging himself with a rope made from strips torn from his blanket. As a result all trials were temporarily suspended while an enquiry was held and the security measures tightened further.

"Pity they don't all top themselves," he said. "Save us a hell of a lot of trouble. Goodbye and good riddance."

Left to my own devices, I was glad to accept an invitation to have a meal with one of the British team, a Major Jones. He voiced the same opinion as the young guard. "Pity he cheated the hangman. Still one less out of the way."

With his sunken eyes and thinning hair, Jones had the haunted look of somebody who had been forced to witness too much horror, a surmise that proved true when he confessed he sometimes had to anesthetise himself with alcohol at night – "Just to blot out what I've had to listen to. And I keep asking myself 'What if?'"

"What if?"

"Yes. Think about it. Quislings in Norway, the Vichy French, Mussolini's followers, they all handed over Jews for the gas chambers. If we'd been defeated and occupied, would we have been the same? That ever occurred to you?"

"No, but it's a depressing thought." I said.

"I'm not going back to my law practice after this," Jones continued. "I never want to see the inside of a court room again.

"What will you do?"

"Emigrate, somewhere far away like New Zealand, take up sheep farming, any bloody thing rather than be reminded of this."

He pushed his half-eaten pork chop to one side. "Whose trial are you here for?"

"A man called Grundwall."

"Ah, yes, the good Doctor, otherwise known as SS Obergruppenfuehrer Grundwall."

"Are you leading for the prosecution?"

"No. Westbury's down for that. Good man. Very thorough. What's your involvement?"

"I was the one who first identified him. I met him by chance, in a bookshop of all places. Seemed harmless enough, a professor at the University in Hamburg. Totally different from the SS types I'd been dealing with."

"Most of them look harmless enough out of their death's head uniform."

"How many of them admit their guilt?"

"I've only come across one," Jones said. "The standard defence is to plead they were just carrying out orders. That doesn't wash with me. The Einsatgruppen squads, maybe, They were usually drawn from infantry units and stood down when the endless killing finally sickened them, or else they were shot like their victims. But the Grundwall's of this world, they're a different breed altogether."

"Will he get the death sentence if convicted?"

"Depends. The majority of death sentences have been commuted of late. That's another reason why I want out. Revenge eats into you. Instant revenge I can understand. Survivors of the camps lynching their guards, yes, but once you institutionalise revenge it becomes one with the crimes that prompted it."

Jones downed his drink and surveyed the empty glass. "That's enough philosophising. This is on me." He took out a wad of dollar notes secured with a rubber band. Seeing my look as he peeled off a few, he said: "Nobody wants our official currency, but they love these. Don't we all? Welcome to the new world."

TWENTY

What struck me on entering the courtroom was how cold it was, as though over long months the litany of horror released had chilled the very walls. I took my seat in the witness section. There were a number of stenographers and translators but only a sprinkling of Press: the trials no longer commanded worldwide media attention except in certain German and Jewish newspapers.

Proceedings were delayed while the President and the four alternate judges heard submissions from the defence lawyers on a series of legal technicalities that were beyond my understanding. When these were completed, the court was declared in session and Grundwall was brought in. I sank down in my seat, anxious to avoid immediate eye contact. He was manacled to a guard, the manacles only removed once he was in the dock. Two American Military Policemen remained on either side of him. I studied his demeanour as he took stock of his surroundings and there was a certain arrogance in the way he held himself. I thought, it was his sperm that made Lisa, this man on trial for his life.

Grundwall took the oath in a low voice. Then Westbury rose and addressed him. "Please state your name."

"Karl Gustave Grundwall."

"Speak louder, please."

"Karl Gustave Grundwall."

"How do you wish to conduct yourself, in German or English?"

"I am willing to answer in English if that is the wish of

the court," Grundwall replied.

"The choice is yours. You can use the facilities of the simultaneous translation. You will find headphones by your side.

"I will answer in English to the best of my ability," Grundwall said. "If I do not understand any question put to me I will ask for it to be repeated in German."

The President then asked Westbury whether Grundwall had been judged fit to plead?

"Yes, your Honour."

"Karl Gustave Grundwall," the President said, "how do you plead to the charges brought against you?"

Grundwall began, "Before I reply, I wish to state..." but got no further before the President interrupted him.

"Defendants are not entitled to make statements at this stage. You must plead Guilty or Not Guilty."

Grundwall lent forward, clutching the edge of the dock. "I enter a plea of innocence. I stand here the victim of a mistake."

"You must answer Guilty or Not Guilty," the President repeated. "No other plea is acceptable to the court."

Grundwall stared around as if seeking help from anybody present, before finally uttering 'Not guilty", first in English, then in German.

The President then addressed him. I had no means of telling whether it was a stock speech which he delivered to all those who came before him, but he delivered it as though for the first time and there was no mistaking the controlled vehemence in his voice.

"Karl Gustave Grundwall you have been brought to this court to be tried under the jurisdiction and authority of the International Military Tribunal, charged with crimes against humanity. The totality of these crimes, which, over many months this court has been forced to hear and will no doubt continue to hear is without precedence in history. You and others before you belonging to the infamous SS have stood in that dock to answer for atrocities arising from a sustained campaign of brutality such as the world has not witnessed since the pre-Christian era. Indeed some of these acts reached such proportions of bestiality that they aroused the sleeping strength of imperilled civilization and acquired a worldwide familiarity. By virtue of the indictment under which you are charged this Tribunal will confront you with incontrovertible evidence of foul and shameful treatment of concentration camp victims over a prolonged period. The prosecution will produce filmed evidence, together with personal testimony to illustrate the methods employed to maim, starve, mutilate and kill. Such methods included male victims being immersed in freezing baths until their body temperature was reduced below 28 degrees centigrade, after which, close to death, they were 'rewarmed' by hot baths and forced to have sexual intercourse with female inmates. Here Nazi degeneracy might be thought to have reached its nadir, but this was not the limit of degeneracy. It will be shown that you and your medical colleagues went further, progressing to experiments on living children as young as two years of age, subjecting them to such unimaginable horrors as to completely refute the universal Hippocratic oath the medical profession is sworn to uphold. In order that you be left in no doubt as to the substance and truth of such crimes as I have described, it is the intention of this court to show you filmed material. Please turn and face the screen."

Grundwall now shuffled around to face the portable screen. The overhead light were extinguished and a court official started the 16mm projector. The film began with a train arriving at the Auschwitz railway siding, then shots of a new intake being disembarked, the packed bodies of men, women and children tumbling out of the cattle trucks and herded into lines by SS dog handlers. They were subsequently divided by sex and age into separate groups, the older women being the first group to be marched away. They filed past musicians in prison garb playing an accompaniment to their last journey. The grainy images had a sickening familiarity for me. The next sequence showed the younger women, now naked, filing past an SS officer who made instant selections, some waved to the right, some to the left. Infant children were forcibly removed from their mothers, any resistance savagely dealt wIth. The footage was without sound giving it an extra dimension of horror. Now, Allied footage, shot post liberation, showed stacks of emaciated dead, pyramids of skeletal bodies layered in grotesque angles to each other, the skulls of some pushed into the sunken genitalia of others. Finally images of a hospital ward where half a dozen small naked children lay in metal beds without benefit of any covering. Three men in white coats partially unbuttoned so that their SS uniforms were clearly visible paused by the bed of an infant girl. Her head had been shaved. While examining her they appeared to be sharing a joke. The film changed to an autopsy room dominated by a stainless steel table and bearing a close similarity to the photograph that had first alerted me to Grundwall's involvement. Another small, naked girl was lying on the table and a man, possibly Mengele himself, administered an injection into her swollen abdomen. The child immediately went into convulsions, her abused body half rising from the table in a violent reaction. And with that the film ended and the main court lights were switched on again.

The President now called Westbury to commence the case for the prosecution. Like Jones, Westbury, by his general demeanour and the tone in which he put his questions, struck me as somebody who would never again believe in goodness. Months later I obtained a verbatim transcript of the trial, and it is from that record that I have been able to relive what took place.

Westbury began with: "May this court take it you are familiar with the scenes in the film we have just witnessed?"

Grundwall gave a mumbled reply.

"I'm sorry, can you please repeat that?"

"Not those exact scenes."

"Others like them then?"

"At the end of hostilities the British authorities forced civilians to attend screenings of such material."

"And did you attend such screenings?"

"Yes."

"What was the general reaction to them?"

"Shock and revulsion."

"Was that your own reaction?"

"Yes."

"And yet they could not have come as a surprise to you, could they?" He opened a file. "From September 1943 until February 1945 we can establish you were a member of the SS staff at the Auschwitz-Berkenau extermination camp. It therefore follows that you must have witnessed at first hand incidents identical to those depicted on film.

"No. That is not true."

"What is not true? That you were a member of the SS?"

"No, that I did not personally witness such incidents."

"Let me ask you this then, did you recognise any of your fellow SS officers shown in the film?"

"No, I did not."

"None of them?"

"No."

"Perhaps these enlargement of frames taken from the film will enable you to reconsider. I must remind you that you are on oath. It might also refresh your memory if I gave you their names." He consulted another paper. "Doctors Mengele, Cleber and Kremer."

The enlargements were handed to Grundwall. He put on his spectacles, I remember, and peered at them for a long time before answering: "I recognise Doctor Mengele, but I am not certain about the other two. The camp administrative staff changed frequently."

"It is known that the said Dr.Mengele arrived at Auschwitz in May 1942 and remained there during the entire period you were also a member of the staff. In that same year, 1942, Dr.Mengele commenced medical experiments on living Jews and others he deemed suitable. He used the pretext of medical science to carry out various painful experiments, mainly on children and with particular attention to twins. Were you aware that he was carrying out such experiments?"

"No, I was not."

"Although technically Dr.Mengele was your superior and you must have had contact with him on a daily basis, you knew nothing of the work he was carrying out?"

"I knew that a separate medical facility existed, but my day to day responsibilities were confined to the health and welfare of the administrative staff families, the majority of whom lived outside the camp."

"Are you asking the court to believe that you never came into contact with Mengele?"

"As I have stated he ran a separate facility."

"And you are stating on oath that you were not aware of the true purpose of that facility?"

"That is correct."

"I find it hard to believe there was no exchange of information between yourself and Mengele. I am seeking to establish how the administration of the camp functioned." Westbury kept his voice even. "Since you were part of that administration, it is not unreasonable to assume that, in order for the daily workings of the camp to function efficiently, there would have been regular exchanges between the various bodies involved. Yes?"

"If you say so." Grundwall replied.

"Let me ask you this, what did you believe was the actual purpose of the camp?"

"I believed it was a correction facility for criminals."

"I will give you time to reconsider your answer since it is patently false and you must know it is false."

"That was the official designation."

"I see. A 'correction facility'. And you had no problem in accepting that?"

"No."

"I put it to you that Auschwitz-Berkenau and other camps of a like nature existed, not as correction facilities but as extermination facilities for the mass murder of Jews, gypsies, homosexuals and others considered a threat to the Reich."

"I had nothing to do with that."

"That is not what I asked you."

Grundwall faltered. "Will you repeat the question, please."

"It was an extermination camp, was it not? One of many facilities built for the express purpose of the Endlosung, the Final Solution."

"The term 'Endlosung' is not one I am familiar with."

"Then let me elucidate. In January 1942, during what subsequently became known as The Wannsee Conference, Reinhardt Heydrich announced his appointment as Plenipotentiary for The preparation of the Final Solution of the European Jewish question. At that conference the means of disposing of eleven million Jews was agreed, and decisions taken to put in place the apparatus needed. Death camps were to be built in remote areas to carry out Hitler's stated aim for the complete annihilation of the Jewish population. Although remote, each site was to be serviced by a railway line. Camps were located at Cilmno, Belzec, Treblinka, Sobibor in the first instance and later the existing facility at Auschwitz was enlarged, an extension being built in the birch wood known as Berkenau. Hence all was in place for the implementation of the Endlosung? Is that now clear?"

Grundwall gave a mumbled 'Yes.'

"Do you wish me to explain further?"

"No."

"Then let me repeat my original question. Will you now agree that the term 'correction facility' is a false description, and that your answer was a deliberate evasion?"

"It was not intended as an evasion."

"Then what was it?"

"I believed what I was told."

"You believed what you were told," Westbury mimicked him slowly. "How often this court has heard that defence. In other words you preferred to believe what you had been told rather than accept the evidence of your own eyes?" He paused for dramatic effect, letting Grundwall wriggle on the hook. He searched for another file, extracting from it a photograph. He moved to the dock and handed it to Grundwall. "Will you confirm that is a photograph of the railway line and siding at Auschwitz."

Grundwall nodded and said "Yes."

"It was here that the line terminated was it not? It was at this siding that trains regularly arrived crammed with new victims for the gas chambers. As we witnessed on the film, a selection process was carried out immediately after they arrived. A number of the healthier young males would be saved for slave labour, but the majority would be gassed within a few hours, cynically led to believe they being taken to a delousing shower whereas, in reality, they were herded into death chambers and sprayed with lethal Zyclon B gas. So," he continued relentlessly, "do you still contend that these processes were unknown to you?"

I leant forward, concentrating on Grundwall's expression during this. I tried to imagine what was going on inside his head; how could he refute Westbury's systematic, clinical stripping away of his supposed ignorance?"

"I had no personal knowledge of those procedures."

"No knowledge?"

"I was never present when such alleged procedures were carried out."

"Physically present or not, let us take it step by step. You knew that trains arrived on a more or less daily basis, did you not?"

"Yes."

"And that they brought new victims – or as you prefer to describe them, 'criminal elements' – to the camp, even though a proportion were infant children and could not be so described."

"I did not believe they were victims."

"Really? What did you believe them to be?"

"I was told they were taking part in a relocation programme for undesirables."

"That is an original way of describing mass murder," Westbury said dryly. "Were you aware that these unfortunates underwent a selection process to determine whether they had an instant or slow death?"

"I have already stated I was never involved in the day to day running of the camp."

"That does not answer me. Were you aware?"

"No."

"Not even as a passive observer?"

"No."

"I find that difficult to believe."

"It is the truth."

"I intend to prove it is less than the truth, since it defies logic. I shall produce witnesses who will testify that your superior, Dr. Mengele, conducted his own selections, compelling victims to parade naked for him in order for him to determine who could further his experiments and that you witnessed this on more than one occasion. Do you wish to reconsider your previous answers?"

"I have stated the extent of my involvement."

"So, when infant children were selected and taken to Mengele's special medical facility, you had no idea why they had been selected?"

"I assumed they were sick children who needed medical attention."

"You assumed. " Westbury drank from a glass of water. "I put it to you that you are lying. Is it not a fact that your superior, Doctor Josef Mengele, who headed The Shutzstaffeln branch of the SS determined what duties his staff performed, and that you were present when his experiments were performed?"

"All senior staff at the facility was compelled to be members of the SS."

"That is not what I asked you. Were you or were you not present?"

"I was aware that he conducted normal clinical investigations in an effort to stamp out epidemics of typhus and spotted fever in the camp. Young children were always amongst the first to contract these diseases."

"We are back to defining the degree of awareness. How aware were you?"

"Typhus was a major cause of death in the camp."

"So was death by Zyclone B. I ask again, were you a witness to the exact procedures used by Mengele?"

"Only as an occasional observer."

"Ah!" Westbury exclaimed. "We are moving closer to the truth."

I sat in admiration of Westbury's adversarial skills, the way in which he had slowly extracted an admission from Grundwall. At the same time I was amazed how long Grundwall had managed to hold out from making any admission.

Resuming, Westbury asked: "Were you then only an 'occasional observer' when Mengele, caused phenol, petrol, chloroform and air to be injected into children he deemed degenerate, causing death, and that subsequently he ordered that the cadavers be boiled so that the flesh could be stripped from their bones and the skeletons sent to the Anthropological Museum in Berlin?"

Grundwall swayed in the dock and one of the guards steadied him. It was the first time I had seen him falter.

"Further, we know from testimony given in previous trials that Mengele's special interest in twins meant that he injected a toxic agent into their eyes in a perverted quest to determine genetic differences. As somebody who trained as a doctor, would you agree that such methods are not usually associated with the treatment of typhus or spotted fever?"

"Even though I trained as a doctor, I had limited practical experience, and therefore never gained any firsthand knowledge of the standard treatment of typhus."

"But presumably during your limited time as a doctor, you had access to medical textbooks?"

"Yes, of course."

"And did any text book you studied recommend an injection of petrol as a standard treatment for anything?"

The chilling sarcasm in Westbury's voice allowed of no answer.

"I am waiting."

Grundwall finally said: "Will you repeat the question?"

"Willingly. I asked if anywhere in your studies you came across textual evidence of petrol being used to cure any infectious disease?"

"No, I did not."

"Therefore were you not appalled to witness, even as a casual observer, Dr.Mengele treat typhus by such a method?"

"I had no influence over the way in which he decided on treatments."

Westbury was not going to let it go. "I ask again, were you not horrified?"

"I thought some of his methods were unorthodox."

"So unorthodox, in fact, they killed rather than cured. How is it then you did not protest about his methods?"

"It was not possible for me to question his actions."

"Not possible? Why?"

"All SS officers were required to swear an oath of obedience."

"But, as a man of medicine were you not bound by a stronger oath – namely the Hippocratic oath?"

Grundwall seemed to be searching for his answer. "I acted as I was compelled to do under military law."

"Therefore, by your passive acceptance of such practices it follows that you condoned such acts."

Grundwall did not respond and the President intervened. "The prisoner will answer the question."

"I submit, it wasn't possible for me to interfere," Grundwall said.

"By that, are you saying you were aware of what was taking place but were powerless or unwilling to condemn such matters?"

"Powerless."

"It is a slender distinction," Westbury said scathingly. "Thus, ibso facto you became an accessory to the crimes committed." He then switched his attack. "Can we establish how you came to be an officer in the SS. Did you volunteer?"

"No. When called to serve I was given no choice."

"Do you accept that the SS was a body feared not only by enemies of the State but also the ordinary general public? That it was brought into existence for one purpose and one purpose only, namely to become an instrument of coercion and terror?"

"It was necessary to keep order in a time of total war."

"But it was in existence before the war, was it not? And you must have known that, from the moment you wore the death's head insignia it set you apart from your fellow citizens. Were you proud to wear SS unIform?"

"Proud?"

"Yes. Did it give you a feeling of superiority?

"I did not think of it in those terms. In any case I had no choice in the matter."

"No, that's right, you did whatever you were told, didn't you? And if you were required to observe the methods used by Dr. Mengele to eliminate typhus, you again did as you were told."

The defence counsel rose and objected. "Counsel is leading."

"I will rephrase that," Westbury said. He took another drink of water. "I put it to you that throughout you have sought to depict your own role as a passive observer, somehow unaware of the real purpose of the camp. Are you still of the opinion that Auschwitz was a correction facility for criminals?"

Grundwall answered slowly. I could see that he was now being ultra careful in his answers. "You have demonstrated that it had a wider purpose."

"And can the court take it that you do not dispute the fact that the woods at Berkenau housed multiple crematoria?"

"I accept that."

"Good. We are making progress. What do you think was the wider purpose of such installations?"

"The most effective way of ensuring a lethal epidemic is contained is by cremating infected corpses."

"Are you saying that the sole purpose was the containment of disease?"

"That was my understanding, although I was aware that not all deaths were the result of disease."

"What were they the result of?"

"In the closing stages of the war the Central Government was forced to drastically reduce the food ration for the civilian population as well as those confined in the camp. The death rate was accelerated by malnutrition."

"You mean the inmates were deliberately starved to death?"

"No, you are twisting my words."

"I apologise." Westbury turned to the bench. "No further questions."

The President consulted his fellow judges, then adjourned the trial for that day.

TWENTY ONE

Grundwall looked relaxed when he arrived in the dock the following morning, as though convinced he had acquitted himself well the first day. The proceedings were opened by the Defence Counsel, a wiry little man named Fraser with a Scottish accent.

"Professor Grundwall, I understand you have a medical degree."

"That is correct."

"Where did you practice?"

"In Manheim, but only for a period of ten months as a locum."

"What does the term 'locum' signify?"

"A doctor who stands in on a temporary basis when the regular practitioner is absent."

"But you only did this for a short period?"

"Yes. I found casual work did not provide enough to support my family. With a child on the way, I took a teaching post with a regular salary."

"I believe that at the same time you also attempted to pursue a literary career?"

"I'd hardly call it a career, but, yes, I was lucky enough to have a collection of my poetry published. Although it was well received, it did not make my fortune."

"And your academic career prospered up until the outbreak of war, is that correct?"

"Yes. By then we had moved to Hamburg and I had been offered a position on the faculty at the University."

"Which you later resumed?"

"Yes."

"Let me turn to your war service. The prosecution has made great play with the fact that you did not serve in the Wehrmacht, but instead joined the SS."

"I did not join The SS voluntarily, I was directed into it."

"Would you have preferred to have joined a fighting unit?"

"Had I been given the chance, yes, like my father in the previous war. But of course I had to go where I was told."

"Did you have any choice where you served?"

"No, I did not."

"And you were sent to the camp known as Auschwitz-Berkenau?"

"Yes."

"Prior to your arrival were you aware that such a camp existed?"

"No. I was informed it was a labour camp for criminals and that I would be responsible for the welfare of the camp staff."

"And those, in fact, were your duties during your entire stay there?"

"Yes," Grundwall answered confidently. He seemed content with the line Fraser was taking.

"Therefore it came as a surprise to you to find large numbers of women and children being brought to the camp."

Westbury was immediately on his feet. "Objection. Counsel is leading."

"Sustained."

Fraser corrected myself. "What was your reaction when you discovered that, in addition to the criminal element, women and children were also present?"

"It troubled me."

The President looked up, frowning, from writing his notes. Quickly aware his response had been inadequate,

Grundwall added: "I thought it quite wrong."

"Did you make your feelings known to Commandant Hoess?"

"Yes, I expressed my concern at the general unsanitary conditions."

"And?"

Grundwall looked momentarily perplexed and Fraser asked: "Did Hoess' implement any changes in response to your concerns?"

"I believe certain changes were made as a result."

Westbury again got to his feet. "May it please the court? I find the accused's answers to this line of questioning deliberately evasive. It is inconceivable that he was unaware that women and children were brought to the camp for one purpose only, namely to be put to death.

"Yes, Mr. Fraser," the President responded. "I do not think the approach you are taking aids the accused's case. I suggest you move on."

Fraser looked temporarily thrown and consulted his papers before continuing. "How long was it after your arrival that you realised the true purpose of the camp?"

Grundwall had been answering quickly and confidently until this point, but now hesitated.

"Weeks, months?" Fraser prompted.

"Within a few weeks," Grundwall answered after a pause.

"And how did this discovery affect you?"

"I was shocked, disgusted."

"Did you discuss your feelings with your fellow officers?"

"No."

"Why was that?"

Again, a hesitation. "Unlike me they were committed SS. I did not embrace their ethos."

"So did you keep your feelings to yourself?"

"Yes. It was dangerous to express opinions that conflicted with official policy, so I did not socialise with my fellow officers more than was necessary. Hoess and the staff did not live on the camp. We were quartered outside the camp perimeter. Some of us lived with our wives and families."

"Your own wife and child, did they live with you?"

"My wife, yes, for a period. Not our teenage daughter. We had sent her to a relative in the countryside to escape the bombing."

"During the period she was with you did you confide your misgivings to your wife?"

"No, I judged it safer for her not to be made party to my worries. The fact that she was the wife of an SS officer did not automatically bestow immunity. Everybody was trapped in a vice of fear from informers. Even letters to loved ones were best 'coded' for safety. Distrust reached paranoid levels. Hoess had one of the staff shot for expressing the view that the war could never be won."

"Was your wife aware of the existence of the crematoriums?"

"I concealed their true function from her."

Westbury rose. "Objection. The court has heard ample verbal evidence that nobody within a wide vicinity could have been unaware of the distinctive smell of burning flesh. The crematoriums operated day and night and day and the smoke from the stacks was clearly visible."

"Sustained."

Fraser then asked: "Did your wife ever meet Dr. Mengele?"

"I think on one occasion, when she arrived and attended a welcoming party."

"Was she ever made aware of Mengele's activities by you or others?"

Grundwall's reply was guarded. "If I discussed him at all

it would have been to explain that he and his team were there to contain the spread of diseases."

"Did the wives gossip amongst themselves?"

Grundwall looked puzzled. "Gossip?"

"Did they socialise with your wife?"

"Yes, I imagine some of them did."

The President interrupted. "Where is this line of questioning taking us?"

"I am attempting to ascertain whether the accused's wife could have learned the true nature of Mengele's role from others," Fraser said.

"Very well. I will allow it. Continue."

"Could your wife have learned from sources other than yourself?"

Grundwall said. "Had she learned such things she would have discussed them with me. She did not."

"After the end of hostilities when the existence of Auschwitz became common knowledge, did you then discuss them with her?"

"Like everybody else we were compelled to attend newsreel screenings, and afterwards she questioned me. I remember she asked, 'Is that why you sent me away?'"

"How did you answer her?"

"I said, 'Yes, it was to protect you'"

"And your daughter. How was she affected?"

I leaned forward to concentrate on Grundwall's reply. "My daughter knew nothing of my time at Auschwitz. This was something my wife and I agreed upon. As far as Lisa was concerned I had spent the war as a translator."

Fraser consulted his junior in a whispered exchange before continuing. "Let us now turn To, Exhibit 764B, the photograph, showing you with Mengele and one other doctor. The prosecution maintain that it establishes you were present when he carried out experiments on children."

Grundwall became animated, thumping the edge of the

dock. "That is untrue. I deny it categorically. I was only ever visited Mengele's special block on Hoess' orders, and I never took part in any of his experiments."

"You realise you are testifying on oath."

"I do."

"Then let me ask you again. Was there any occasion when, under orders or not, you actively took part in the inhumane experiments instigated by and performed by Dr. Mengele?"

"No, I did not."

I thought, am I listening to the lies of a man fighting for his life, or should I believe him? If I had to sit in judgement, which way would I vote?

"Thank you. No further questions," Fraser said and sat down.

The President said: "Are you ready to call your first witness, Counsel?"

"Yes," Westbury said. "I call Captain Seaton."

I got to my feet, and walked to the witness stand to take the oath. Grundwall never took his eyes off me.

"Please give you name and rank."

"Alex Charles Seaton, Captain, Intelligence Corps."

"Captain Seaton, in April of this year were you serving as a member of a Field Security unit based in Hamburg?"

"Yes, I was."

"What were your duties?"

"My main duties consisted of seeking and interrogating ex-members of The SS, Gestapo and other proscribed organisations who were still at large."

"And what was the object of such interrogations?"

"To identify the perpetrators of war crimes." Then I added: "It was often a question of sorting the wheat from the chaff."

"How would you define 'the wheat?'"

"Those who had so far escaped detection by assuming bogus identities."

"And the chaff?"

"Those who, after interrogation, were given a clean bill of health and allowed to resume their civilian occupations."

"In which category did you put the accused?"

"Neither, for the reason he was never brought before me for interrogation. From his file I understand that he was questioned by others, and given clearance, but I had no knowledge of it."

Westbury handed the vital photograph to me. "Have you seen this photograph before?"

"Yes, I have."

"Please tell the court the circumstances whereby it was first brought to you attention."

"It formed part of a batch of material passed to us from the War Crimes department of the United States Army for cross-reference."

"Did you examine it personally?"

"Yes."

"And what was the result of that examination?"

"It was my belief that one of the men shown was the accused."

"Karl Grundwall?"

"That is correct."

"On what did you base your identification?"

"I had met the accused on several occasions."

"Under that name?"

"Yes."

"How did that come about?"

"I had made his acquaintance by chance some months earlier in a second-hand bookshop where we discovered a mutual love of literature. Later he invited me back to his home."

"Why did you accept such an invitation?"

"The rules regarding fraternisation had been relaxed. I thought he was an intelligent, cultured man and up until then

I had had no opportunity to socialise with ordinary German civilians and I welcomed a chance to discover how they had lived under the Nazi yoke."

"That is what you believed him to be, an ordinary civilian?"

"Yes."

"During these meetings did you have any reason to suspect that he was in fact an ex-SS officer who had chosen to conceal the role he played in the war?"

"None whatsoever. He had introduced himself as being a Professor of Philosophy on the faculty of Hamburg University. Mindful of my responsibilities, I checked this and found he was indeed a member of the faculty and had resumed his academic career shortly before the end of hostilities."

"Prior to that photograph being brought to your attention did the accused, by any casual remark or action cause you to change your first impression of him?"

"No. My duties demanded that I remained suspicious of anybody I came in contact with until satisfied of their innocence. , I met with the accused on several occasions, but he never gave me any reason to doubt his sincerity. During talks we had together he convinced me he was genuinely horrified by the revelations of the Final Solution."

"He talked about the Final Solution with you, did he?"

"It would be untrue to say that he used the term 'Final Solution' to me, but he questioned me closely about the concentration camps, in particular Bergen-Belsen since my unit had taken part in the liberation of that camp."

"Did that seem odd to you?"

"No. I believed he wanted to be convinced that I had first-hand knowledge that the camps existed and his interest was motivated by the shame he felt."

"Following your examination of the photograph, what action did you take?"

"After further examination of it, I made my opinion known to my commanding officer, Lt.Colonel Machell. He in turn returned the photograph to the American authorities and asked them to carry out further verification checks. Subsequently he was informed my initial identification had been substantiated by the Jewish War Crimes Bureau who had obtained positive identification from ex-inmates of Auschwitz."

"Armed with this confirmation, did you confront the accused?"

"No, I did not."

"Why was that?"

"By then the matter had been taken out of my hands. I had no further contact with him."

"Thank you."

Fraser rose to cross-examine. He began immediately with the line Machell had said the defence would use.

"Captain Seaton, what is your relationship with Lisa Grundwall, the daughter of the accused?"

"That of a close friend."

"A close friend. Wouldn't it be more accurate to describe it as a relationship of an intimate, sexual nature?"

Westbury was quickly on his feet. "Objection. Irrelevance."

"Sustained." The President addressed Fraser: "Counsel, I will allow a certain latitude if you pursue this line of questioning, but I must warn you I will rule out conjecture."

"Thank you, my Lord." Fraser turned to me again. "Captain, you have admitted that you accepted the accuser's hospitality and visited his home."

"Yes."

"On how many occasions?"

"Two to the best of my recollection. Perhaps three, I am not sure."

"And on each of these occasions did you give him and his family gifts?"

"Yes."

"What kind of gifts?"

"I took them some coffee, cigarettes, soap and chocolate."

"Black market gifts in other words?"

"No. They were gifts, I did not sell them. They were part of my own legitimate entitlement and supplementary to my own needs."

"Did you use such gifts to progress your relationship with the daughter, Lisa Grundwall?"

"Not consciously."

"You did not think of them as bribes which would advance your cause?"

"No. I did not. Indeed when I first visited the accused's home I had no idea he had a daughter."

"Even so, would I be correct in saying that Fraulein Grundwall was grateful for the gifts you brought her?"

"Of course. She had been deprived of chocolate for a long time."

"Can we turn to a leave period when Fraulein Grundwall accompanied you to a Gasthof in Krumpendorf, Austria. Did you occupy the same bedroom on that occasion?"

"Yes."

"Did intimacy take place in that room?"

"We were in love."

"I must ask you to answer the question."

"I prefer to say we made love."

The President chimed in at that moment. "Counsel, I fail to see where these questions are leading us. We are not here to consider the morals of the witness, nor his relationship with the daughter of the accused. This is not a divorce court. Please confine your examination to matter pertinent to the indictments."

Flustered, Fraser leafed through his papers. "Captain Seaton, you have stated that the accused expressed a sense of shame at the Nazi treatment of the Jewish population."

"Yes. He spoke of collective guilt, which I took to mean that the entire German nation shared that guilt. He spoke of it taking a hundred years for Germany to atone and that, even then, the crimes should not be forgiven."

"Were you convinced of his sincerity?"

"At the time, yes."

"Having heard his testimony in this court, do you continue to believe in that sincerity?"

I turned to the bench for guidance. "The witness is not required to answer," the President pronounced.

"Let me rephrase that," Fraser said. "You have heard the accused say on oath that he played no part in the crimes he is standing trial for. Did his answers convince you?"

"They were consistent with his general defence."

"You believed him then?"

"I do not think it is up to me to believe or disbelieve. That is the function of those sitting in judgement."

"But you must have formed an opinion."

I looked to the bench, but the President was writing and allowed Fraser to continue. "May I remind you that the prisoner is accused of crimes which, if he is convicted, carry the maximum penalty of death by hanging. I would also remind you that you have stated that, prior to his arrest you did not consider him capable of such crimes. That is true, is it not?"

"Yes. At that time I had no reason to suppose he committed any such crimes."

"So I am asking you, if your opinion has altered after listening to the prisoner's testimony."

"My opinion is immaterial."

Fraser pursued this course, attempting to draw me out, but I resisted and was finally allowed to stand down and the court was adjourned for lunch. As Grundwall was taken down to the cells he gave me one last, hard look.

TWENTY TWO

When the court reassembled for the afternoon session Westbury called the first of his other witnesses, a small white-haired man of indeterminate age who walked to the witness box with the aid of two sticks. Seeing him brought back vivid memories of the time I had been at Belsen; I found I was choked with emotion. He was sworn in with the assistance of an interpreter. Both Grundwall and I donned headphones.

"Please give your name."

"Josef Rajzman."

"What is your nationality?

"Polish."

"Are you Jewish?"

"Yes."

"You have a number tattooed on your wrist, do you not?"

"Yes."

"What does that tattoo signify?"

"That I was number 7568 in Auschwitz."

"How long were you in Auschwitz?"

"Four months."

"When was that?"

"December 1944 until we were liberated."

"And previous to that?

"Treblinka."

"Was that another concentration camp?"

"Yes."

"Have you any explanation why you survived while so many others perished?"

"God looked down on me. "

"What was your function in the camp?"

The word 'function' confused Raizman, and Westbury changed it to: "What were your duties in the camp?"

"I buried the dead."

"And did the dead you buried die from natural causes?"

Raizman listened to the translation, and then became agitated. "No, no, no! They were murdered."

"How were they murdered?"

"Gassed. Sometimes shot. "

"Including children?"

"Many children. "

"And women?"

"Yes, women. Many. Everybody was murdered."

"Where did you collect the bodies from?"

"The gas chambers. "

"How about the medical block? Did you have to collect bodies from the medical block?"

"No, not allowed. Verboten!" Raizman suddenly shouted, using a single word of German.

"Will you please face the dock and tell me whether you recognise the prisoner. Take your time."

Rajzman peered hard at Grundwall.

"Take your time," Westbury repeated.

"Yes, that is him. "

"Can you be more explicit, please?" Again he was confused by 'explicit' and Westbury put the question another way: "Can you name the prisoner?"

"He was SS. Officer."

"What name did you know him by?"

"Grundwall. "

"You are quite certain?"

"I never forget. Not their faces. Not anything. Never."

"And you confirm that he served as a member of the SS staff at Auschwitz during the time you were held there?"

"Until the last month. Not after. The SS left. Only the ordinary guards stayed."

"Why do you think they disappeared before the camp was liberated?"

"Why?" Rajzman repeated loudly, swinging around to glare at Grundwall. "Why do you think? They were saving their skins."

"Did the prisoner leave the camp with the others?"

"Yes, all of them went. I don't see him again until now."

"Thank you."

Fraser cross-examined briefly. "You have stated you were never allowed to enter the medical block."

"I have said that, yes."

"So therefore you cannot know whether the prisoner ever worked in the medical block or not, can you?"

The question had to be put to Rajzman three times before he fully understood. "Verboten I have said it was verboten for me. I am never inside that place."

"Thank you. I will take that as No."

Westbury's second witness was a Jew named Zeitlen, who came into the court wearing his prayer shawl. Painfully thin, more a walking skeleton, his physical frailty was not evident in the robust and dignified manner in which he gave his Testimony. He admitted to having been a Kapo, and that he had witnessed SS guards snatching infant children from their mothers as soon as they got off the trains.

"When mothers resisted, they were shot," he testified. "The babies were taken by the legs and smashed against a wall until only a bloody mess remained or else thrown into buckets of water and left to drown. Dogs would be set upon the men and would tear them to pieces. Women were stripped naked and strung up, left to hang until they died."

"Did you witness such events on a regular basis?"

"Every time a train arrived."

"And the rest. How were they killed?"

"Gassed. At first they used trucks and gassed them with the fumes."

"How did they do that?"

"They backed up the trucks to an opening in the wall of a block close to the Commandant's office. So that he did not hear the screams they revved up two motor cycles outside."

"How long did it take them to die by this method?"

"Twenty minutes. Longer sometimes. That is why they made use of the Little Red House."

"Tell the court what you mean by that."

"It was a house in the fields at Birkenau. Just a little house, which they made into a gas chamber. Later, they needed more room still, so they did the same to the Little White House."

"Are those the names the SS called them?"

"Yes. Don't worry, they would say, you are going to the Little Red House."

"And afterwards, when they were dead, what happened to them?

"We dragged them to big ditches. To Lazaretto."

"Lazaretto? What does that mean?"

"It was the nickname they gave it. Meaning, the 'Infirmary.'"

"I understand that those like yourself who carried out the task of disposing the bodies wore armbands. Is that true?"

"Yes."

"What sort of armbands?"

"They had the Red Cross sign on them."

"The Red Cross?"

"Yes. It was a Nazi joke."

"A joke?"

"Yes."

"Are you saying that they made jokes about these things?"

"Yes."

The President asked Westbury; "Counsel, where is this line of questioning taking us?"

"May it please the court I am seeking to establish that given that the accused was present in the camp when these atrocities took place on a daily basis, it stretches incredulity to believe he was unaware of them. I also wish to demonstrate that SS personnel viewed these hideous events with indifference, as matters of no consequence. They took the view they were not dealing with human beings, but creatures of a sub-species."

The President conferred with his fellow judges before saying, "Very well, we will allow your argument."

Westbury asked Zeitlen if he recognised Grundwall. Unlike Rajzman, he did not hesitate and gave an immediate identification.

"Let me ask you this. In the course of your work were you ever compelled to take live infant children to Dr.Mengele's medical block?"

"Yes."

Westbury said: Let me ask you that again. You took live infant children."

"Yes."

"What age were these children?"

"Some two years old, maybe, others older, maybe four or five, I can't be certain. They did not look like children. They looked like old people."

"Do you know why you took them to the medical block?"

"No, I never saw them again."

"The accused has told the court that the reason these children were selected was to find a cure for the typhus epidemic raging throughout the camp. Do you agree?"

"Typhus was always present."

"That is not what I asked you. I will put it another way. When you delivered children to Dr. Mengele's, did you believe they would receive normal medical attention?"

"I don't know. You didn't ask questions if you wanted to stay alive."

"Is that why you became a Kapo, to stay alive?"

Zeitlen lowered his head before answering. "Yes."

"Were you given a choice?"

"Yes. A choice between life and death."

"Did the other inmates hate you?"

"They didn't stay alive long enough to hate us," Zeitlen said with chilling honesty.

Three further witnesses were called, all three anxious to have their moment of retribution. They all identified Grundwall and there was little Fraser could do to dent their evidence. One of the three, a woman named Salomea Kaplan, who spoke good English, gave a detailed description of the selection process carried out by Mengele.

"He was always there early to meet the death transports, as if he could not wait to find new victims. And he made the same speech to those herded in front of him. Always the same. 'Ihr geht's jetzt baden, nachher werder ihr zur arbeit geschickt.' Every time the same, that is why it is fixed in memory. He pretended to give them hope. "Now you are going to the bath house and afterwards you will be put to work" Then he would begin to choose. The old, who meant everybody over 40 and the young, meaning those under 15, were sent to the left. I was healthy then, so I was sent to the right. Special children, were kept back."

"What do you mean by 'special' children?"

"Any twins."

"I see. Please continue."

"While this was happening, while we were standing there in lines, ash was falling from the chimneys. Of course

161

nobody knew it was human ash. And all the time the camp orchestra played. Then the majority were marched to a building with a sign over the entrance in large letters: Bade und Inhalations raume." People believed what it said. Two hours later they were dead."

"How was it you escaped?"

"Because I was young and able, I was put to work digging graves."

"Was the accused ever present when the selection took place?"

She turned and regarded Grundwall. "I think so, but they looked different in their uniforms, fatter, well fed." She continued to study him. "Yes, he was the one with glasses, like now. Sometimes he was there."

"Thank you. Your witness," Westbury said to Fraser, but Fraser declined to question her. Leaving the witness box she rounded on Grundwall and cursed him in her native tongue.

Westbury called his final witness, a ten-year-old girl in a wheelchair who testified she had been experimented on by Mengele without anaesthetic and left paralysed below the waist. Although she was unable to swear that Grundwall was present during her ordeal, she identified him as somebody she had seen in the medical block.

Again Fraser did not cross-examine. The President announced he would hear closing statements at ten the next morning and adjourned the proceedings.

TWENTY THREE

I took my seat for the final session uncertain as to the eventual outcome. Studying Grundwall as he was brought into court, he again did not give the appearance of a man expecting the worst. On the contrary he seemed composed.

Westbury rose to deliver a surprisingly short closing statement.

"The Prosecution contends that the charges levelled against Karl Gustave Grundwall have been proven beyond all reasonable doubt, and we therefore do not intend to burden the court with a recapitulation of the entire evidence. The accused is a scholar, a university Professor of Philosophy, and a poet... hardly a role model for a typical SS officer, yet it has been clearly established that for three years and one month he was an officer in that proscribed criminal organisation, as determined under Control Council Law No.10. Although he has repeatedly contended that he did not join the SS voluntarily, but was conscripted and had no choice in the matter, it is the prosecution's view that this is open to doubt. What is not open to doubt is that he served as an SS officer on the medical staff at Auschwitz-Birkenau extermination camp; that, further, he could not have been unaware of the true purpose of that camp, and that his evidence that he believed it to be a correction facility for the criminal element must be treated with the contempt it deserves. Central to his defence is that he had no personal involvement in the monstrous crimes committed in Auschwitz as part of the Final Solution and that he had no option but to be a reluctant, passive observer.

Throughout he has maintained that he was ignorant of the perverted practices carried out by his superior, the infamous Dr.Mengele, but again this strains credulity. It beggars belief that a man of Grundwall's undoubted intelligence and medical knowledge would accept that Dr. Mengele sought cures for typhus by injecting sufferers with petrol. His testimony on this point must therefore be treated as a deliberate lie. The question that must be asked is why then, just before the end of hostilities, did he deliberately falsify his records, fabricating a history of having spent the war elsewhere? These were not the actions of an innocent man, but rather the actions of a man with much to conceal. Had it not been for the vigilance of the joint Anglo-American Intelligence services, and in particular the initial identification by Captain Seaton, he would have continued to escape detection. He has never at any time shown the slightest remorse, but instead offered the plea that he was compelled to be a passive witness. Passive acceptance of crimes against humanity has already been ruled as no defence. We therefore ask for the maximum sentence this Tribunal is empowered to hand down."

I made eye contact with Grundwall as Westbury concluded. He held my look for a few seconds before lowering his head. Fraser them commenced the closing statement for the defence.

"I submit," he began, "that the prosecution's case is not proven. No conclusive evidence has been produced to establish beyond reasonable doubt that Karl Grundwall was ever actively involved in the collective crimes for which he stands accused. He has admitted being one of the medical staff at Auschwitz-Berkenau and that his service there as an officer in the SS was mandatory, in the same way that a it would be mandatory for a British doctor serving with the Army Medical Corps to be commissioned and compelled to serve where directed."

The President was quick to interrupt. "Counsel, I cannot allow you to draw such a parallel. The Army medical Corps is a humanitarian section of our armed forces and cannot be compared with the SS which was primarily a quasi-police force within a police state, given extraordinary and virtually unlimited powers which it exercised without regard to the laws of a civilised society."

"What I seek to establish, my Lord, is the dilemma of an educated man compelled to accept a commission in a proscribed organisation and drafted to serve in Auschwitz. He had no choice since the concept of conscientious objection was not allowed in Nazi Germany."

"Even so, your reference to a parallel situation between the SS and the British Medical Corps will be struck from the record. Proceed."

"Thank you. On the first count in the indictment I submit that it has not been conclusively proved that the accused played any active role in the experiments carried out by Dr. Mengele. I further submit that the photograph which first prompted his arrest shows him as an observer only and that none of the witnesses could state positively that he was anything other than an observer. The prosecution failed to produce either still images or filmed footage showing the accused taking an active role in such experiments."

Fraser painted a picture of Grundwall as a man who had been forced to remain silent in order to protect himself and his family. It was hardly an inspired defence, but given the weight of evidence against Grundwall, possibly the only course he could take. "It is common knowledge that, during the Nazi regime, those who criticised the policies of the State or questioned the actions of their superiors were liable to the severest penalties, including death. Should the court so require, I will produce evidence that many members of the SS were imprisoned and executed for refusing to carry out orders. The credo of blind obedience was drilled into them from the moment they were sworn in. The accused's failure to protest at the actions of others may be taken as cowardice to be treated with contempt, but it does not of itself imply or prove guilt. The Prosecution alleged that the accused has shown no remorse, but I would draw the court's attention to the evidence given by Captain Seaton, who stated that the accused did expressed shame and a sense of collective guilt for the crimes committed by the Third Reich. I therefore respectively submit that, on the main counts of the indictment the case against Karl Grundwall has not been proven beyond reasonable doubt and that, justice demands a verdict of Not Guilty."

He sat down. I had watched Grundwall intently during this, but he had betrayed no emotion one-way or the other. The President now addressed him. "Before this court retires to consider its verdict, I must draw your attention To Article 24, under which a defendant can make a final, unsworn statement. Do you wish to exercise your right to make such a statement?"

"Yes, I do." Grundwall said. "I would like to emphasise once more that I am innocent of taking any active role in the execution of the so-called Final Solution. Until its meaning was explained to me, I did not know that such a plan existed, any more than I knew the uses made of the Little Red and White Houses at Birkenhau. I am not a brave man and I knew that the fate of my wife and daughter always hung upon my actions, that any disobedience in obeying orders on my part would mean they would suffer grievously. Such dangers to them did not end when the war ended, for there were many elements, both foreign and domestic, intent on taking revenge. That is the sole reason I took steps to conceal my past when I resumed by academic career. My behaviour has been described as cowardice. I admit to this and I will carry the burden of that cowardice to my grave. For the rest of my life I must accept my share of the collective guilt, but from my clear recognition of the causes, the terrible methods and consequences of the war, I pray there will arise a new future for the German people which will one day obliterate this stain. I therefore throw myself on the mercy of this Court."

The President merely nodded in acknowledgement, thanked the Prosecution and Defence for their conduct of the trial and ordered Grundwall to be taken down to the cells.

TWENTY FOUR

At the end of the proceedings I went in search of Major Jones, eventually finding him in the large communal office where half a dozen stenographers were busy typing up the evidence.

"Can I ask you a favour?" I said. "Am I permitted to see Grundwall now?"

"What would you want to see him for?"

"It's a personal reason."

"I'd need more than that to be of assistance."

"In the course of giving evidence I admitted that I have been having a sexual relationship with his daughter."

Jones frowned. "I see. Yes, well you can't get more personal than that, I suppose, but it's not up to me. The Provost Marshall will have to rule. Normally it's not allowed, but now the trial's over, he might stretch a point in your case. I should warn you, he may not after the recent suicide."

While I waited I tried to decide what I was going to say to Grundwall if I got the okay. Jones came back into the office and gave the thumbs up. "He said, yes, except he'll deny it if anybody ever asks, so keep it short."

"Understood. Thank you."

A Military Police Sergeant conducted me to the holding cells below the court. "Rap on the door when you're through," he said as he unlocked the cell. "I'll be out here the whole time."

Grundwall was sitting on the edge of his bed. He had the

look of an exhausted man washed up on a beach. When I entered he searched for his spectacles and put them on. "I expected you might appear," he said. "Do you have a cigarette?"

I proffered a packet. "Of course. Here. Keep them."

"You were always generous to me and my family." There was no mistaking the sarcasm in his voice. I lit the cigarette for him. "Have you come to commiserate or gloat?"

"Neither," I said.

"Pity me, then?"

"I'd be less than human if I didn't."

"I thought that was what has just been proved? That I'm less than human."

"Look, this is a difficult meeting for both of us." I said. "Shall we try and not make it more so?"

"Perhaps more difficult for me than you."

"I haven't come to discuss the trial. It's Lisa I want to talk about."

"Ah, Lisa, yes. How is my Lisa?"

"I'm taking care of her."

"Are you? Should I be glad about that? And my wife? How is she? I haven't been allowed to communicate with either of them."

"As far as I know your wife is well. I sent her some money via Lisa, and I intend to go on taking care of both of them."

"Your consideration knows no limits," Grundwall said.

"I know you must hate me."

"Is that surprising?"

"I've just listened to you justifying your actions, saying you had no choice. I had no choice either in what I did."

"Then that's the only thing left we have in common."

"I came here in the belief that the one thing we still have in common is love for Lisa. So I ask a favour for her sake. I know you love her and she loves you. I also love her and I believe she returns that love. I want to marry her, but our marriage would have no chance if she ever learned of the part I played in your present situation."

"I imagine not," he said. "So what is the favour?"

"That when next you see her or are allowed to communicate with her, you find it possible, for the sake of any happiness we might have together, not to reveal my involvement."

Grundwall took a long draw on his cigarette, and then ground it under his heel when only half smoked, as though to show me he regretted accepting it from me. "It's perhaps a mistake to mix happiness and love. They don't always go together."

"Is that something you teach in your philosophy classes?"

Grundwall ignored this. "And if I don't grant your request?"

"Then I imagine there's no future for me and Lisa."

"It's not something I can promise," Grundwall said finally. "I must think about it. When am I likely to be granted contact with my wife and daughter?"

"I've no idea, but now the trial's over I imagine conditions will be relaxed."

"And having sat through the trial, how d'you think they will deal with me?"

"I'm not a judge."

"The prosecutor asked for the maximum penalty."

"I thought your defence counsel put forward a forceful plea in mitigation."

"He did his best, such as it was. But you heard the evidence. Do you believe me to be guilty?

"I think you are guilty of deception."

"Ah, deception. That's the game we're both in, aren't we? After all, you deceived me with your friendship."

"No. I took you for what you said you were until you proved me wrong."

"And now, you want me to lie for you?"

"If you choose to call it a lie. But if you care anything for Lisa's happiness I am asking you not to reveal the one thing that would destroy it."

"Perhaps I would prefer her not to marry somebody like you," Grundwall said slowly. "Did that not occur to you? That might be the kindest thing I could do for her. And even if I were generous enough to lie for you, how can you be sure that at sometime, somewhere, somebody won't whisper the truth in her ear? Can you live with that time bomb, as I have lived with it, always wondering when the blow would fall?" He arranged his features into something approaching a smile. "And when that happens, as happen it will, what price happiness then?"

"I love her," I said, "and that's the risk I must take. The choice is yours, I can only beg."

"I may not have a choice. If the court is not inclined to mercy, then what you are asking becomes academic. Dead men are not in a position to grant favours, are they? So we must both wait and see. Philosophy has taught me able to face those events which are forced upon us, but not to foresee the outcome of those events."

He lay back on the bed and closed his eyes, signalling that our discussion was at an end.

I stared down at him. "You asked if I pitied you," I said. "I pity both of us."

He did not reply and I went to the cell door and rapped on it. The Sergeant let me out.

TWENTY FIVE

Boarding the train to Hamburg, I carried sadness with me like unwanted luggage, thinking what a fool I've been, what a fool to think Grundwall would do me any favours, what a fool not to have thought it through.

Opposite me in the carriage reserved for Allied personnel was a middle-aged Army Chaplain with the beginning of a paunch and a smooth complexion that looked as though it had never been near a razor. I've always been uneasy in the company of gentlemen of the cloth and I'm not sure why. It may have something to do with my atheism or because I just cannot comprehend how anybody could spend their lives justifying what to me is a lot of nonsense. That and the fact that they seem to know all the answers to life and I know none.

As we settled into our seats he remarked on my Intelligence Corps shoulder flashes, and then asked in a soft West Country accent whether I was permanently stationed in Nuremberg.

"No, Father. I was just here to give evidence in a trial."

"I'm not a Father in any sense of the word. Just a Church of England vicar. I'm Daniel, Daniel Saunders." He undid his jacket, produced a silver hip flask and unscrewed the small drinking cup that capped it. "Would you care for a taste? Single malt. My sister included it in her last parcel."

"Alex Seaton," I responded, accepting the offer of a drink. The neat malt burned the back of my throat when I swallowed.

He took a measure for himself and replaced the cap, then

seamlessly resumed: "When I think about these trials I remember something Talleyrand said. He held that war is not a condition between one man and another, but between state and state, in which individuals are only accidental enemies and therefore cannot be held responsible for the crimes they commit. You've been giving evidence you say?"

"Yes."

"Not an enjoyable experience I'm sure."

"No." I suddenly felt the need to confide in a stranger. "Certainly not in this case because I was responsible for this particular man's arrest. He was somebody I had previously trusted. An accidental enemy, I suppose you might say."

"German?"

"Yes."

"You say you trusted him at first?"

"Yes," I said. "I'd met him and his wife socially, and he deceived me into believing he was a untainted by the Nazi years, a cultivated academic, one of the silent minority who had opposed Hitler. How wrong I was."

"What made you change your mind?"

"A photograph came to light. A photograph taken at Auschwitz, showing he had served there as an SS officer." I broke off. "Look, forgive me, I can't think this is of any interest to you."

"It obviously weighs heavily on your mind." He proffered the hip flask again. I shook my head.

"Well, because it isn't cut and dried. The fact is that when I got to know him and his family, I fell hopelessly in love with his only daughter."

"Did she know of her father's past?"

"No. And I believe that."

"What was he accused of?"

"Being part of the infamous Dr. Mengel's unit at Auschwitz. Mengele was the monster who carried out experiments on children."

"Dear God, dear God," he murmured and stared out at the desolate landscape we were passing through. "Does she know that you were the one who exposed him?"

"No, not yet," I said. "But it can't be concealed forever. And then, will she ever forgive me?"

"Worse things have been forgiven," Daniel said. He was silent for a while. "I suppose for a long time now the love of God has been sufficient for my needs, so I'm hardly the best person to offer advice. Love, such as you have confessed to, is an unknown country to me. Not that I ever took the vows of celibacy... there was a moment when my life might have taken a different path, but it passed..... . Do you have faith? Faith in God, I mean?

"No, I don't."

"Well, even without faith, God sometimes provides the answer. He doesn't withhold his love from anybody."

"It must be comforting," I said, "to have such certainty."

He shook his head. "If I had certainty, I wouldn't question why God divides his mercy, why He lets a single child die of starvation in a world of plenty, why He allowed such a place such as Auschwitz to exist, why creatures such as Mengele aren't struck down like Lot's wife." He fingered his dog collar. "Wearing this doesn't bestow any special wisdom. If it did I might be able to offer you a solution."

For the remainder of the journey he talked about less sombre topics. I only half-listened, my turning over in my mind the best course of action and by the time we parted at the Hamburg terminal, I had steeled myself to what I had to do. Instead of changing platforms and boarding the connection to Berlin, I went to the Military Police post.

"Sergeant," I said, producing my identity card, "I need to get somewhere urgently, but I don't have transport. Can you help?"

He fixed me up with a spare Jeep and a driver who knew his way around and drove me to Lisa's address. When we arrived outside the apartment block, the driver said: "This area can be a bit dodgy, sir. Sergeant gave the okay for me to wait and bring you back."

"Thank him, but that won't be necessary. I'm not sure how long I'll be."

I followed an alley round to the entrance and mounted the dirty concrete stairs to the second floor. There was a smell of cabbages that took me back to the first time I had visited the Grundwall's.

Greta, not Lisa, opened the door to me.

"Ah, Greta," I said. "It is Greta, isn't it?"

"Yes."

"Is Lisa in?"

"No, she is still rehearsing."

"Can I wait for her?"

"Bitte, as you wish," she answered without enthusiasm. As she stepped back into the light I studied her face. It wasn't a beautiful face, too hard for that, good bone structure, but a mouth not made for charm and the small dark eyes suspicious.

"You like coffee?" Greta asked.

"Yes, if you can spare it."

"Your money bought it." There was a hint of resentment in her answer, a hint, too, of insolence. "Only black. We have finished the sugar."

"Black's fine and I don't take sugar."

I watched while she boiled water in a saucepan on a small gas ring.

"It's cold in here," I said.

"Yes. Always. There is no heating in this block. We put on an electric fire at night, but it uses too much money."

Now she took down a decorated tin and an earthenware jug from a shelf over the sink and carefully measured one tablespoon of coffee grounds into the jug.

"Are you going to join me?"

"No, we save ours for breakfast."

"How is Lisa?"

"She manages." She poured the boiling water onto the coffee.

"Did she get my letters?"

"I think so, yes."

"And you, do you have any work?"

"I am lucky. I work some days. Translating for the Commission."

I held out my packet of cigarettes. She took one and I lighted it for her.

"Have things improved here?"

"A little."

"D'you have family?"

"My home was in Flensburg, but my father and brother are *tod*."

"What about your mother?"

"She was killed in an air raid."

"I'm sorry."

The conversation petered out, until she asked: "What d'you think will happen?"

"To Lisa's father? I don't know what the verdict will be."

"Will your people execute him?"

"I hope not, but of course he is charged with very serious offences. If he's found guilty, he'll face a long prison sentence. He was given a fair trial." I immediately realised my slip in using the past tense.

"You mean it's over?"

"I believe so," I lied.

Greta smoked half of her cigarette, and then carefully put it out and to one side. "I hate what the war did."

"Yes. It was bad for everybody."

"Not so bad for you. We are left with nothing."

"Well, it wasn't one sided," I said evenly, "and we are trying to put Germany back on its feet."

"Half of Germany," she replied.

"Because you invaded Russia and now it's pay back time." I sensed that she would never be completely won over whatever I said. We sat in silence as the light outside the single window faded and it was another fifteen minutes before Lisa appeared. She stood in the doorway, amazed at finding me there, then rushed forward and flung she in my arms.

"Why didn't you tell me you were coming? I've missed you so much. Do you have news about father?"

"He told me the trial's over," Greta said, confirming she had picked up on my chance remark.

Lisa stepped back. "Over? It's over? Have they let him go free? Tell me they've let him go."

"Darling, they haven't reached a verdict yet."

"I know they'll find him not guilty. A woman in the cast reads cards. Today she did mine and said good news is on the way."

"I'm sure the cards were right," I said. "I thought perhaps, if it's all right with Greta, I could take you out for a meal before I have to leave again."

"Oh, yes, please," Lisa said, then caught herself and turned to Greta. "Do you mind?"

Greta shrugged. "Do what you want, it's all the same to me."

I felt I had to make some gesture towards her and took four cigarettes from my packet and lay then on the table. "To make amends for us leaving you."

"Danke."

On the way down we encountered a young man on crutches. He had one leg missing and was wearing a battered Wehrmacht cap. I stood to one side to allow him to pass, but I heard him hawk and spit as we left the building. Lisa held my arm tightly, her head resting on my shoulder as we walked to a nearby restaurant in the annexe to a partially ruined building. A commissioner in shabby regalia stood outside and saluted me. We were shown into a vaulted room decorated with pastoral murals and an over-obsequious Maitre 'D conducted us to our table.

"Would the Herr Captain and his lady guest like a cocktail?"

"We'll have some wine," I said.

"Wine, of course, Herr Captain." He produced a wine list.

"What d'you prefer?" I asked Lisa. "Red or white?"

"You choose," Lisa said. "I don't know anything about wine."

I studied the modest list. "A bottle of number seven."

"An excellent choice Herr Captain." His oily manner grated on me. He smirked at Lisa when spreading the napkin on her lap.

"I'm so happy," Lisa said, reaching for my hand across the table. Her hand was cold. "I know they won't do anything to father because he's done nothing wrong. My mother would have known, wouldn't she? And if she'd known, she wouldn't have kept it secret from me. We've never had secrets between us. So I'm still sure that, like the cards said, it's going to be good news in the end. She's very good, this woman. Things she's told other people have come true."

"Well, that's a good omen," I said, hoping she would not detect the note of doubt in my voice.

"When I woke up today everything was so black and hopeless. And now it's all changed and I'm here with you."

"I want you to be happy." I reached in a pocket for my cigarettes. "I noted Greta smokes," I said, "have you succumbed?"

"No. I'm tempted, but I can't afford the black market prices."

"Are you getting enough to eat, did I leave you enough money?"

"Yes, more than enough. You're so good to me."

"Greta was telling me she works as a translator. Does she have a boyfriend?" I was conscious I was making small talk, to keep away from the danger area.

"Somebody in Control Commission dated her once, but she doesn't believe in fraternisation. She was married to a bomber pilot who was killed."

A waiter arrived with the wine, which he poured with a great flourish as though it was Premiere Cru. I raised my glass. "To us," I said.

We studied the menu. "Is that going to be enough for you?" I asked when she had made a choice.

"Yes. I don't eat much these days."

"You should."

"I tried to get permission to see father but it was refused," she said, immediately reverting to the subject uppermost in her mind.

"I'm sure you'll be able to see him soon."

"D'you believe in what the cards tell you?"

"I've never had mine read."

"I believe in them. When my friend laid them out she said there wasn't a single bad one." The trust in her face destroyed me. I thought, how to begin what I have to do? I started to say, "Darling, whatever happens," but at that moment our first courses arrived. I took a few mouthfuls, then put down my knife and fork and began again. "You know I love you, don't you?"

Lisa looked up from enjoyment of her food, puzzled but smiling. "Of course I do."

"And that whatever happens I shall always love you."

Her smile died. "What could happen? When father's released, as he will be, everything will be right again."

"What," I said slowly, "if he's not released?"

Now she stopped eating. "Don't say 'what if', don't say that."

179

"Sweetheart, I broke my journey instead of going straight back to Berlin, so you'd hear certain things from me rather than anybody else."

"What sort of things?" Her voice, her whole being, had changed.

"You once told me that during the war your father worked as a translator. That wasn't true. He was an officer in the SS."

All the colour drained from her face. "That's not possible."

"I love you, I wouldn't lie to you. The reason he was arrested and put on trial is that he was part of the administration in the Auschwitz concentration camp."

"No," she said. "No, they made that up."

I shook my head. "Darling, I was at the trial. Survivors from the camp identified him."

Her face seemed to dissolve in front of me. She suddenly stood up, clutched at the tablecloth and sent her food and wine glass clattering to the floor. Unbalanced, she stumbled backwards, knocking her chair over. I was just quick enough to catch her as she fainted. The Maitre 'D hurried to the scene.

"Something wrong, Herr Captain?"

"Yes, my friend suddenly felt faint. Bring a glass of water."

"Of course, at once." He clicked his fingers at one of the waiters. "Wasser Schell! I hope it was not to do with the food."

"No, The food was fine." I took the glass of water and held it to Lisa's mouth. "Sip this, darling." When she had taken some I dipped a napkin in the glass, and patted her forehead with it.

One waiter righted her chair while another started to clear the broken crockery.

"Get me the check," I said to the Maitre 'D. "And I need to use your telephone." I helped Lisa back onto a chair. "Sit there until you feel better, darling."

"This way, Captain." He led me to the office. "We have a good record for the food we serve."

"Don't worry, I've said it was nothing to do with the food." I dialled Machell's number.

"To what do I owe this honour?" Machell asked. "Where the hell are you ringing from? Berlin?"

"No, I'm in town, sir and in trouble. I need a pad for the night. Is there any chance I could use yours?"

"What sort of trouble?"

"Personal."

"Girl friend personal?"

"Yes."

"Same girl friend you told me about?"

"Yes, only now it's desperate. I've just come back from Nuremberg and her father's trial."

"I see. Right. Get the picture. Yes, okay. Borrow my place."

"You're a real friend, sir. Are you sure?"

"Well, strange as it may appear to you, I still manage to sow the occasional oat. I'll rest my head on a friendly female for the night. Doubtless she will greet me with open arms."

"There is one other thing. I don't have any transport."

"Now you're pressing your luck. Where are you?"

I gave him the name and address of the restaurant.

"Stay put. I'll come and fetch you."

"How can I thank you, sir?"

"You can't," Machell said. "I'm too good to be true."

TWENTY SIX

Machell's set of rooms on the second floor of a rare unscathed building was surprisingly opulent for somebody who went to some pains to shun any public ostentation. He showed me where to find everything before he left. Naturally he had provided himself with a well stocked bar, and in addition the kitchen had an American fridge which worked and was full of basics. The main room was had some good pieces of antique furniture plus a pair of comfortable armchairs. As for the bathroom, that was marble and piping hot water came out of the taps while his bedroom was the lair of a sybarite – an inviting, French-style double bed covered with a fur rug. I felt guilty about turning him out.

"Help yourself to anything you want," he said, "especially the bar. I've always found drink to be the great panacea." He had been discreetness itself on the journey, making no comment about Lisa's obvious distress.

Once we were alone, I led her into the bedroom, made her lie on top of the bed and covered her with the rug. "I'll make you some tea with plenty of sugar," I said. No longer crying, she stared at me as though a stranger. Returning with the sweet tea, I helped her to a sitting position, then propped pillows behind her before steadying the cup in her hands. She took a few sips, then gave me the cup and sank back.

I could not read her. There was nothing in her expression, not despair just blankness. I felt her hand. It was cold. I went to the small kitchen and poured the rest of the tea away. There was a tin of Huntley and Palmers biscuits on the shelf over the sink and I stared at the familiar wording, thinking what a long way from home I had come to give unhappiness to somebody else. Then I helped myself to a Scotch from the bar. I had eaten little since leaving Nuremberg, but the neat shot had no effect. I could think of nothing but Lisa's pain. There was a photograph of a younger Machell in a silver frame on a side table, showing him in tropical gear with his arm around a dusky Indian girl. The print had a crease dissecting it suggesting it had once been folded and kept in his wallet. I stared at it, wondering if this was the mother of the love child he had once confessed to. Returning to the bedroom, I found Lisa had undressed and got under the covers. I shed my own clothes, climbed in beside her and cradled her as one cradles someone injured.

After a long time, she said, "I wish I could die."

"Don't say things like that, darling. There's always hope."

"You don't believe that," she said. "I can tell by your voice. If they put him in prison, I shall die."

"I won't let you die. I love you and I'm going to marry you."

"Why would you marry me now?"

"Because nothing's changed between us. Nothing. We still love each other."

"And that makes it all right, does it?"

I bent over her and put my lips on hers, but she did not open them to me. Then she started to cry again. "Why?" she said between sobs. "Why did it happen?"

"The war," I said. "The war did things to people. Everybody changed. I changed; it did things to me too. Nobody escaped, only those who died."

"You said... they brought evidence against him. What evidence? I want to know."

Still holding her close, I searched for the words that would not wound her further. "Your father claimed that because he had previously trained as a doctor he was given no choice, but was posted Auschwitz and made responsible for the health of the staff and their dependents. Your mother joined him there for a time. Did she ever tell you that?"

"No."

"Auschwitz and other camps like it existed for one purpose only. Hitler had decreed that the entire Jewish race, men, women and children, was to be exterminated. That is why all those who worked in such places, especially those in the SS, were held responsible for the crimes committed there."

"I know father didn't commit any crimes, he couldn't."

"But he was there, darling, while others did. He was there in the wrong place at the wrong time, a time when the killings happened every day."

"The Russians killed Greta's husband, your planes bombed us, what difference is there?"

"There is a difference between armies killing each other on the battlefield and killing people in cold blood simply because they are Jewish."

As I stared into her innocent face I knew that if ever she was to understand the horror and misery of events beyond her comprehension I had to tell her something I had long buried, something I had never before revealed to anybody.

"I killed once," I said.

"You?"

I held her closer. "Not on the battlefield, I wasn't in a fighting unit. But in another camp, the one we liberated at Belsen. I killed a young Jewish woman, not much older than you.... The day before we got there, the guards had murdered her two small children before her eyes. She had begged them to kill her too, but instead they had left her to go insane with grief. She begged us to shoot her... but we couldn't do that. Her poor mad face haunted me, so later that same day when I was on my own, I searched for her, finally found her behind the crematoriums kneeling in the filth beside piles of the unburied dead. While I watched I saw her pick up a piece of broken glass and attempt to hack at her wrists. . We all carried morphine in those days... I knelt down beside her and injected a lethal dose into her bare arm. I stayed with her until she died. It was all over very quickly and nobody saw me, not that another death meant anything amongst so many..."

Lisa's had begun to tremble long before I finished and now she shook as though in a seizure. Holding her nude body to mine I was immediately aroused and in Machell's borrowed bed, I made love to her in an attempt to blot out both the past and present. As I entered her I realised, all too late, that I was not wearing a condom, but by then I could not have stopped. When the moment came it was so intense, bordering on pain, that it obliterated all else. I lay with my head nestled into her damp neck, spent with passion. Our bodies slowly relinquished each other, our heartbeats slowed to normal, and we drifted into merciful sleep.

We said little the next morning. I made breakfast for us and then walked with her to the stage door. When we kissed and parted, she said: "I only feel alive when I'm with you. I know you'll make everything come right in the end."

"What I'm going to do," I said, "as soon as I get back to Berlin is rent an apartment for us. Then I can take good care of you all the time." I foraged in my jacket for some money. "Meantime I want you to have this."

"I can't keep taking your money."

"Yes, you can. Don't German husbands keep their wives?"

"I'm not your wife."

"But you will be." I pressed the notes into her hand. "No goodbyes," I said. "We don't say goodbye, you and me."

I walked away from her quickly. I didn't look back, but I knew she would still be standing there, believing in me.

TWENTY SEVEN

Rawnsley looked up from reading his copy of The Times and said: "Was Nuremberg fun?"

"Fun? No, I wouldn't say that."

"How did your war criminal do?"

"He's not 'my' war criminal.

"Sorry, excuse me. I thought you had a propriety interest in him. Did they decide to hang him?"

I wondered what Graham had told him of my situation. "No," I said. "I left before they arrived at a verdict."

Graham joined us at that moment. "Ah, you're back, Alex. Does the name Chivers ring a bell with you?

"Yes."

"A Major in the Control Commission?"

"Yes. Why?"

"While you were away the Military police pulled him in during a brothel raid. He was in civvies, and turned very truculent, said he was there carrying out an official survey on morals. Absolute bollocks, of course, and they passed him to us to check him out. He gave your name as a close friend, said you'd vouch for him."

"He's certainly not a close friend," I said emphatically. "I first clapped eyes on him in Hamburg, thought he was a pompous little prick, very full of himself. Told me he'd spent the war in some, hush hush place... Bletchley I think he called it. Meant nothing to me."

"Have you seen him since?"

"Yes, but not intentionally. Once at the docks when I

was going home on leave. Then here, in a nightclub, just before I went to Nuremberg. Always seems to be chasing some dodgy business deal. The last time it was a scam involving Leica cameras."

Rawnsley came out from behind his newspaper. "Doesn't take long for the spivs to start crawling out of the woodwork." He got up and left the room.

"How did you deal with Chivers?"

"He went back to Hamburg with a flea in his ear," Graham said. "Swore he'd put in a complaint at the way he had been treated. I'm interested that he claimed to have been at Bletchley. I shall follow that up."

"Was Bletchley something special?"

"Yes. Very special and still on the top secret list. Blabbing about it is not encouraged."

At that moment an orderly joined us and handed me a Telex. "It's from one of the prosecuting team at Nuremberg," I said, "telling me that the man I gave evidence against escaped the death penalty, but was convicted on the secondary indictment and given thirty years."

"The right verdict in your view?"

"I don't know," I said. "Maybe thirty years is a death penalty at his age."

"So where does that leave you with your girl friend?"

"I don't know. Obviously it came out that I was the first one to identify her father, and the defence made much of my relationship with her."

"So her father now knows it was you who sprang the trap, but she doesn't. Or have you told her?"

"No."

"He will, presumably?"

"I imagine. Well, yes, I'm sure he will."

"How will she react to that? Or don't you care? In the circumstances perhaps you'd welcome ending the relationship? That might be the best solution. Pity they didn't give him the drop. One can forget the dead in time, but never the living. 'He who forms a tie is lost, the germ of corruption has entered his soul.' Conrad." Then Graham became businesslike again as though quoting Conrad had embarrassed him. He handed me a thick folder. "Decode this lot, will you and let me know if anything requires immediate action. And if you're at a loose end, let's have dinner tonight."

I spent the rest of the day logging the contents of the folder. It was for our eyes only and dealt with Project Backfire, set up to locate, and send back to England any German scientists who had worked in the nuclear field. The Yanks were likewise shipping home anybody with the same credentials they found in their sector. We were to disregard any questionable Nazi histories; all that mattered was their potential worth to us. The race was on to discover how advanced the German nuclear programme had been and to commandeer any knowledge.

Graham treated me to a meal at the Officers Club, where his conversation, far from discussing my ongoing situation with Lisa, was immediately dominated by his own demons.

"Never thought it would revert to the law of the jungle so quickly, Alex," he said as soon as his choice of Burgundy had been swirled, tasted and accepted. "We're on the back foot again, the ball's no longer in our court," he continued, always prone to mix his metaphors. "Naturally Whitehall is urging restraint, blocking any attempt for us to move up into another gear and get real. The word is, don't make waves, wait and see which way Moscow jumps. In other words do nothing until it's too late. Our pursuits have always been regarded with distaste by the F.O. We're meant to stay off their sacred patch. I've invested my entire life in this game, Alex, and you know what I've ended up as? – a pen pusher, a bloody pen pusher."

I thought: what the hell have I got myself into? As with

Miller, the old guard seemed to singing the same dirge in the same key of disillusion. I couldn't take the spying game seriously. Real enemies used conventional weapons, mowed you down with machine guns, and blew you skywards with booby traps. Dead-letter drops, clandestine meetings, talk of the 'Firm', 'Control' and 'moles' remained the stuff of the nursery – as though those who practiced the dark arts were still trapped in a Winnie The Pooh world inhabited by middle-aged Christopher Robins. I broached the subject cautiously because one never knew how Graham would react. "Do you ever question whether the whole business of espionage and counter-espionage has a touch of futility about it?"

"Futility?" Graham was immediately on the defensive.

"Well, put it this way, what in the last analysis has it ever achieved? It hasn't stopped any wars. It changed nothing when the wholesale carnage in Flanders was claiming half a million casualties in a single day. It was hopelessly adrift at Arnhem."

"You're confusing intelligence with espionage," Graham answered tetchily. "Not the same thing at all. There'll always be failures; we don't practice an exact science, but that doesn't negate the need for us to exist. We were put on this earth to thwart those who pose a threat to our values and our way of life." He was silent for nearly a minute, eating nothing but fiddling with his steak knife, then looked up and smiled. "Don't mind me. I have to defend my reason to exist. Of course I question the whole mad business, never more so than today. While you were in Nuremberg learning the fate of your once prospective father-in-law, the cull that began with the murder of my girl, accelerated. We've started to haemorrhage agents, Alex. In Belgrade first. Somebody I turned, blue chip investment with access to top level Soviet thinking. Gone. Then a second in Warsaw, part of the same network. Somebody in the know is cleaning our stables. But where, that's the question?"

"Miller is convinced it has to be London."

"Perhaps he's right. He maybe a piss artist, but he's a canny old bastard. Perhaps we do have to start thinking the unthinkable." He cut the fat from his steak and pushed it to one side. "Maybe it's not so unthinkable at that. You don't appreciate how some of us came to be in this game, Alex. Nobody asked me what I wanted to do; it was taken for granted that I would go into the diplomatic, like my father and his father before him. I was slipped into the family tradition like drawing on an old glove. Nobody vetted me properly. Why would they? I looked right, spoke with the right accent, and wore the right tie. Somebody who knew Daddy took me out to dinner at Rules, made small talk about Len Hutton and the best way to tie a fly, anything but the actual reason for the meal. Well, I tell a lie. There was a moment when he casually enquired whether I had shed my Communist tendencies. Since I had no idea what was behind the question, I said I was working on it. I suppose he thought I was being flippant and dropped the subject."

"Were you ever a Communist?"

"Never a card carrier but, yes, I flirted with the idea like most of my year, went to a few meetings held by speakers like D.N.Pritt and Maurice Dobbs, both confirmed Marxists pushing the Popular Front. It was fashionable to be radical in Cambridge during the Thirties. We bought the idea of revolution, it felt dangerous and daring, like having your first French letter hidden in your wallet. Most of us despised Baldwin and Chamberlain. Those on the Left were the only ones actively fighting Fascism in the International Brigade. Despite that affinity, I wasn't a convert for long. I found something so infinitely dreary about the comrades parroting the official line. Anybody with a modicum of intelligence had to reject the crap they spouted. So in my case it was just a phase and I drifted away. But some didn't, they even managed to rationalise The Nazi-Soviet Pact. I mean, that was the ultimate test, wasn't it? If you could swallow that without vomiting, you could swallow anything – the show trials, the deliberate starvation of the Russian peasants, the purges, murders and Siberian prison camps. Some did, some were able to justify everything to themselves." Graham lit a cigarette but immediately thought better of it and laid it on the edge of an ashtray. "When the war came we were all scattered into various branches of the Services, but who knows where some of the committed ended up? Some, like me, must have been absorbed into the SIS. Who bothered to find out where their true loyalties lay? Are some still in place? After all, what body could be more perfectly designed to harbour traitors, given that the prime object of a secret service is to remain secret?" Graham allowed himself the faintest smile. "You know, of course that, officially, we don't exist, have never existed since the day old Kell was given the job of inventing us. No statements are ever made to Parliament, our budgets never debated." He retrieved the cigarette, holding it between his thumb and first fingers like an actress unfamiliar with a prop. "God, I'd like to get legless tonight."

"Why don't you? I'll see you safely back to the billet."

"Because I can't, Alex. No matter how hard I try, drink only dulls me, never obliterates. Maybe one day they'll pack me off home in disgrace, a security risk."

I liked Graham, he was the professional and my boss, but I couldn't read him with any accuracy. Just when I thought I was tuned in to his wavelength, the signal became corrupted. I suppose the truth was he was a victim of love, like me. In addition we were both trying to make sense of a peace that was still a war. I sat opposite him, listening with half an ear to his wandering dialogue while all the time trying to imagine what Grundwall's next move would be as he began thirty years incarceration. What had he got to lose by revealing my part in his fate to Lisa? Nothing. It was the only revenge left to him.

I did see Graham safely home to his billet that night and when we parted he apologised for being such a morbid companion. "Pity you didn't meet me in my best years, Alex," he said gravely. He wasn't drunk or maudlin, just icy cold.

First thing the following day I rang Major Jones asking him to let me know in which prison Grundwall would be serving his sentence, so that I could pass the information on to Lisa. Then went in search of Staff Sergeant Webb who ran our Transport pool and was generally regarded as the font of all knowledge and was noted for slagging off the system that held us captive. He was in his usual form that morning, greeting me with: "Sir, what Whitehall tosser decided we should now drive around in these?" He pointed to two gleaming new Humber Snipe saloons he had been servicing. "That's a really brilliant stroke, given they're the only ones in Germany. They might as well gone the whole hog and painted 'Secret Service' on the door panels."

"Still, more comfortable than what they replaced," I said. I was anxious to send Lisa some good news. "Tell me, Harry, where could I start looking for accommodation?"

"You want to move out of your billet, sir?"

"No. I want somewhere safe for my girlfriend." I winked.

"Great minds think alike, sir. I've just done the same for my own little fraulein. The place I found which might suit you. Owned by an elderly geezer who lives in the basement and lets out the rest of his house. I happen to know he's got one flat not spoken for. I pay him in stuff – bottle of vodka, some Balkan Soprano baccy every week. Suits him, suits me."

"Can you take me there?"

"Pleasure, sir. But let's not use a Humber, they haven't been road tested yet, so if you don't mind, we'll take the Bedford."

On the way he asked: "You married, sir?"

"No."

"Funny old business sex and marriage. My divorce papers came through finally. I got a Dear John letter the night before we crossed the Rhine. Tried to get myself killed that night, but my number wasn't on a bullet. And here I am, ready to dive in again head first."

He eventually pulled up in front of a detached house in Ploener Strasse, a house partially hidden from the road by a screen of damaged trees with a faded grandeur about it.

"Who else lives here?" I asked.

"Apart from my girl? There's an old bird on the top floor, who keeps herself to herself. Then a bloke who teaches piano. I think the landlord must be some sort of aristocrat. Got a Von in his name. That's classy over here, isn't it?" He led me down a flight of stone steps to the basement doorway and rang the bell. There was a wait and then a stooped old man wearing several cardigans and a scarf wrapped around his throat opened the door. His face, under thin, yellowed strands of hair brushed sideways across his skull, had the quality of parchment.

"Guten tag, Herr Von Krenkler," Webb said.

"Guten tag." Krenkler stared past Webb to me.

"This is one of my officers, Captain Seaton. He's interested in looking at a flat if one's still available." Webb's German left much to be desired, but Krenkler got the gist.

"Bitte" he said. "Bitte," and shuffled to one side allowing us to enter. He led the way through his quarters to the upstairs hallway. As we climbed to the first floor I we heard the strains of Beethoven's Moonlight Sonata being picked out on a piano. The wooden stair treads were worn, the patterned wallpaper faded and peeling, yet redolent of a opulent past. Kenkler stopped outside a door on the second landing and produced a bunch of keys, studying them carefully before selecting the right one and unlocking the door. The room I entered was panelled, alternate panels decorated with bunches of flowers on a faded blue background. There was a marble fireplace flanked on both sides by empty bookshelves. The furniture was sparse, formal: a sofa and two matching armchairs covered in floral silk that had seen better days. A chandelier with some of its glass drops missing hung from the centre of the ceiling and the plaster cornice had gaps in several paces. I went through into the kitchen, a much smaller room, which in turn led into a bathroom. The bedroom was larger with a double bed in the French style like Machell's, together with an ornate wardrobe and side table.

"Yes, fine," I said in German. "I'll take it. What rent are you asking?"

"I am open to negotiation," Krenkler replied. "Will you be paying in cash or in other ways?"

"Cash."

"Dollars?"

"No. British Army currency."

He shrugged, obviously disappointed. Nobody wanted the Monopoly-style notes we had put into circulation. I named a figure which he agreed without argument and I gave him a month's rent in advance. "I won't be living here myself, I'm taking it for a lady friend, Fraulein Grundwall, but I will be responsible for all the outgoings."

"It's no concern of mine," Krenkler said, "as long as you don't turn my house into a brothel." As he pocketed the cash he gave me a sly smile. "Do you ever have any spare coffee?"

"Possibly."

"I can always give it a home," he said, freeing two keys from his bunch. "One for the main door and one for this apartment."

I came away excited, feeling I had acted positively.

"Cunning old sod, slipping in that bit about spare coffee," Webb said. "Can't blame him, I suppose. He must have seen better days."

On the return journey I asked: "Are you going to marry your fraulein?"

"Yeah, I expect so. Just worried if she'll fit in back home. I found Blighty totally foreign even to me the last time I went back on furlough. Not that I had much to go back to with the wife getting shagged by the local Air Raid Warden. I came across him in a pub while I was there. A right ponce and I thought about decking him, then decided he was welcome to her. One thing's for sure, whatever happens I won't be going parking my heavy pack in Huddersfield. Might even pitch my tent here, learn the lingo properly, and find a decent job, because bet your life we'll put fucking Germany on its feet before we sort out our own fucking problems. What d'you intend when you get out, sir?"

"Tell you the truth, I don't know."

Listening to him considering his future, it was brought home to me that my own would be decided by Grundwall. I wondered whether during his university lectures he had ever quoted Gauguin's 'Life being what it is, one dreams of revenge.' As he faced thirty years behind bars, what else was left for him but revenge?

The next few weeks passed slowly. I wrote to Lisa every other day, describing the apartment I had rented and reiterating that I wanted to marry her. A further Telex from Major Jones informed me that Grundwall's defence had lodged an appeal with the Allied Control Council. That body interpreted its duty as limited to considerations of mercy linked to a possible reduction of sentence, its members being judged not competent, in legal terms, to override the Tribunal's verdicts. In due course word came back that the appeal had failed and That Grundwall was being transferred to a prison outside Hamelin and would be allowed one visit a month. I saw that my only course was to confess my involvement to Lisa before her father got in first.

I began a new letter and after four drafts, I finally settled on this: 'My Dearest Lisa, I have just been told that your father will shortly be moved from Nuremberg to a prison in the Hamelin area and will now be permitted visitors once a month. I know that you want to see him as soon as possible, even though it is a long journey from Hamburg. I will find out what documents and permissions you and your mother need and help with the fares.

Sweetheart, I realise that many of the things that happened during the war are incomprehensible to those who did not take part. The role your father played can only be understood if one accepts that the world is not black and white. Sadly, none of us can live life backwards and what happened, happened. Perhaps there is a God who will forgive all our actions. I wouldn't know, because I stopped believing in Him when one of my friends was blown to pieces in front of my eyes.

I told you the story of the young Jewish mother I helped die so that you might understand that we all had to make terrible choices and that the one I had to make at Belsen will always haunt me, just as what I have to now tell you may well end any love you have for me. I must take that risk because if we are ever to have a life together you must learn the truth from me and nobody else.

Because of the job I had to do during and after the war, it was my fate to be the one who first discovered your father's past. In the course of my duties, I examined a photograph taken at Auschwitz. To my horror I recognised your father in the photograph and saw that he had been an SS officer. At first I put my love for you before my duty and said nothing of my discovery, but then I realised that if I said nothing it would be a total betrayal of that poor Jewish mother girl and thousands like her. I also realised that by exposing your father, your love for me might not survive. You now know the choice I made and I can only ask you to try and understand that I owed a debt to the dead. Now you will make your own choice and I will have to live by your decision. I love you very much, and always will, but perhaps that will not prove enough. I pray it will, for to lose you is unthinkable."

When I read it the following morning I saw all its inadequacies, but I knew I had to post it and risk everything. I sealed the envelope and handed it to the clerk in the Mail Room on the way to the office I shared with Rawnsley. He was already at his desk and waved a languid hand in my direction as I entered. "That character was never there," he said.

"What character was never where?"

"That Control Commission bod. Chivers. A complete bloody phoney, never set foot in Bletchley. It really chokes me. We win the war against all odds and then entrust the peace to ghastly little shits like him." He picked up his pipe, pointed it like a pistol and mouthed a silent 'Bang!' "Shoot the buggers, that's what I'd like to do."

"I'm all for that. What's the perfume you're wearing?"

Rawnsley, immediately aggrieved, said, "It's not a perfume, it's an after-shave I bought in the Yank PX. Don't you like it?"

"Not over much."

Hurt, he began to fill the pipe from a leather pouch. "Our leader wants to see you. Been in twice looking for you so don't keep him waiting any longer. He's become increasingly irritable, I find. Probably male menopause."

"We could be about to fish in muddy waters," Graham began as soon as I entered his den. "Word is that somebody wants to come across."

"Who?"

"We're giving him the codename Vanya. Maybe he'll prove to be a useful uncle, maybe not. Ever seen a production?"

"I'm sorry?" I said, all at sea. I could never get used to

the way in which he jumped from one topic to another without drawing breath.

"The play, Uncle Vanya? You've seen it, surely?"

"No, I haven't."

"Then you've missed the best Chekhov by far," Graham pronounced. parading his knowledge. "It gives a unique insight into human frailty."

"You're saying this 'Vanya' is a possible defector?"

"Yes. Possible. One of our scalp-hunters in Bern made the contact and he sounds hopeful. He met Vanya at a Soviet Trade Mission and during a heavy drinking session put out a feeler. Got a good initial feeling and subsequently engineered a one-on-one on safer ground."

"Who is Vanya?"

"Heavy hitter apparently. Colonel in the KGB, learned his trade in the Cheka. During the war ran a network of partisans behind German lines. His only son was a tank commander who was shot during one of the purges. Vanya was lucky to escape the same fate. That sort of sob story can be suspect, but our man believes his disillusionment to be genuine. With his tongue loosened, he boasted he had plenty to sell and after our man had helped him demolish a second bottle of Stolly, named his price, always a good sign they're serious. Our man played it deliberately vague, said he didn't have the authority to take it further without getting back to London, but said we would be in touch if we got the okay. So, who knows? Could be a plant. On the other hand, could be a boost to our fortunes. We need a success after the recent failures. I thought you might like to cut your teeth on him, handle the next stage."

"What's that?"

"Vanya's coming to East Berlin in three weeks for a Trade Fair. Always good pickings to be had at such events – new Western contacts, opportunities for blackmail."

"Blackmail?"

"Yes. God you're naïve. Classic KGB technique. Hone in on a likely target, get him legless, put him in a hotel room with a tart or rent boy, take a few incriminating snapshots and apply the screws. I want you to go to the fair, meet him and form a judgement. Is he the genuine article or a dummy? We'll thoroughly brief you and provide you with a new identity. My first idea is to make you a salesman for British motorbikes. Know anything about them?"

"Nothing. Never ridden one."

"Ah, well, I'll think again."

"How will I recognise him?"

"We have photographs. Think you can handle it?"

"Hope so."

Digesting this new development, I went back to my office and found some mail on my desk, two letters, one from home, and the other with a German postmark. I tore this one open. It was short, written on the back of a theatre call sheet, the handwriting uneven.

'Mein Leibe Alex, please don't be angry, but I think I'm pregnant and I'm so scared what you will say. Tell me what I should do. I will wait at the stage door every day at one o'clock for you to ring me. Please ring as soon as you get this. I love you. Lisa.' The last sentence was heavily underlined.

"You look as though you've seen a ghost", Rawnsley said. "Bad news from home?"

"No." I walked to the window and read her note again.

"By the way, did you see the Labour government intend to cut our budget?"

"I haven't read the papers for a couple of days."

"It's vital to keep up with the real world."

I thought: the real world isn't in *The Times*, it's here in this note. I rushed back to the mailroom.

"That letter I handed in a little while ago," I said to the post clerk. "Can you give it me back, I need to add something."

"Sorry, sir, already collected."

"How long ago?"

"At least half an hour, sir."

"Where does the mail go from here?"

"Couldn't say for certain, sir."

"Well, who would know? They must go somewhere, man. Find out."

He disappeared for a while, but returned to say: "No joy, sir. Nobody seems to know exactly."

I agonised until it was lunch time, then rang the theatre stage door at exactly one o'clock only to hear the engaged tone. I redialled every two but it was permanently busy. I had the number checked, all to no avail. Later the same day, around the time when Lisa usually finished rehearsals, I tried again. This time the surly stage door keeper male agreed to fetch Lisa and I finally heard her voice. "Darling," I said, "I tried to phone at lunch time as you asked, but the line was always busy."

"Everybody uses it." She sounded flat. "Are you angry with me?"

"Why would I be angry? Of course I'm not. I'll be thrilled if it's true."

"It is true," she answered. "I saw a doctor yesterday. I'm so frightened, I wish you could come back."

"I will as soon as I can, darling, but it isn't that easy..." The connection went dead and although I redialled immediately, now it was busy. After several tries with the same results, I gave up. My life was in a code I could not decipher. I tried to rehash what I knew about pregnancy, but my limited knowledge was a collection of dubious old wives' tales. I buttonholed Graham just as he was leaving the building.

"How long before Vanya comes to East Berlin?"

"Eighteen days, why?"

"I know I shouldn't ask this, but can I have your

permission to go to Hamburg for a quick visit, forty eight hours at the most?"

"Why?"

"My girlfriend's just told me she's pregnant."

"Don't go. Send her the money for an abortion," Graham said coldly.

"I can't do that, she means too much to me."

"D'you really want a child by her, given the background? Children last a long time, Alex."

"She still has no idea of the part I played in her father's arrest. A letter's in the post in which I confessed everything, and I need to get to her before it arrives if I'm to save our relationship."

"Don't' save it, save yourself from future grief," Graham said.

"I have to try."

He studied me for a few moments. "Well, if you're intent on ruining your life, obviously nothing I say will have any effect, so you'd better go. But, be back in forty eight hours. Any longer and you're in trouble."

"I really appreciate it, Graham."

"You must have realised by now that my steely exterior hides a sentimental fool underneath. Go before I change my mind."

I used a WAAF contact in Air Control to get me a bucket seat on one of the daily Dakota flights. It was dark when we landed in Hamburg and once again I pulled rank and requested a car from Military Police to Lisa's address. She opened the door to me this time instead of Greta. She was in a dressing gown, bare footed, her face blotched from crying. "I thought I'd never see you again, "she said. "I thought you'd hung up on me," as I held and kissed her

"Don't be silly. The phone went dead and although I tried I couldn't get through again."

I could feel she was naked under her gown.

"And you're not angry?"

"Would I have come if I was angry? I'm going to marry you, aren't I?"

"You still want to?" She was close to tears. "Why are you so nice to me?"

"I don't know. It must be that I love you."

While we hugged each other, over her shoulder I scanned the room but, to my relief, I couldn't see my letter anywhere. I produced a bottle of wine I had brought with me. "Come on, we're going to celebrate. You gave me good news about the baby and I've got some for you." I uncorked the wine and poured two glasses. "Come and sit on my lap." She did as I asked and we clinked glasses. "You remember I said I wanted you to leave here and be with me in Berlin? Well, I've rented an apartment for you."

"Really?"

"Really. Once you're there I'll take more care of you." I put my hand on her stomach. "Both of you. "

It was only then that thoughts of her father surfaced. "And have you been able to find out more about father? Have they given a verdict?"

"Yes," I said. "I put everything in the letter you haven't got yet."

"And they're going to set him free. Is that what's in the letter?"

As gently as I could, I said: "No, sweetheart, they're not."

Her face crumpled. "Not?"

"They found him guilty."

"How could they?" She wriggled off my lap and stood facing me. "He's not guilty of anything, it's all lies."

I held out my arms to her, but she did not respond. "The evidence against him was damning, sweetheart. He was convicted and given thirty years."

She swayed, uttering a cry like an animal and rushed to

the sink where she bent over and retched. I went to her and supported her head until the spasms subsided, then helped into the only armchair. Her dressing gown gaped open, exposing her nakedness, but she made no attempt to cover herself, but rocked backwards and forwards. She was shivering and I fetched my army greatcoat and draped it around her shoulders. Reaching for her clenched fist I gently loosened the fingers one by one and held her hand in mine. Speaking slowly as to a child, I said, "I've told you everything in my letter. When you get it you'll understand."

"I want to understand now."

"All right. I'll tell you now." I began to tell her the contents of my letter, telling it in a way that softened the blows. She said nothing until I had struggled through to the end, but her nails gradually dug into my palm. "That's the whole story," I finished. "I've kept back nothing."

She pulled her hand away. "And the part you played, does Vater know that?"

"Yes."

"And you believe he's guilty?"

"The court found him guilty."

"But what do you believe?"

"Is that important any more?"

"To me it is."

"I believe he had a past he had to answer for."

"You betrayed him," she said. "Why?"

"I've just explained why."

"Because of that one Jewish woman?"

"Not just her."

"Would you have done the same if it had been your own father?"

"Darling, that's not a fair question."

"It is to me. Whatever he did or did not do, he'll always be my father. I shall never abandon him."

"I'd never want you to." I tried to reach for her hand

again, but she would have none of it. "We have a life, too, don't we?" She did not answer. "Don't we?" I repeated. "Doesn't the fact that you're carrying my child count?"

"I don't know," she said. She was calm now, calm and cold. "I don't know anything any more. When I see Vater, he'll decide for me."

"Well, I'm certain he hates me, so I can guess what his answer will be. The only thing that matters to me is what you decide."

"He will decide," she said again.

"You say I betrayed him, but he was guilty with or without me, and he betrayed you by what he kept hidden. Of course you mustn't abandon him, I wouldn't want you to, but does that mean you're going to throw away what we have?" I waited. "Does it? I have to know." I searched her face for any sign that would give me hope. "I haven't changed because of what has happened."

"Perhaps I have," she said flatly. "How could it ever be the same again? Always between us."

"Do you think I came here today believing we could turn back the clock and wipe out the past? We have to live with what's handed to us. Life isn't a dance floor you can walk off if you don't like the tune they're playing. I came dreading what I had to tell you, but I thought that what we feel for each other could overcome everything. This pain will pass, I promise."

"Don't make me any more promises. I'm tired of promises. You gave me something and then you took it away," she said in the same remote voice."

"You mustn't believe that," I said, but I might as well have been talking to a stranger.

"What else is left for me? My father's life is over, he'll die in prison."

"It's the life he made for himself, but there's another life to think about now, the life of the child inside you."

204

"I shall do whatever Vater decides," she said like a mantra.

"Am I no longer in the reckoning? Look at me. Look at me. I thought you loved me."

"I do I love you," she said, "but it's not enough any more." She took my greatcoat from her shoulders and handed it to me like a hotel cloakroom attendant. It was a dismissal.

"I'd rather you hated me, than this," I said. "One can live with hate." I put on the greatcoat and picked up my hat from the table. I waited, but she gave me no last minute reprieve. "I'll see that you and your mother get the necessary permissions to visit. Have you enough money for the fares?"

"We'll find the money somewhere."

"Tell me if you can't" I leant forward and kissed her cheek. It was like kissing a statue. "Just take care of yourself."

The same disabled war veteran we had encountered before was coming up the stairway and I stood to one side to let him pass. I felt as crippled as him, the sense of loss hollowing me like somebody who has been told he has a terminal illness.

TWENTY EIGHT

Graham never asked me about the outcome of my visit, nor did I volunteer anything. Preparations for my coming trip to the Eastern sector occupied me during the following weeks, but I made time to track down the various permissions Lisa and her mother needed to visit Grundwall. I sent these together with the location of the prison in Hamelin. Every day I searched the mail for her handwriting on an envelope, praying she had had a change of heart, but nothing ever came.

Having decided what my new identity should be, Graham provided me with a passport in the name of Alex Wilmot, a salesman for farm equipment, born in, Boston, Lincolnshire. "Better not to change your Christian name, avoids making any inadvertent slip. Likewise I settled on farming as an occupation so that you're on familiar territory. I take it you still remember your bucolic childhood?"

"Yes."

"We'll be supplying you with a bunch of current Trade brochures for tractors, combine-harvesters and other agricultural equipment, together with price lists and delivery schedules."

"What happens if I actually take orders?"

"You accept them. The Firm has a covert department that will deal with them, but don't expect any commission. Practice your new signature; you're bound to have to sign in at the fair, and on any order forms. Remember, Vanya will be looking for any chink in your armour, just as you must be ultra aware of any in his."

"Is Alex Wilmot married?"

"I thought not. Means another layer to remember."

"But presumably he was in the war?"

"Yes, we gave that a lot of thought. He served in a home ack ack Battery and never went overseas."

"What rank?"

"Sergeant, Royal Artillery. It'll all be in your file."

He and Rawnsley put me through several mock sessions rehearsing me in the dialogue I could expect from Vanya, whose real name was Sergheyevich Vassiltchikov.

"The priorities you must quickly determine are (a) is he a plant? (b) has he got anything of value to sell? and (c) should we buy? Remember, if he tumbles you, Alex Wilmot is dead in the water, a non-person, nothing to do with us. As far as we're concerned you never existed."

"Tell me the bad news," I said as cheerfully as I could.

"Make doubly sure you carry nothing on you that connects you to your real self. When you smoke, smoke the British commercial brands not any Army issue. Above all, don't sound keen, let him make the running. You play the role of somebody who's been there before and knows the dangers for you both. Happy so far?"

"No, but go on."

"Okay, let's walk it through step by step. Let's assume you've just met him. First you make certain it is Vanya."

"How do I do that?"

"Our man in Berne gave him the passwords. At some point Vanya will ask whether you ever have snow in England. You'll reply, 'Sometimes, but nothing like you get in Russia.'"

"God, real schoolboy stuff."

"Yes, well, schoolboy stuff, as you put it, is important," Graham, said with a hint of annoyance. "Don't mock it. Get it wrong and it's curtains. Right. Assuming you've got over that hurdle and had an initial discussion about the products you're promoting, then you suggest you go somewhere more congenial for a drink, and hopefully he'll take you to a bar or restaurant, preferably somewhere noisy where you can talk. Even so, there could still be bugs. Has he got a flower in his buttonhole? Good place for a mike. A vase of flowers on the table or bar top, or fixed to the underside of the table."

"Understood. Can I go back a bit? You said we'd have an initial conversation about farm machinery. Will he be knowledgeable about that?"

"He'll probably pretend interest for appearances sake. He's playing the same game as you, don't forget. His cover is he's attending the fair as an official of their Trade Ministry. The fair's genuine enough, they're anxious to get their hands on Western technology."

"Does he speak English?"

"Yes. And German."

"Since he's a hardened pro," I said, "surely he'll know we wouldn't send a tractor salesman to recruit him."

"Of course. What's your problem? He'll know you're not the genuine article. He's not interested in that, all he'll be looking for is proof that we've taken him seriously and taken it a step further. His main concern will be to be satisfied we can protect him once we've got him out. That and the financial consideration, of course. Money speaks louder than loyalty. If you're satisfied with his answers, you are authorised to assure him on both points. We will protect him once he's with us, give him a new identity and a payment of fifty thousand sterling in Swiss francs."

"Christ!" I exclaimed. "I wouldn't mind a deal like that."

"The fair lasts three weeks," Graham said, ignoring this. "If you come back with a positive reaction, we'll bring him across on the last day."

"I don't care for you saying 'if'."

"Okay, when you come back."

"How will you bring him across?"

"Once again it's all detailed in your file. You will instruct him to be in the loading bay area at noon on the final day. We're anticipating there'll be maximum activity on that day with everybody packing up. A white truck marked Mayflower Refrigeration AG driven by our Sergeant Webb will arrive with a consignment of American refrigerators, invoiced for the personal attention of Vanya. He will inspect them and pass all but one. The ones he accepts are then off-loaded, and the faulty one he has deemed unacceptable returned to the West. During his inspection he will have found a British passport complete with photograph naming him as Albert Chamberlain, electrician. This will be inside the ice compartment of the faulty fridge, sealed in the packet containing the guarantee together with five thousand dollars on account to give him confidence that we're on the level. Then he gets into the cabin beside Webb and they drive out."

"Will that work?"

"There's bound to be chaos on the last day and we've timed it so that, if all goes to plan, Webb will reach the checkpoint just after the guards change over. All the paperwork will be in order and the new guards won't know that there was only one man in the truck when it came in."

"Fingers crossed."

"Once we've debriefed him and extracted our pound of flesh, we'll hand him over to the Yanks. They'll ship him out on a cargo flight, to live happily ever after. Or not as the case may be. Who cares?"

He and Rawnsley took me through the plan several more times before they were confident I had mastered everything, paying particular attention to Vanya's photographs. My travel kit consisted of a second-hand English suit, shirt, tie and shoes, a well-scuffed wallet containing items such as a railway ticket stub, a Farmers Union membership card and a picture of Vera Lynn cut from a magazine. I still had a feeling of taking part in a fantasy with sinister undertones; Graham had left me in no doubt that if the operation went belly up, I would be abandoned to my fate. 'Abandoned' was a word that inevitably led me back to Lisa. 'I shall never abandon him' she had said and I tried to imagine what had taken place when she and her father had finally been reunited. What had his decision been? Had he insisted that she terminate the pregnancy? Abortion was a criminal offence in Germany; at his bidding would she resort to some dangerous backstreet job?

The morning I was due to go in I carefully checked the interior of the car I was driving. "It's clean," Harry Webb said. "Been over it twice, sir. False number plates, full tank and the brakes are shit hot. But don't take my word for it, check it out and test it yourself."

There was a scuffed fibre suitcase on the back seat packed with some toiletries (a bar of Yardley soap, spare razor blade. toothbrush and toothpaste), a change of shirt and socks with British laundry marks and a quantity of Trade brochures. The suitcase had a label attached to the handle giving my name and an address in Boston, Lincolnshire. I had also been issued with currency in used notes – the equivalent of a hundred pounds in Occupation notes and three hundred US dollars.

"Watch your back, at all times, sir," Harry said, "and don't forget Stalin is holier than JC."

Feeling naked without my uniform and gun, I tested the brakes before moving off. Webb had done a great job and the engine was tuned to perfection. I followed the line of the canal then turned north onto Friedrichstrasse, heading for the American checkpoint. The GIs on duty enquired the reason for my visit and examined my passport before waving me through. Leaving them I preceded across the uneven surface of Zimmerstrasse to the G.D.R. barriers. The frontier police ordered me out of the car and took my passport into the control hut. Another demanded to know how much money I was carrying. I produced the notes, which were spread out on a table and counted twice. Before handing them back the policeman pocketed some of the dollars. It was quite blatant, no attempt to conceal the theft.

"We like dollars," he said.

"Don't we all?" I wasn't going to argue.

"Do you have camera?"

"No."

"Radio?"

"No."

"The purpose of your visit?"

I indicated the brochures. "I'm a salesman going to your great Trade fair."

He searched the car's interior and boot, opening my suitcase and rifling through the contents, then made me release the hood catch and examined the engine. Finally he trundled a mirror under the chassis, only then was my passport returned by his companion. I noted the passport had been marked on one page with a coloured pencil.

When I was allowed to proceed I drove around the concrete blocks until stopped by a Vopo. He too demanded to examine my passport before waving me through. An armed soldier raised the barrier and I entered East Germany for the first time. The Trade Fair was being held in a giant warehouse half a mile from The Friedrichstrasse railway station and had been given a makeover for the occasion. A large banner proclaiming the event stretched across the facade. I parked my car where I was directed, retrieved my stack of brochures and walked to the entrance and purchased a ticket, paying for it in dollars. Inside I was greeted by two uniformed, hatchet-faced women manning a stall extolling the virtues of life in the G.D.R. and accepted the leaflets they thrust at me. I toured the fifty or more exhibits and although some displayed Western exports, most held products from the Communist bloc with a distinctly antique appearance, reminding me of items in rural museums devoted to the dawn of the industrial revolution. I thought it politic to do the rounds while keeping a weather eye open for Vanya. Martial music blared from loudspeakers, punctuated every now and again with official announcements, as watchful Volkspolizie circulated in pairs amongst the crowds. Playing my bogus role, I distributed some of my brochures to the officials on the agricultural stall and was gratified to find that I could do a passable job of salesmanship. There was a refreshment area offering free food and drink and while introducing myself to my first dollop of caviar, I was suddenly tapped on the shoulder and turned to find Chivers alongside.

"How about this, sport?" he boomed. "Haven't seen Beluga for years." He spooned a generous mouthful, a few eggs dropping onto the lapel of his shiny suit. "Must tell you, just pulled off a humdinger of a deal. Fifty Practikas at a price you wouldn't believe."

"Do me a favour and fuck off," I hissed.

Chivers jaw dropped, traces of caviar on his lower lip. "I beg your pardon, who d'you think you're talking to, soldier?"

"It's not soldier, it's Captain, and I said, fuck off. You don't know me and I don't know you. Understood?"

"No, I don't."

"Use your loaf for fuck'sake. I'm here undercover."

I quickly walked away. Unnerved by the encounter, but thankful it had happened before I made contact with Vanya, I went back to the agricultural stall and found the same man I had approached earlier.

"Any interest?" I asked.

"It's possible we might be interested in tractors at the right price." "What d'you consider the right price?"

"Less than you quote here."

"Well, I'm sure we could better it, depending on how

212

many you order." Beyond him I suddenly spotted Vanya making his way towards us. "Give me some idea how many you're thinking of."

"That will be decided by the Ministry. I merely pass on the information."

The moment Vanya joined us the man became deferential. Vanya was wearing a superior blue serge suit with the ribbon of the Order of The Red Star in his buttonhole.

"We are discussing tractors, Comrade Commissar," the man said. He handed my brochure to Vanya as I introduced myself.

"Vassiltchikov," he responded and shook my hand firmly. Examining the brochure, he said: "No Fordson's? I'm told the Fordson is a good machine."

"We are agents for Massey-Fergusson's, equally good, but I'm sure we could supply Fordsons if they're your preference."

"Who's to say what preference I have until I know the price?"

"Exactly, Comrade Commissar," the other man said. "I made the same point. The price is all important."

Vanya said: "We know you capitalists make a big profit whatever the price. Are the ones you sell reliable?"

"Very reliable."

"In all conditions? We have very bad weather in Russia. Have you any idea how cold it gets? Minus thirty degrees some years. You're from England, yes?"

"Yes."

"Do you get snow in England?"

"Sometimes," I answered slowly, "but nothing like you get in Russia." I saw Vanya's eyes give a slight flicker.

"Nothing is like Russia," he said. "Everything in Russia is bigger than anywhere else. Perhaps you and I can do business, perhaps not. No guarantees, but let's have a drink and find out." To the salesman he said: "Leave this to me, comrade. I know how to bargain with capitalists. Come, Mr. Wilmot, let us find the vodka."

As we walked towards the hospitality area we passed Chivers gesticulating to three dour-looking types. He broke off and glared at me.

"Who is that man?" Vanya asked, catching the look.

"Which man?"

"The one I saw you talking to a few minutes ago."

"No idea. He came up and tried to sell me some cameras."

"Is he one of yours?" he asked.

For a second he caught me off guard. "If you mean, is he British, yes I think so, but I've never seen him before."

"One should always be careful not to talk to strangers, don't you agree?"

"I agree." At the refreshment table he did not wait to be served but grabbed an open bottle of vodka by the neck and poured two generous shots. "To the German Democratic Republic," he said.

"The German Democratic Republic."

"And tractors," Vanya said. "May they soon be ploughing our fields."

"Is the fair going well?"

"We have a lot of ground to make up. Our war brought terrible hardships."

"Let's hope we can be of some help." Mindful of Graham's advice, I started carefully, determined to sound and act the professional. "Tell me, what is the average acreage of Russian farms? Are they in hundreds or thousands? I ask because I need to point you towards the right size of engine."

"Tens of thousands."

"I see. That's big by our standards."

"As I said, in the USSR everything is on the heroic scale."

"Like your war effort."

"What did you do in the war, Mr. Wilmot?"

"I was in the Artillery."

"Where?"

"In England. I served in a coastal ack ack battery. And you?"

"Infantry," Vanya said. He took out a leather cigar case containing three dark cigars and offered one to me.

"I'll stick to cigarettes if you don't mind." I produced a packet of Passing Clouds. "Would you care to try one of these?"

"They're not strong enough for me."

He lit a cigar and offered the burning match to me for my cigarette. "So, let's get down to business. How many and how soon can you supply us?"

"Well, like you, many of our factories were badly bomb damaged, but we're getting back to normal. We would of course give any order from you top priority. Delivery times would depend on the size of your order."

"No, it would depend on the price. Quote me for two hundred."

"Two hundred! That would make my company very happy. If you're thinking in those numbers I'm sure my bosses would come back with a very attractive price. I'll put it to them and get back to you.."

"How are your bosses? Do they grind the workers into the ground?

"No those days have gone. Look, since I'm sure we are going to strike a deal, can I take you for a meal? It would give me great pleasure, but you choose where. I don't know East Berlin at all."

"Sure, I know places. You want company?"

"Company?"

"Female company."

"Oh, I see. I thought we would be talking business."

"That is business," Vanya said. He laughed, his face partially obscured as he exhaled a cloud of acrid smoke from his cigar. "But I insist you will be my guest. I will show you real Russian food. The Germans only know how to cook one thing. Their goose." He waited for me to react to his joke and I dutifully laughed.

"That's very good," I said. "I must remember that one."

Vanya led the way out of the warehouse, waving aside the officials at the door when they asked for me to show my ticket. A uniformed driver was waiting beside a black limousine and Vanya gave him instructions in Russian. We sped through empty streets at high speed, with Vanya giving me a running commentary. "Already we are rebuilding all this in our image and then we will repopulate it. Before long it will become Russian. Germany will never rise again, we will see to that. Our beloved Stalin made sure we got here first."

"It must have been bloody at the end," I said.

"They destroyed Stalingrad, we erased Berlin."

We drew up outside what appeared to be a large private house and the driver hastened to open Vanya's passenger door. A Russian soldier snapped to attention and saluted as we entered. I had a sense of foreboding. Inside, the circular marble hallway, dominated by a portrait of Stalin, opened into a small anteroom. This led into a much larger room which was the restaurant. We were conducted to a side table in one of the alcoves. Remembering Graham's warning, as I sat down I dropped my sheaf of brochures. Bending to retrieve them I checked the underside of the table for a bug, but could see nothing untoward. "This is very impressive," I remarked as a waiter immediately brought a carafe of vodka. There were no flowers on the table.

"What shall we drink to?" Vanya asked when he had poured two glasses of vodka.

"How about 'to happy conclusions?'" My hand was clammy and the glass almost slipped out of my grasp.

"Or 'Journey's End'?" Vanya responded with a straight face.

Now the cat and mouse proceedings begin, I thought. Both of us watching for chinks in the armour, as Graham had put it. Vanya was sure to be an old hand at mind games. I faced somebody who had spent his entire life keeping one step ahead of others.

"You say things are bad in England. How bad?"

"We're virtually bankrupt, having pawned the family silver to pay for the war."

"Sold to the Yanks, yes? What they called Lend Lease. What d'you think of the Yanks?" Before I could answer, he gave his own opinion. "They take everything."

"Well, they give a lot back too."

"Soon we will be spoken of as God's own country instead of them. Soon we will overtake everybody. Comrade Stalin will see to that. He switched abruptly to another subject. "What are conditions like for workers in England?"

"The new Labour government is bringing in measures to improve their lot."

"Your Labour party is imitation socialism, a half-way house."

"Change is always slow in England, and everything is in short supply. We still have food rationing."

"In Leningrad they ate rats and dogs during the siege," Vanya said. "That's what we call short supplies. You don't get shorter than that." The waiter returned and hovered. "Let me order for you. Dog is not on the menu today." He gave the orders rapidly in Russian.

"So, shall we talk tractors?" I asked after he had poured more vodka.

"All in good time. One should never be in a hurry to take important decisions. Agreed?"

"Except I have to make a living. My employers want results." My response seemed so weak. I thought: are we both going to talk in riddles? "Just a suggestion, but perhaps, it would be a good idea for you to visit England and inspect the product before placing an order? As our guest, of course. Is it easy for you to travel abroad?"

"It can be arranged. Not easy, but possible. Everything is possible if the will is there. Would I be paid for this visit?"

"Paid?"

"A commission?"

"Sure, that wouldn't present any problem," I answered, trying to keep my response casual. "Is the idea of such a visit attractive to you?"

"It could be if it holds benefits."

We were served hot Borsch with coarse black bread and we both ate in silence for a while.

"This is excellent," I said. "I've never had it before."

"Did I not tell you? Russian food is good for the soul."

After I took the last mouthful I asked: "What sort of benefits would you be looking for?"

"Certain assurances."

"As well as a commission?"

"Of course."

I found myself floundering, knowing that now I had to move the dialogue onto a different level. This, together with the knowledge that I was on enemy territory – the restaurant was so obviously the preserve of top Party officials – there was always the possibility that I had been led like a lamb into a trap. Even if the table wasn't bugged, hidden cameras could be filming everything. Toying with my spoon, and pushing calm at him, I said: "We're just fencing with each other, aren't we?"

"Are we?"

"Oh, I think so. But I'm used to that," I continued, attempting to give the impression we were equally matched. "If we meet your demands, my company usually looks for a long term business relationship benefiting both parties. That inspires confidence. If I go back and ask them to grant you favourable terms, it would be reasonable, would it not, for them to expect a return gesture?"

I waited as the soup plates were removed and we were served with generous helping of meat and cabbage. "It comes down to mutual trust," I resumed.

"So, how do we go about achieving that trust?"

"It begins here at this table," I replied. I was feeling more confident. "So you lead. Tell me what you would want."

"No, what would they give?"

"Luxuries."

"Such as?"

"Enabling you to enjoy a different life style."

"And where would I enjoy that?"

"Your choice." He stopped eating and took out his cigar case. "But the first question they'll ask, of course, is whether your credit is good."

He bit off the end of a cigar. "One accumulates a lot of credit in twenty years. It would a relief to cash it in and buy some security for one's old age."

"Can you show them an indication of what you've accumulated? Something I could take back with me?"

His cigar case was lying between us on the table. "I thought you might ask that," Vanya said. "Help yourself to my last cigar, but don't smoke it until you get home. It will remind you of our pleasant meeting."

I extracted the last cigar, held it to my nose as I had seen others do, and rolled it between my fingers before carefully tucking it into a breast pocket.

"Let's talk about specifics," Vanya said. "Assuming I have provided your people with enough to convince them of my credit rating, what is the next step?"

"Well, we deal in a variety of other goods. One of our subsidiary companies exports American refrigerators. It so happens a consignment of these is due to arrive here at noon on the final day of the fair in a truck with the name 'Mayflower' on it. In your capacity as a Ministry official you could make it your business to inspect them."

"Why would I do that?"

"To make certain they're all in good condition. You could reject a damaged one."

"You think one might be damaged?"

"I'm sure of it. Delicate things refrigerators when they're transported over rough roads. The ice compartments always need careful scrutiny."

"The ice compartment?"

"Yes. Where they put the guarantees and instruction booklets. You never know what you might find."

I felt reasonably pleased at the way in which I had explained the plan.

"Guarantees are important," Vanya said. "Is there a time limit on them?"

"No. They're good for life. I think you'll find ours very generous."

Vanya flicked his drooping cigar ash onto his plate. "And what happens to the faulty refrigerator?"

Now I took the biggest risk. If he was playing with me then I was dead in the water, as Graham had put it. If, on the other hand, he genuinely intended to defect, then the final step of the plan had to be put to him. "Eventually," I began slowly, "it will be returned to the factory in the United States. The delivery truck will be driven in by one man. When it leaves just after the guards at the checkpoint have been changed, he could be accompanied by a second man as he drives out." I paused to let this sink in. "The new guards will not think anything odd about this, since they didn't check the van's arrival."

"So who is the second man?"

"I leave that up to you."

"Noon on the last day of the fair, you say?"

"Yes."

Vanya signalled a waiter for the bill.

"Whatever you decide I enjoyed meeting you," I said. "Thank you for your hospitality."

"Oh, this is your hospitality," he said, pushing the bill across the table. "We need all the hard currency we can get."

"Of course." I settled in dollars. It was a small price to pay to bring the ordeal to an end.

Vanya's car drove me back to the parking lot at the fair where we parted without ceremony.

TWENTY NINE

"Lucky," Graham said suddenly.

"Sorry?"

"I've just remembered the name of the cat."

"What cat?" I said, baffled. It was entirely typical of Graham to break off in mid sentence and introduce a completely new topic. "The one we had when we were first married. A tabby. Did you ever have a cat?"

"We had dogs. There was a cat, yes, a Tom, but you don't keep cats as pets on a farm. He was a good ratter, went feral in the end. What made you suddenly think of that?"

"Association. You playing cat and mouse with Vanya."

"The only time I felt he was serious was when he said it would be a relief to cash in twenty years credit. For 'credit' read information."

Graham said, "Old pro's like him are figure skaters who judge the thickness of the ice under their blades before striking out. The microfilm he gave you was middle grade stuff, nothing special. Still I wouldn't expect him to pass over the crown jewels at this stage. So now we must wait and see if he shows on the day. You did well from all accounts. Bringing somebody in from the cold is never easy."

"There is one other thing. Guess who turned up at the fair? Chivers. Isn't that a coincidence? I told him to piss off before he blew my cover."

"I always hate coincidences," Graham said. "They're seldom what they seem.

"Did anything else emerge about him?"

"Well we already know he was never at Bletchley. He was called up in 1942, only did his six weeks initial infantry training with the Essex Regiment, and was then discharged on medical grounds. Shaved his armpits, maybe, who knows? No record of him every applying to be a fighter pilot. That was another piece of bullshit he gave you. The trail goes dead after that until he surfaces over here in the Control Commission and turns up too often for comfort where you're concerned. I've sent word to Machell at your old unit, to keep close tabs on him."

Waiting for the last day of the fair, I remained consumed by the loss of Lisa. They say true lovers never accept finality. Over and over again I relived our last meeting, examining everything she had said like a forensic scientist searching a cadaver for clues to a death. More than once I weakened and phoned the stage door number, and although I got through once, I was told she was not available. The shell of my life had been removed.

On an impulse I went to find Harry Webb. He and his team were readying the truck he was to drive to the East sector. A stencil of the 'Mayflower' logo had been applied to both sides of the vehicle and half a dozen refrigerators were waiting to be loaded.

"Got a spare vehicle I can borrow?"

"Of course, sir. Take one of the Humbers," Webb said.

I drove myself to the apartment I had rented for Lisa. As I pulled up in front of the house I saw a small boy sitting on the porch steps attempting to mend a crude wooden replica of a bomber plane. He scrambled to his feet as I approached, hiding the plane behind his back.

"Let me see," I said in German.

He handed it to me. One wing hung loose from The fuselage. "You need glue," I said. "Do have any glue?" he shook his head. "Here." I held out some money. "Buy yourself some." Fear was replaced by surprise on his face as

223

his hand closed over the notes. Without a word, he ran off.

Letting myself in, I heard the same Beethoven sonata being practised. I mounted to the second landing and entered the empty apartment. Looking around I thought, this could have been our bedroom, here she could have cooked us a meal, this small room could have been the nursery. I slumped down in a corner of the main room, my back pressed against the flaking plaster and stayed there for over an hour, chain-smoking, wondering what her days were like now, whether by now she had visited her father and what had passed between them. Was she still carrying my child or had Grundwall ensured that he had the last word and persuaded her to abort? Above me, as though by thought transference, the unknown pianist began playing the song from The White Horse Inn. I felt cut off from everything and everybody – the recent encounter with Vanya seemed to belong to a doppelganger masquerading as me.

I stubbed out my last cigarette, exited the apartment and walked down to the basement. When Krenkler shuffled to the door at my summons, I handed him both keys.

"I'm returning these," I said. "My friend will not be coming after all."

Krenkler said: "I cannot give you back your money."

"That's okay, spend it on vodka."

Krenkler expression changed; he had obviously been expecting me to insist on partial repayment, but I had no stomach for a fight, I just wanted out.

Returning the car to the garage I found that Webb was still working.

"Care to join me for a night on the town, Harry?" I said.

"Never say no, sir. I'm your man, soon as I've cleaned up and made myself respectable."

We ate in a restaurant Webb had sampled before where the food was indifferent but the beer good. He drained his second stein and asked: "This trip I'm going to make, sir. Fancy he'll show?"

"We're hoping he will"

"Can't imagine what it must be like to take a step like that. Here I am wondering whether to put down roots here and he's about to turn his back on his homeland."

"Are you worried about bringing him out"

"Yes and no. Makes a change from routine, and something to talk about in years to come. Can't be as dangerous as Caen." He veered off the subject and said: "Forgive me asking, sir, but has your girlfriend moved in yet?

"No. She's not coming after all. I returned the keys today. It didn't work out," I said, cutting off further discussion. "Let's go on somewhere. Got any suggestions?"

"Depends what you're looking for."

"Oblivion."

"Sorry, sir?

"Don't keep calling me sir. We're off duty. My name's Alex. What am I looking for? Somewhere a bloody sight livelier than the Nuffield Club."

"Right, Alex." He used my Christian name awkwardly. When I had paid for the meal, he took me to nightclub in a side road off the Kurfurstendamn. Here the décor looked as though the designer had given up halfway through the makeover, the walls painted in lurid colours and decorated with Klimt prints. The tables had miniature flags of the three Allies on them and were grouped around a small dance floor where a few couples were gyrating slowly to recorded music. The waitresses were dressed in scanty outfits with pink bows in their hair. The Manager advanced on us.

"Guten abend, mein Herrs." He escorted us to a table one the edge of the dance floor. "You wish champagne?"

"No. Bring a bottle of Scotch," I said.

"Of course, mein Herr."

When my eyes became accustomed to the dim lighting, I could make out half a dozen women of indeterminate ages at the bar, dressed to impress the punters. A couple of them glanced in our direction.

"This okay?" Webb asked.

"Sure."

The Scotch, when it came, had a label I did not recognise. I poured two measures that old Machell would have approved of.

"To your safe return, Harry." It burnt my throat as it went down. Two women joined us.

"You wish company, gentlemen?" She was brunette, her companion a mousy blond.

"Why not?"

The brunette sat down next to me. "I'm Inga," she said, and my friend is Marlene." Her friend, a fairly obvious dyed blond displaying eye-stopping cleavage made sure that Webb didn't miss it as she joined him.

"Well, Inga, would you like a Scotch?"

"D'you have champagne?

"Is that the house rule?"

She glanced to the Manager. "Champagne is very nice."

"Well, we mustn't deny you." I signalled to the Manager who was already half way to us. "Champagne, mein Herrs?"

"How did you guess?" I said.

"You are British, ja?" Marlene said. She had a lisp.

"British to the core," Webb answered.

"British are always so polite. We like British very much."

"Marlene, eh?" Webb said. "They wrote a song about you. Do you know Lily Marlene?"

"Oh, ja."

"Big favourite of ours too." Webb launched into a few bars, and the girls clapped their hands in exaggerated delight. Then Inga followed him in German.

"Sounds better in German," I said when she had finished."

"Bitte?"

"Much sadder,"

"Ah, yes, very sad," she agreed.

"Shall I give them 'We'll hang out the washing?'" Webb said.

"Maybe not." The champagne arrived and was opened with a flourish despite the cork coming out with a plop rather than a bang. "Bottled yesterday, was it?" I said. He took this with a smile.

The girls raised their glasses. "Down the hatch," Inga said.

"Ah, you've said that before, haven't you?"

"Bitte?"

"Never mind. Skol."

Neither of them were great lookers, but they were pleasant enough. I listened as Webb chatted them up in his fractured German, which produced giggles. He was entirely at home, the typical British squaddie who knew his way around. I envied him.

"You are very quiet, you do not like me?" Inga said.

"Yes, I like you.

"You wish to dance? Is good music, I think."

"Very."

I took her onto the cramped dance floor. She immediately pressed herself against me and I felt the warmth of her body and caught a whiff of the cheap cologne was wearing. Whether it was just the whisky or holding a woman in my arms for the first time in weeks, I found I was aroused. When the number came to an end we remained on the floor waiting for the next record.

"Are you lonely?" she asked.

"I've been lonelier."

"I like you very much. Do you like me?"

"Yes, you're a very nice girl. Where are you from?"

"Before I am living in Leipzig. You know Leipzig|?"

"No."

227

"Is a beautiful city, but no work there."

The next number was a slow waltz and again she danced wIth the lower part of her body pressed into me. When the music ended and we returned to our table I said to Webb: "Shall we divide and conquer?"

"Sounds good."

"The evening's on me, Harry." I put some notes down on the table. "Here, this should handle it. Have a good time. Let's go someplace else," I said to Inga.

She took me to a house half a mile from the club where she lived in the basement. The living area had a divan bed in one corner covered with a fur throw, and in one corner there was a curtained-off kitchen area. The moment we were inside she killed the overhead light and switched on a small bedside lamp which filled the room with an orange glow, which she doubtless thought was erotic.

"Do we settle the money first?" I asked.

"As you wish. I trust you. The British are always generous. Bitte, make yourself comfortable." She disappeared into the bathroom.

I sat on the bed and noted a packet of condoms and a German Bible on the small table beside it. I removed my clothes, folding them neatly and placing them over the back of a chair. Naked, I got under the fur and waited for Inga's reappearance. When she reappeared from the bathroom she was wearing a pink robe which recalled the candlewick bedspreads my mother's generation thought the height of fashion. She let the robe drop to the floor, revealing a figure that owed more to the art of corsetry than to Nature. The contrast between her body and Lisa's immediately weakened my ardour. Inga joined me under the fur and reached down to fondle my flaccid penis before sliding down to fellate me. I willed my body to respond and her practised ministrations eventually produced the desired result. As soon as I was hard, she reached for a condom and expertly rolled it down my penis, then sat astride me and guided me inside her. For a few moments it seemed that I could perform, but then my erection collapsed.

"I'm sorry," I said.

"You don't find me attractive?"

"On the contrary, and it's nothing to do with you. I've had too much to drink," I said, wishing that was the real reason. The truth was the moment she had begun to writhe above me in simulated passion, disgust had replaced desire.

"You rest, then we try again. Yes, next time I make sure it is good."

I lay back on the thin pillow, but when she again tried to rouse me I gently lifted her head from my groin. "Don't," I said. "It's not your fault. I'll still pay you, don't worry."

I swung myself off the bed, desperate to escape. I removed the limp condom and put on my clothes. Inga watched me impassively. I handed a generous amount of money to her.

"Danke," she said twice.

Once outside I relished gulping in fresh air, happy that I had not betrayed Lisa, even though it was an act she would never learn of.

THIRTY

"What time is it now?" Graham asked, wiping the eyepieces of the field glasses with a handkerchief.

"Just gone twenty past one."

We were sitting in one of the Humbers with a clear view of the East German Control point. There was a fair amount of traffic coming and going, but so far no sign of our white van.

"How far is the drive from Fair to here?"

"It took me roughly half an hour," I said.

"They should have appeared by now if everything went to plan." Graham refocused the glasses and swept the checkpoint again. "More than the usual number of Volkspolizie around. Not a good sign." From long habit he spoke softly, as if there was a danger of being overheard, then handed the glasses to me. "Take a look."

I adjusted the range to my own eyesight and zeroed in on the border guards marching stiffly along the line of the sandbag emplacement, carbines slung. A battered Opel had been stopped at the first control hut. The driver was ordered out and directed by the Vopos into the command hut while they searched the car. He eventually reappeared and was given a body search before being allowed to go.

"They're being extra thorough today," I said.

We sat in silence for another fifteen minutes staring straight ahead. There was a lull in the traffic; a few cyclists came through, but no vehicles.

"Difficult race to understand, the Germans," Graham said suddenly.

"In what way?"

"They're such a mixture. Brahms Cradle Song and Wagner. And think how quickly that lot over there have accepted Uncle Joe in place of Adolf. Change of unIform, change of philosophy, no problem. Four years ago those goons would have been proudly wearing SS gear and herding Communists into the gas chambers . . . " He was about to launch into one of his philosophic monologues when I interrupted him.

"Our van's just appeared." I handed him the field glasses and he fiddled with the focus, exclaiming, "Jesus! Can't see a bloody thing. Your eyesight must be lousy." He adjusted the glasses to his own vision and studied the scene. "Yes, it's just been halted at the first barrier."

"Can you make out Vanya?"

"Yes. They've both got out and are going into the hut. All very casual. Guards seem relaxed. One has gone to the rear of the van and is looking inside. Wait, wait!"

"What is it?"

"Another car has pulled in front of our van. Black saloon, standard KGB issue. Came from behind the hut, obviously kept in readiness there. Three characters getting out of it. Doesn't look good."

I took the glasses from him and quickly refocused. The three men in dark suits Graham had mentioned were grouped to one side of their vehicle. Webb came out of the hut first, followed by Vanya. "Both Webb and Vanya have reappeared," I reported, "and are walking towards our white van." As they got closer the three men made their move, closing in on either side of Vanya and bundling him into the saloon. I saw Webb react and run to the van. Jumping in behind the wheel he gunned the engine and accelerated towards the barriers. The guards started shooting out his tyres. Although the van immediately veered crazily, Webb managed to keep going and crashed through the first barrier.

The sound of a siren carried to us and a further burst of gunfire came from the observation tower. I saw the windscreen on the van suddenly become opaque. Two more guards ran out and dropped to a kneeling position, pumping sustained automatic fire into the van which finally spun out of control and crashed onto its side by a bank of sandbags. The Vopos rushed to it and pulled Webb out.

"They've got Harry," I shouted. "The bastards have killed him."

Webb's body was quickly dragged out of sight and the black KGB saloon backed out and drove away. It was all over as quickly as it had begun.

"Oh, Jesus!" I said. I felt as though I had been watching a cinema trailer which didn't reveal the plot but showed the action highlights.

"That was all staged for our benefit. They knew we'd be watching," Graham said. "Let's go."

I turned the ignition key and swung the Humber's wheel.

"What happens now?" I asked.

"They'll lodge a complaint about a violation of their border controls. We'll deny any knowledge or involvement. End of story."

"That's it?"

"That's it." "

"Are you saying we're powerless to do anything?"

"Webb knew the risks. He knew nobody plays by the Queensbury rules. The body might be returned to us in due course. Maybe not."

"Don't you care?"

"Of course I bloody care. I sent him in."

I drove in silence for a while, reliving Webb's last moments, thinking to the night we had spent on the town with a couple of whores. Thinking, too, of a second flat in Krenkler's building that would now be vacant.

"Who d'you think blew the whistle?" I said finally.

"Could have been Vanya. Maybe he never intended to go through with it, just baited a trap which we fell into. Wouldn't be the first time. Then again he might have been serious, but got careless. We shall never know. Or, the worst scenario, somebody on our side gave them the tip off. However you look at it, we fucked up."

"Who knew except us?"

"London had to know and give approval."

"So it could be that there is a mole?"

"Alex," Graham said Tersely, "don't ask me questions I can't bloody answer. I'm as sick as you are. Webb was one of the best. But he took the job knowing he wouldn't get any help if it went wrong. And it went wrong."

"How can you live with that?"

"I live with it because the game we're in requires me to. I do what I'm told to the best of my ability until they put me out to pasture. Then I'll have the rest of my life to mull over the insanity of it all. What you witnessed this afternoon is the dirty end of a dirty business, and if that doesn't sit with your conscience, get out while you can."

"I might just do that," I said slowly.

THIRTY ONE

As predicted, the Soviets lodged a strongly worded condemnation about the incident and, in turn, our authorities blandly denied any knowledge or responsibility.

"How will we ever know whether Harry's dead or alive?" I asked.

"We won't unless they deign to tell us," Graham replied. "And we can't enquire about a man whose existence we've already denied."

"Oh, bollocks, he was a serving British soldier."

"No. The day they shot him he was a civilian working for a bogus refrigeration company."

"We're talking about a man's life, for God'sake. What d'you tell his next of kin?"

"That he was killed in a car crash. His life will go into the Marie Celeste file, end of story. MI6 doesn't award posthumous gongs."

"It's all madness. Madness."

"Alex, I agree, but the object of the madness is to keep secrets. Take that away and the whole edifice collapses and we're out of a job."

"God," I said "you're such cynic"

"Am I? I prefer to call myself a realist."

That night I made an effort to get seriously drunk, seeking to obliterate some of my demons, but the alcohol barely dulled me. The recurring image of Webb's dead body being dragged out of the van made me realise that I was a fool to believe I could ever share Graham's values. Harry hadn't given his life for a cause, he had been a pawn sacrificed in some perverted game of chess. Graham might be able to accept the outcome without questioning the morality, but I couldn't.

The following morning he said: "I've been thinking about your own situation in view of what happened. It's a dead cert they got you on film either at the Trade Fair or the restaurant Vanya took you to, which renders you a liability here. If I were you I'd put in for a posting elsewhere, some cushy desk job in a warmer climate."

"What if I want out altogether? Didn't you say 'if your conscience troubles you, get out?"

"And does your conscience trouble you, Alex?"

"Yes. Yours doesn't I take it?"

"I cannot afford a conscience, Alex." He smiled as he said it.

That last remark decided me. Without telling anybody of my intentions, I packed an overnight bag and had one of our drivers take me to Templehof. I hung around at the airport until I managed to secure a seat on the last flight out to Hamburg. It was dark when the DC7 touched down and this time, since I was technically AWOL, instead of bumming a lift from the Military Police, I took a taxi to Lisa's flat and instructed him to wait.

Greta opened the door to me.

"If you were expecting to see Lisa," she said, "she isn't here"

"Is she at the theatre?"

"No. She no longer lives here, thanks to you."

I ignored the antagonism. "So where does she live now?"

"With her mother."

"Where? In Hamburg?"

"No."

"Where then?"

"I cannot tell you."

"Cannot or won't?"

"She told me not to give it to you." There was a note of satisfaction in her reply.

I said: "It's vital I see her."

"Maybe not to her."

"Just tell me where she is. Please."

"I can't help you." She went to close the door.

"Well, tell me one thing: was she well when last you saw her?"

"As well as could be expected. You should know about that."

Now a young man appeared behind her. "Anything wrong?" he asked In German.

"No," Greta answered. Then to me: "Don't waste your time looking for her, Englishman. She's finished with you." The door was slammed shut.

For minutes afterwards I remained on the stairway, my back pressed against the peeling wall, trying to decipher what Greta had meant when she said 'as well as could be expected.' Did she mean Lisa was still carrying the baby or that she had aborted it?

I had the taxi driver take me to the theatre where I questioned one of the production staff.

"Ja, Lisa, she left," the man told me.

"Any idea where she went?"

"No. We don't see her any more."

I asked the stage door keeper whether she had left any address, but again drew a blank. Wanting the comfort of the familiar, I walked to my old hotel. Since I was last there the Kronprinzen had been patched up and the adjacent bombsites cleared, but there were no rooms available and I tried the Atlantic officers' club next and there I was successful. When I had parked my gear and had a wash I went down to the bar. There was a noisy party in progress in the adjoining dining room and the raucous behaviour of others enjoying themselves grated, punching home the bleakness of my own situation. I sat at the bar nursing a drink; memories of Lisa swirling around in my mind, my body remembering too much.

I looked up to find the ubiquitous Chivers standing beside me and anger resurfaced as I remembered our last encounter at the Trade Fair.

"Well, fancy," he said, "look who's here. I was hoping our paths would cross again."

"Why was that? Thinking of flogging me a dodgy Leica?"

"You know why. I didn't care for your attitude the last time we met."

"You didn't?

"No, it was totally out of line. You were bloody offensive and I want an apology."

"Oh, piss off, you boring little man, or I'll tell you what I really think of you."

"Let me remind you, I hold a superior rank."

"Really? You mean the one you bought off the shelf?"

"I'm warning you, Captain."

"Okay, you've warned me, now go away and let me enjoy my drink before I get really offensive."

"I'm not leaving until you apologise, otherwise I shall take the matter further. I don't intend to let it rest until I have satisfaction."

"Is that supposed to frighten me?"

"If you know what 's good for you, you'll do the decent thing."

I said: "Don't threaten me. You forget it's my job to suss out dubious pricks like you, and I sussed you the first time you came into my orbit. You were never at Bletchley, that claim is as bogus as your put-on posh accent." From Chivers' changed expression I saw that this had struck home. "And for your information, I wasn't in East Berlin for my health and you probably blew an undercover operation. As a result one of my best men bought it."

"How was I to know that?" Chivers blustered, no longer so sure of his ground.

"No, you were too busy with another of your scams. What's it going to be next? Flogging diluted penicillin? I hear there's a killing to be made there."

"I don't have to listen to this and, by God, I'll have you for slander."

Faces were turned in our direction as he raised his voice.

"Oh, get knotted you pathetic cunt," I said as I stood up and pushed past him, spilling the remains of my whisky on his immaculate uniform jacket.

"You did that deliberately!"

"If only," I replied as I left.

"I have witnesses," Chivers shouted after me.

There was a knock on my bedroom door an hour or so later and I answered it to be confronted by two Military Policemen. The Sergeant saluted.

"Captain Seaton?"

"Yes."

"Sir, we have to ask you to accompany us to the Provost Marshall's office."

"What for?

"A charge of assault has been laid against you, sir."

"Assault?"

"Yes, sir. By a Major Chivers, sir."

"He's not a real bloody Major. He's in the Control Commission." The Sergeant fidgeted, uncertain as to how to proceed.

"Right, you have your orders, so we'd better go." I picked up my beret and they stood to one side to let me to exit first.

The Provost Marshall was a huge Scot called Reid who spoke in a gravelly Glaswegian accent that was difficult to penetrate. "I gather you ran into a bit of trouble with one of our Control Commission johnnies. Bloody bane of my life. He's charged you with making slanderous remarks to a superior officer in front of witnesses and deliberately throwing a glass of whisky over him."

"I wish it had been deliberate, but I wouldn't waste good Scotch on somebody like him. As to the slander, this is a character we've been investigating. He alleges he spent the war in some hush hush establishment, which we've discovered isn't true. I last saw him in the Russian sector of East Berlin while on an undercover operation which went wrong. It's possible his presence there at the same time was the reason it went belly up and one of my team died as a result. So you can imagine I wasn't over pleased to see him again."

"His statement says you abused him with foul language."

"I called him a cunt and a prick, if that's what he's referring to.. Nothing foul about that, just giving him a choice." I was surprised how relaxed I felt about the whole thing.

"Had you been drinking, Captain?"

"Yes."

"Heavily?"

"Not more than usual. I walked out of the bar without falling over and went to my room, where your men found me."

"Look, Seaton, between you and me, having met the man I wouldn't disagree with your description of him, but he's pressed charges and I haven't got any option. Are you stationed here in Hamburg?"

"I was. Now I'm in Berlin."

"Field Security?"

"Not any longer. I'm MI6 now."

"Ah!" Reid made a grimace. "Well, you'd better return to Berlin, report the incident and await developments. I'll pass the papers to your superior and let him deal with it. Give me his name."

"My head of station is somebody called Green."

"What rank does his hold?"

"He doesn't have one. He's Foreign Office." I gave Reid the details of our headquarters.

"Fine. Officially, I've advised you of the charge and possible consequences. Do you want to give me a statement of your version?"

"Maybe not. Never say anything that can be used against us, isn't that right?"

"Fair enough, I agree, laddie. I can't wait to show a clean pair of heels to this country and get home to Falkirk. Ever been there?"

"No, sadly I haven't."

"Well, good luck, laddie."

"Thank you, sir."

"Not at all. You're one of us and we look after our own."

I saluted and left.

Later, when the charge papers eventually arrived on his desk. Graham asked: "Couldn't you have steered clear of him? What on earth possessed you to get involved in a fracas with that character?"

"He started it. Demanded an apology for the way I treated him at the Trade Fair. That got me on the raw, and I more or less accused him of being the cause of Harry Webb's death. Which may not be too far from the truth, because Vanya spotted him and asked questions."

Graham studied the papers. "The charges are (a) conduct unbecoming of an officer in that you used obscene language and (b) you threw a glass of whisky in his face."

"I accept the former, but as to throwing whisky in his face, that's bollocks. I accidentally spilled some on his jacket. Actually, I should have decked me. I was itching to."

"He claims to have witnesses. Obviously I'll have to pass

these papers to London."

"Will I be taken out at dawn?"

"You'll certainly get your wrists slapped and it'll count against your advancement. However, my accompanying report will give our assessment of Chivers and the extenuating circumstances."

"You assume I want advancement. I don't. Harry Webb's death has concentrated my mind. He was sacrificed for what? So that we could bring some bloody defector over to our side, pick his brains and keep the spy industry going? Well, fuck that. I can't take Harry's death in my stride like you. I've made the decision. I want out."

"Sleep on it, Alex."

"I already have. I'm not a natural for this game like you. It's all so bloody pointless and cynical: we win one war then start organising for the next."

Graham said: "Are you sure the reason you want out isn't because of Grundwall and his daughter? Be honest with me if nobody else. Isn't it that, in your heart, you're regretting having turned him in?"

"No, that isn't the reason."

"I think it has a lot to do with it, whether you admit it or not."

"I didn't have a choice," I said. "The choice was made for me way back, in another place. That American war correspondence made it crystal clear to me."

"Which American war correspondence?"

"The woman you asked me to take sightseeing. She said, 'God left early in Buchenwald, if He was ever there.' That summed it up for me."

"Show me a time in this war when He didn't leave early," Graham said.

THIRTY TWO

The necessary formalities went more smoothly than I had imagined. I received a reprimand and was docked a month's pay as a result of the charges Chivers had levelled against me, and the incident was duly marked on my record sheet. Parallel to this, I was required to have an interview with the General commanding Group before my application to resign my commission could go forward. From the start, the General, who was in his late forties and wore a black eye patch, treated me as a wayward son who had strayed, but could be saved.

"Apart from this recent and isolated incident, Captain Seaton, I see your conduct has been exemplary throughout your service. You're exactly the sort of officer we want in a peacetime Army, so why do you wish to chuck it in because of one small blip?"

"My request was not influenced by the reprimand, sir."

"What prompted it then?"

"Personal problems, sir."

"The Army is always here to help. I'm here to help. If you have a personal problem, let's discuss it confidentially. It won't go further than this room, but I may be able to provide a solution. Do stand at ease. What you're proposing is a very drastic step. I see from your records you were promoted in the field, which is highly significant. Your present rank is not substantive, but I could help there. In the normal course of events you could expect to make Major within five years but who knows how far somebody with your qualities could go?

You have the profile we badly need if we are to consolidate the peace. Have you considered what you would be throwing away?"

"I have, sir, yes."

"I would be failing in my responsibility if I didn't persuade you to think again. Personal problems, you say? Are you married?"

"No, sir."

"Family?"

"My mother and father, sir."

"And they're still alive, are they?"

"Yes, sir."

"Any money problems?"

"No, sir."

"Do you have a job waiting for you?"

"No, sir."

He fingered his eye patch. "So you would be launching yourself onto an unknown sea. Until now your life has been cocooned by the Army, has it not? It's natural, inevitable, that after coming through a long war, you should feel uncertain as to the future. Many share the same feeling. The way ahead is certainly going to be a challenge, but that is why people such as yourself are needed for the task. That's not flattery, just a statement of fact. A career in the Regular Army should not be dismissed lightly. It offers security, a superior life style that separates you from the humdrum."

The rosy prospect he was dangling in front of me had the reverse effect from what he intended. The more the he rattled on the more I wanted to test the waters of that unknown sea he had described.

"I appreciate the wisdom of everything you're saying, sir and I'm most grateful to you, but my mind is made up. I'm sorry to disappoint you, sir."

The General's expression hardened. "As long as you don't disappoint yourself," he said.

An uneasy month later my discharge papers came through. With my gratuity and some back pay I was entitled to, I departed the Army with £345, more money than I had ever possessed. I delayed telling my parents what I had done; I wanted some time to adjust without pressure and I knew what their reaction would be. Instead I lied, writing to them that I was taking up a new position which would mean I would be out of contact for a few weeks.

I accepted Graham's invitation for a farewell dinner in the same restaurant in the French sector where our relationship had begun. "So, the deed is done," Graham, said, raising his glass. "You've chosen this moment to leave what will probably become the only growth industry in the West. Have you made any plans for what comes next?"

"No."

"None at all? Doesn't that scare you?"

"Not yet, but I'm sure it will. Like you, I made plans once but they didn't work out."

"Well, let's keep in touch. You've taught me a lot, Alex."

"Me? What could I have possibly taught you?"

"That principles count. The required Establishment teaching is that principles are for those without ambition. If you want prosper in the corridors of power, never give a straight answer when an obscure one will suffice. Dissemble until such time as questioner has forgotten what he originally asked."

"But you've always spoken out."

"No, seldom, and on the one occasion I did it worked against me. So let that be my last piece of advice to you. By the way, I've never asked you this, did you vote Labour?"

"Yes. Yes, I did. Although I thought it a pity they couldn't continue with a National government that had held up well during the war, I decided that a change might be a good thing."

"Do you still feel that?"

"Not sure."

"Wait until you get home and sample it. Both major Parties are only interested in absolute power in order to be corrupted absolutely."

"I shall miss your cynicism, Graham. It's been a breath of fresh air."

"Or flatulence maybe? I've gone beyond mere cynicism, I'm now totally disillusioned with everything and everybody," he said with one of his enigmatic smiles.

And on that note we parted for good, because we never did keep in touch. I saw his name once in a copy of *The Times* I picked up in a doctor's waiting room. He had been awarded a knighthood.

Before leaving Germany I made last attempts to discover Lisa's whereabouts, but again drew blanks. I wrote to her care of the theatre asking for my letter to be forwarded. Whether it was, or whether, on receipt, she chose to ignore it I have no means of telling.

When I arrived in Harwich I was quickly made aware that my life had irrevocably changed. Dragging my heavy duffle bag, I made my way to the Custom sheds. Overhead the gulls swooped low in the grey sky as they too searched for booty. A middle-aged Preventive Officer with an apology for a moustache singled me out. "Anything to declare, Captain?"

"I don't think so."

"You don't think so? No cigarettes or booze?"

"No booze, just a few cigarettes?"

"What d'you call a few?"

"Fifty."

"How about cameras?"

"No," I said. Outside a departing ferry sounded its mournful claxton.

"Open your duffle bag, please, Captain."

I obliged. He rifled through the contents and took out a

package wrapped in brown paper. "What is inside this, Captain?"

"An inkwell."

"Inkwell? Show me, please."

I opened the package and explained: "A souvenir I took it from Josef Kramer's desk at Belsen. He was the camp Commandant there."

He turned it over in his hands, at a loss to make anything of it. "Are you on home leave?"

"No. Happily I'm being demobbed at last."

"And you have nothing else? No jewellery for a girl friend?"

"No jewellery, no girl friend."

Thrusting his arm down to the bottom of my duffle bag and rifling around, this time he came up with nothing of interest. "Right," he said curtly, "You can go, Captain."

"Thanks for the welcome home," I said, but the sarcasm was lost on him.

I made my way to the platform where the London train was waiting. A cold wind blew in from the sea, swaying the chains hanging from the giant cranes. I bought a copy of that day's Express at the newsstand and was surprised how thin it was, before walking the length of the train until I came to a First Class carriage, thinking to myself, may well be the last time you enjoy a bit of privilege. Stowing my gear, I was joined by a 2nd Lieutenant my own age wearing the wings and red beret of the Parachute Regiment. He immediately put his feet up on the opposite seat, loosened his battledress jacket and offered me a cigarette. "On your way for demob?"

"Yes," I said. "You?"

He nodded. "Thought it would never come. Are you looking forward to it?"

"Yes, I suppose so, though I guess it'll feel odd not to be wearing a uniform after all this time. A leap into the unknown, like your first jump."

"Nothing's like your first jump. Mind you, the second is the worst because by then you know what to expect. Can I take a look at your paper?"

"Sure, go ahead."

He glanced at the front page headlines. "Oh, great! Old Bevin promises we'll all get a job. Give me a break. Is there one waiting for you?"

"Not really."

"Me neither. I'm going to blow my gratuity taking my girl to the seaside for a dirty week."

The Guard's whistle sounded and a few seconds later our train pulled out of the station, gradually picking up speed. We passed rows of identical houses such as a child might draw, just basic boxes. Their small back gardens all had sunken corrugated iron air-raid shelters sunk into the patch of lawn, the flower beds now given over to vegetables. There was little evidence of bomb damage in that part of Essex and it wasn't until we reached the outskirts of Colchester, that I saw fields scarred with bomb craters, here and there a ruined building, a church with its steeple chopped in half, a burnt-out warehouse. The roads seemed like narrow twisted ribbons compared to the autobahns I had left behind. Our train sped through country halts and in the patchwork of fields small children on top of concrete blockhouses paused in play and wave. The passing scene mesmerised me, my head lolled against the grimed carriage window and I lapsed into an uneasy cat nap, only waking when we were entering the grey outer rim of the metropolis. Here everything was uniformly drab, the pedestrians in the streets like Lowry stick figures. I felt I was coming home to a foreign city that had been left unfinished, that those who first designed it had lost heart halfway and settled for a formless chaos. I opened the carriage window and gulped in sooted air.

"Where's your home?" the Lieutenant asked as we both began to gather up our belongings..

"Lincolnshire."

"Coventry, me. Ever been there?"

"No. Coventry took a pasting, didn't it?"

"And how. My mother and little sister were both killed when the house bought it. So I'm going to my girlfriend's place in Oxford. Handy if I ever get to university."

"Well, I wish you luck."

"Likewise. Good to meet you. Least we made it, didn't we?"

The train pulled in beneath the shattered glass dome of Liverpool Street station, our carriage stopping in front of an old, defaced poster warning that Careless Talk Costs Lives. I walked with the throng to the barrier, past a Nestle chocolate machine empty now of the penny bars I had bought as a child. A crowd of relatives and girlfriends were waiting to greet the passengers and I felt a tinge of envy as a pretty blond rushed forward to embrace my travelling companion.

I had a railway warrant entitling me to travel to the Aldershot depot and there complete demobilisation, so I took the Tube to Paddington and caught another train. Once in the depot, my measurements were taken and I drew a suit, a pair of shoes, a shirt, pairs of socks, a tie a Trilby hat, a food ration book and another of clothing stamps.

Outside the depot touts were offering to purchase the entire collection for a few pounds. I gave one of them the Trilby hat for free, having decided that I looked ridiculous in it.

Then it was another train back to London at the end of a long day. I checked into the YMCA at Tottenham Court Road, which even in those far off days was known to be a favourite haunt of sexual predators, but by then I was too tired to care. The following morning, having made some complicated calculations, I figured that my nest egg of £345 would give me three months in which to find a suitable job if I lived frugally. I had no experience of fending for myself, but that morning I discarded my uniform at last and put on the demob suit. Setting out in search of the new life, my first need was to find cheap lodgings, but I had no idea where to start. A policeman suggested I try the Bayswater district. "Look in the shop windows," he told me. "Most of them have cards advertising what's available." He gave me directions how to get there.

I had the feeling I stood out like a sore thumb in my civilian clothes and by the time I reached the Bayswater Road my new shoes were crippling me. Taking the policeman's advice, I scoured the windows of every shop I passed, but the majority of the small ads were for ACCOMMODATION WANTED. After an hour's fruitless search, I felt hungry and chose a café close to Paddington station where all the customers still had war-time faces, lined and tired. There was a vacant seat at a table occupied by an elderly man poring over the racing form, his fingers holding a stub of pencil were stained almost black with nicotine. The sparse menu was written on a blackboard behind the counter: Fried Spam and chips, egg and chips, steak and chips. The inclusion of steak surprised me

"Can you tell me if I need this to eat here?" I produced my ration book.

The old man, disturbed from his deliberations, looked at the book, then at me. "I bloody hope not," he said ambiguously.

I ordered the steak and a cup of tea, but got a shock when I took my first bite; the meat had an unfamiliar sweet taste.

"Horse," the old man volunteered, seeing me pull a face. "Ain't you had horse before?"

"No."

"Where you been living then, at the bloody Ritz?"

"I just got out of the Army."

"Well, it won't poison you. Horse is a bloody sight cleaner than cows. They don't have shit around their arses."

He laughed at his own description, and the laugh developed into a choking cough."

His illuminating piece of information was not exactly reassuring and I settled for the greasy chips and my cup of tea. Now that the ice had been broken and a certain bond established on the merits of horse meat, the old man asked if I was interested in a dead cert for the three thirty at Kempton Park?"

I didn't catch on at first and he repeated, "Kempton Park, race course. Gee gees, like on your plate. I could get you on at seven to one."

"That's kind of you, but I don't know anything about racing."

His offer refused, he lost interest in me. I paid and left to resume by search for accommodation, finally spotting a card in a greengrocer's shop window. FURNISHED ROOM SUIT SINGLE PERSON SOBER HABITS NO PETS REASONABLE RENT APPLY WITHIN.

I enquired inside and was shown the room by the shopkeeper's wife, a petite woman who spoke in whispers who introduced herself as Mrs Drane. The room on the first floor was furnished with ill-matching items, a section partitioned off to provide a small kitchen area with a sink and gas ring. She showed me a cupboard where the bare essential crockery and cutlery were kept together with a frying pan and kettle.

"You share the bathroom on the landing with the other tenant," Mrs Drane informed me. "He's a commercial traveller, goes out early so you shouldn't be inconvenienced with your ablutions. Were you thinking of staying long, Mr.Seaton? quickly adding, "we only let for a minimum of a month, payable in advance."

"What do you charge?"

"Four pounds a week, plus you're responsible for your own light, heat and bed laundry."

I saw that the heating consisted of a single element electric fire fed by a shilling meter, and took my time before responding – some instinct telling me it was a mistake to readily agree to terms.

"That's the going rate," Mrs Drane said.

"I don't disbelieve you, but having just come out of the Army and without a job at the moment, I have to be careful with my money."

"Well, things are hard for all of us right now. I could stretch a point and reduce it to three fifty. Can't go any lower."

I looked around the room again. "Okay," I said, "I'll take it for a month, see how things go."

As I counted out fourteen pounds, she said: "Is there a Mrs Seaton?"

"No."

"Just asking. One strict house rule, no women in the room after nine o'clock at night."

It was the first time I had come across the conviction amongst some landladies that fornication only took place during the hours of darkness. "Of course," I said.

"Do you have any luggage?"

"I left it at the YM."

She gave me a key for the separate entrance by the side of the shop and after retrieving my belongings from the YMCA, I christened my ration book and bought a loaf of bread, half a dozen eggs, a tin of Spam, butter, milk, tea, sugalr and a bottle of beer. Returning to the room, I arranged my things, then made a sandwich from the rough, National loaf, and drank my bottle of beer. There was none of the feeling of adventure I had once imagined, and the prospect of spending the remainder of the evening in the room was infinitely depressing. I went back into the streets and eventually found a cinema showing a French film, *Mayerling* starring an actress I had never seen before,

Danielle Darrieux. Compared to the usual Hollywood product, nobody in the cast seemed to be acting; they were so real, so human, devoid of artifice.

That night I dreamed I was lying in bed beside Lisa, both of us dressed like the doomed lovers in Mayerling and I had my service revolver pressed against Lisa's temple. I awoke before I pulled the trigger, sweating and disorientated, unable to get my bearings for several minutes.

THIRTY THREE

I applied for half a dozen jobs during the next two weeks, having first signed on at the nearest Labour Exchange. I was sent after a vacancy at a Royal Mail sorting office, but it had been filled by the time I got there. A sympathetic foreman told me he had heard a nearby brewery was looking for a Security man. "Should be right up your street from what you've told me of your Army career," was his strange reasoning, adding, "And you get free beer."

I went to the brewery and was interviewed by a sceptical manager. "I don't know that we're looking for somebody like you, young man. No offence, but we're after more of a dogsbody, to check the padlocks and stuff. Suit an old aged pensioner who wants some pocket money."

Next I went after a job as a salesman in the household department of a large general store, only to find that they needed somebody with practical experience of electrical goods. I trudged back to the Labour Exchange and this time was directed to an insurance office wanting a ledger clerk. It didn't sound promising but, much to my surprise, the Manager immediately offered me the post.

"I understand you held the rank of Captain, Mr. Seaton."

"Yes."

"I couldn't do active service because of a dickey leg." His mauved cheeks suggested he gave the sherry bottle a regular thrashing. He had a gold pocket watch on a chain which he swung with hypnotic precision throughout the interview.

"Can I ask what the job entails?" I asked.

"Very basic," he said. "Piece of cake for somebody like yourself. When the reps report who they've signed, you open a separate ledger page for every new customer, name, age, address, etcetera, type of insurance they've agreed to, the weekly amount they have to pay. If they get behind with their dues, you inform head office and they issue a warning. If they're more than four weeks in arrears, we write them off and close the page. We don't take prisoners."

"What kind of policies are usual?"

"Nothing big. The majority are for death benefits. what we call Whole Life, which is a bit of a misnomer when you think about it. Our typical policyholder doesn't want to die a pauper. They want to leave this world with a bit of class, an oak coffin with brass handles, not a cardboard box. When the policy pays out they're guaranteed a decent departure."

"Are they expensive?"

"No, no. Just a few shillings a week. Our collectors take the money on the doorstep, rather like the milkman. People prefer the personal approach."

"Seems fair enough," I said, trying to keep interest in my voice.

"Now, as to salary. We start you with a month's trial at eight pounds a week, which with regular increments could rise to twelve, all thing being satisfactory. Two weeks paid holiday per annum, plus a Christmas bonus. Let me introduce you to the rest of the team. You'll find we're one big happy family here."

He led me into a back room where two middle-aged women were sitting at their desks.

"This is Elsie, who'll be your superior and will hold your hand and show you the ropes until you become familiar. Elsie, this is Captain Seaton, one of our returning war heroes."

Elsie was of diminutive stature with thin hair scraped back into a tight bun and having her hold my hand was not the most attractive proposition. She gave me a watery smile, exposing a fearsome set of dentures. Her companion, introduced as Betty, was younger but both had the pinched look of condemned spinsters.

"Nice to meet you both," I said. Betty gave me a flustered look and quickly resumed typing. The room reeked of mothballs.

"You'll find that Elsie runs a tight ship, isn't that so, Elsie?"

"I do my best," she answered primly.

"So, can I take it, Captain, that you'd like to accept?"

"It certainly sounds a very challenging job," I said, trying to convey an enthusiasm I did not feel.

"Two things never go out of fashion, births and departures, "he said. "We're basically in the departure end." He swung his pocket watch with renewed energy. "I once saw a sign outside a cleaners which said "We Dye To Live and Live To Dye" – die spelt dye – clever don't you think? I've often thought we should have a variation. You know "We live for you to die."

"Maybe a bit off-putting," I suggested.

"Elsie agrees with you, don't you, Elsie?"

"It's just my opinion, Mr. Addison."

"So, Captain. Can you start tomorrow?"

"I've got one other offer I'm considering," I lied.

"Well, I can't hold it open for long. Let me know first thing in the morning."

"Of course. I look forward to seeing you again, ladies."

Oh, God, I thought as I left the building: is this what I relinquished my commission for? On my way back to the Labour Exchange I prepared an explanation for the official. "I'm sure it's a very good career opening," I said, "but I don't think I'm the right man."

"Mr. Addison rang us to say he thought you were ideal," the official said peevishly. "It would seem to be an idea position for somebody with your limited qualifications. We can't keep sending you after good jobs if you persist in turning them down. People like you must accept that you've come back to a very competitive market."

That night, I again berated myself for what now seemed a hasty and ill-judged exit from the security of Army life. The prime reason, I acknowledged, had been to put distance between myself and Lisa, but sitting there in the bleakness of the rented room, I wondered if eventually I would be forced to admit defeat and take up my father's plan.

I embarked on renewed efforts, gave the Labour exchange a miss and struck out on my own, scouring the small adds in the three London evening papers. One that caught my eye advertised the job of Manager for a second-hand bookshop. I located the premises in one of the alleyways between Charing Cross Road and St.Martin's Lane. The shop window was crammed with an eclectic selection ranging from sets of Dickens, Carlyle and the Waverly novels to copies of Beano and Magnet annuals. Entering the dim interior I made out the figure of a bearded gnome behind the counter, wearing what appeared to be a hand-knitted suit. He was drinking from a chipped mug and made no attempt to acknowledge my presence. Perched on top of a stack of books a ginger cat regarded me with malevolent eyes.

The gnome finally said, "Do you know what you're looking for?"

"I came about your ad," I said. "Has the position been filled?"

"I've had a number of enquiries."

"Have you made a choice?"

"I'm considering." He brought his hands together and held them in front of his mouth as though praying for divine guidance. I could only guess at his age, for under the greying hair he had the features of somebody younger. His eyes suggested he had spent his life peering at print in inadequate light. The shop was crammed to bursting point, the shelves bowed from the weight of books; in every spare space, piles of them leant crazily.

"Know anything about the second-hand book trade, do you?"

"No, but I'm well read and love books. If you gave me the job I'm sure you could teach me very quickly."

"Wouldn't depend on that." He picked up a book, blew dust off it and handed it to me. "This for example. What would you price this at? First edition Huxley's *Antic Hay*. Know it, do you?"

"Heard of it," I said, "but never read it."

"Not that rare, but collectible in this condition with dust jacket and no foxing. Know what foxing means?"

"Faded?"

"Discoloured. They used good paper before the war. The wartime stuff was rubbish, little better than toilet paper. It'll self-destruct very quickly."

I handled the book carefully. "Ten pounds?" I ventured.

He allowed himself to smile for the first time. "If you can get three pounds for it, I'll make you a partner on the spot. I'd let it go for thirty bob to make a sale." He took a match and started some deep excavation work on his teeth. "What's your name?"

"Alex Seaton."

"And what other jobs have you had, Mr. Seaton?"

"None. I've just been demobbed from the Army."

He stroked the cat's ear. "Well, if nobody better turns up during today, I'll give you a trial. It's a lonely trade. Some days nobody comes through that door. Then again, you have days when you sell a book you've had for years and never thought you'd see the back of it. Plus you have to have a nose for book thieves."

"Do you get many?"

"I get my share. They nick books from Foyle's then try and flog them here.

"Really?"

"Oh, yes. Then there are the wankers looking for smut. I don't have any truck with smut. Some do, I don't." There was a slight thawing in his attitude. "If I was to take you on, what sort of money are you looking for?"

"I've no idea what bookselling pays."

"Not a great deal is the answer." He probed his teeth again with the match. "I could go to ten pounds for a six day week, nine 'til five."

"That's more than I've been offered elsewhere."

"Well, there's a reason for that. Often you'd be left here on your own. I travel around the country a lot, covering house sales, auctions. That's where I find the bargains. So, I have to be careful who I leave in charge."

"Well, I'd be happy to take the job if you offer it to me."

"Let me sleep on it. I think better in bed."

"Shall I come back tomorrow then?"

"Yes. Tomorrow."

"Right. Thank you for considering me."

I walked to Soho when I left him, mingling with the drabness of others on the crowded pavements, for in my cheap pin-stripe suit I was as anonymous as the next man. In Shaftsbury Avenue I studied the front-of-house posters of one of the theatres. They were advertising *The Winslow Boy* by somebody named Terence Rattigan. The playwright's name and the cast list meant nothing to me and I was conscious how many holes there were in my education. Crossing the road I came across a small eatery called Taylor's. The prices on the menu were within my budget and the food, if basic, was well cooked and tasty. Seated at the counter and listening to the buzz of idiosyncratic chatter around me it became obvious that most of the clientele were theatricals, some in work, some bemoaning the injustice of being out of work. Their dialogue was peppered with mentions of 'Binkie', 'ghastly old Sherek' and 'Wolfit' – names which again conveyed nothing to me but seemed to be the epicentre of their universe. In contrast to most, they were animated, full of life and dressed with peacock originality. They fascinated me.

Mr and Mrs Drane were shutting up shop when I returned and the wife asked if I'd had any luck with job hunting.

"I've got the possibility of one in a bookshop. Nothing definite, but fingers crossed it seems hopeful.

Her husband, spoke to me for the first time. "Where've you been looking?"

"All over the place. The Labour Exchange sent me after several possibilities, but none of those were suitable."

Little did I know then that the mere mention of anything concerned with Labour sent him into a fury. Now he launched himself into a long non-sequitur, predicting the certainty that the current government were set on doing away with the Royal family. "Happened in France and Russia and it'll happen here, mark my words," he finished before humping a box of apples into the shop. "Such a deep thinker," Mrs Drane confided with quiet pride. "His mind has untold depths."

When I returned to the bookshop the following morning there was an ambulance in St.Martin's Lane at the entrance to the alleyway.

A small crowd of onlookers were gathered by the shop and as I joined them a policeman came out followed by two ambulance men carrying a covered body on a stretcher.

"What happened?" I asked.

"Bloke had a heart attack, I think."

As the policeman started to close and secured the premises the ginger cat flew out and disappeared. "

"Excuse me," I said to him. "I was hoping to start work here this morning."

"Your bad luck then," he replied cheerfully. "That was the owner they took out."

I sat on the steps of St. Martin's in the Fields and had a cigarette, watching grey clouds of pigeons in Trafalgar Square rise and settle again while I reflected on the unexpected turn of events. Afterwards I spent the rest of the morning in the National Gallery before going to take my place at the lunch counter at Taylor's. I found myself next to a dishevelled man of indeterminate age with obviously dyed blond hair, wearing a florid plaid shirt with matching tie and had a camel hair coat draped over his shoulders. He was having a loud conversation with two young men further along the counter.

"I said, 'Daphne dear, I don't give a flying fuck if he is the bloody director, I'm too old and, frankly, too talented to be spoken to like that. Either he apologises or it's goodbye Yours Truly.'" He forked a piece of sausage and waved it in the air for emphasis.

"Good for you, Chris," one of the young men applauded. "And what did she say to that?"

"Oh, Daphne's such a devious cow, so far up Binkie's arse she's disappeared. She'd piss on her own grandmother for a free meal at the Ivy."

Then, suddenly conscious of me beside him, he turned and smiled. "Sorry about the language."

I said. "I've heard worse." At close range I noticed he had a cold sore on his upper lip.

"We've met, haven't we?" he said.

"I don't think so."

"You're an actor, though?"

"No."

"I could have sworn you were the one who gave such a marvellous performance in that strange piece Peter Brook put on last year."

"'Fraid not."

"Well, forgive me, my naughty mistake. I'm Christopher Weight, pleased to meet you."

"Alex Seaton"

"With your looks you should be an actor, Alex."

"You're all in the theatre, I take it?"

"These two budding stars are actors, but I gave up treading the boards a hundred years ago. Now I design sets and costumes for my sins, which are many. Tony, Keithy, meet Alex."

We all exchanged greetings.

"So, if you're not an actor, duckie, what d'you do?"

"Nothing at the moment." It was an odd feeling to be addressed as 'duckie'.

"Join the club," Tony said. "We're resting, too."

Christopher said, "I was born Mrs Curious. You must do something."

"Until recently I was in the Army in Germany."

"Oh, silly me, I should have guessed. That suit you're wearing, dear, is the giveaway. You should burn it, dear, at the first opportunity."

"That might be difficult. Right now I don't possess another."

"You're so bloody cruel, Chris," Keithy said.

"Oh, well, can't change the habits of a lifetime." He ate another piece of sausage. "To make amends, Alex, I happen to have a lot of spare clothing coupons which you're welcome to. I also happen to know the most brilliant little tailor who'll run you up something in a flash. And very reasonable, dear. After all, somebody as good looking as you doesn't want to give the impression he's a displaced person."

"What d'you call 'very reasonable'?"

"I push a lot of work in his direction, duckie, so he owes me."

Tony interrupted at that point, saying that he had to cut and run. "I'll see you at Terry's tonight, Chris. Nice to meet you, Alex. Don't let him lead you astray."

When they left I changed the conversation from my appearance and asked Chris if he was working on anything at the moment.

"That's a very good question. I was meant to be designing the frocks for a new production of *A Winter's Tale* for Tennent's, but the director's a major drama queen who thinks she's Coco Chanel, and we had a little difference of opinion this morning. I'm not sure my name will still be in the programmes when it opens. Do you live in London?" he continued without pause as though this was a natural progression.

"At the moment, yes, but depends if can land a job. I was due to start somewhere this morning, but the man who was going to employ me dropped dead overnight."

"How inconvenient of him. What sort of job are you looking for?"

"Problem is I don't have any skills."

"What did you do in the Army?"

"Interrogating Nazis."

"Yes, that does rather limit one. Though, mind you, dear it might suit if you became a theatrical agent. Just kidding. But look, I've got a lot of contacts. If you're not busy, come back to my flat and I'll make some calls."

"Really? I'm sure you've got better things to do."

"Duckie, I never intended to go back to the bear pit this afternoon. Let them sweat."

Chris put his hand on my check when it came. "Allow me. Always a privilege to treat a soldier."

We took a bus to Knightsbridge then walked to his flat in Pont Street. The front door nestled between two shops and opened into a narrow corridor with a flight of stairs at the end. The walls of the stairway were lined with theatre posters and the first floor main room was stuffed with bric a brac and furniture of conflicting styles: a gilt Louis XV console next to a contemporary sofa covered in floral chintz and strewn with needlepoint cushions, several small tables piled high with art books, a white baby grand piano, the closed lid cluttered with a dozen silver photo frames.

"Make yourself at home, Duckie," Chris said, "while I put the kettle on and make us a cup of decent coffee. One of my lovers sent me a tin from New York."

Left to myself I looked around his crammed bookshelves and then studied the photographs on the piano. I recognised a few famous faces – Charles Laughton, Anton Walbrook and Sally Gray, the latter two I remembered from the film *Dangerous Moonlight*. Pride of place was given to a portrait of a young sailor.

"Admiring my hall of fame?" Chris said when he returned with the coffee.

"Yes. Do you actually know Sally Gray? I fell in love with her when I saw her in that film about a Polish pianist."

"The one starring Mrs Walbrook you mean? Yes, I gave her some help with her frocks."

His frequent use of the female gender when referring to men struck me as odd, but I pretended not to notice. "The music from the film made a great impression on me. It made me start to listen to the classics which I'd never done before."

"Oh, yes. Of course the Warsaw Concerto was terribly derivative, but dear Dickie Addinsell got away with it. I'm glad you liked the film because it was directed by a great friend, an outrageous old queen called Brian Desmond Hurst. You'd love him, so wicked. Likes to refer to himself as The Empress of Ireland."

By now I was totally out of my depth. "This photo – I pointed to the one of the young sailor – "Is he your brother?"

"No, I've never gone in for incest, dear. A friend. A very close friend who was killed on the Hood," he said and turned away. " How d'you take your coffee?"

"Milk and one sugar, please. You've got a very nice flat."

"Bit of an old curiosity shop. I shall turn into Miss Haversham one day. Except there won't be a wedding cake. Sit yourself down and tell me more about yourself. Were you very brave? I expect you were, you have that look about you."

"Not really. I had a lucky war compared to most."

"Do take off that frightful jacket and relax. I haven't forgotten about ringing around on your behalf. Do you type?"

"Two-fingered variety."

"Just asking because I know of somebody who's looking for a Man Friday to sort out his life, secretary cum chauffeur. He's an actor you might have heard of – Roger Glennon?" I shook my head. "No? Well we won't tell him, don't want to bruise his ego. Would something like that be up your street?"

"Well, I'm willing to give it a try." What am I getting into? I thought.

"Now then, forgive me for plunging straight in, but let's get it over once and for all. Are you straight, dear?"

"Straight? In what way?"

"Yes, you're straight, dear. As you've probably guessed, Yours Truly isn't, but don't look worried I'm not going to jump on you. My trouble is I always fall for the straight ones. It's a sad failing, leads me into all sorts of pickles. I did try it with a girl the once. Disaster, dear. Even if I'd lashed my dick to a toothbrush I still couldn't have performed. Not offended by my asking, were you?"

"No."

"That's a relief. Some people react very violently. I was on tour in Manchester once and after the curtain I went trolling." Seeing my blank look, he explained: "Trolling, duckie, is when we go looking for a bit of rough trade. I was in a pub and saw this gorgeous matelot having a drink with a really rugged old geezer. When he went to the cloaks for a piss I followed him and stood next to him. I said: "What d'you want to go about with that old rat for? He turned to me and said, 'that old rat happens to be my father' and gave me a punch that broke my jaw. Didn't cure me, of course."

I listened to the story with my mouth open, but Chris seemed totally unabashed. "More coffee?" he asked. "No, I tell you what, even though the sun isn't over the yardarm, let's have a touch of Vera Lynn instead."

"Vera Lynn?"

"Mother's ruin, dear. Gin."

I began to relax, sensing that, whatever Chris' original intentions towards me might have been, I was not in mortal danger. He didn't mention phoning his actor friend again, but turned the conversation to his own life, confessing that he had escaped any form of war service. "They even rejected me as a Land Army Girl," he said. The unaccustomed slugs of gin he kept pouring made me lower my guard and I found myself revealing more of my own experiences. Eventually I got around to Lisa, and slowly described the way in which my entrapment of her father ensured the end of our affair. I faltered at that point for it seemed surreal to be making an intimate confession to somebody I had met only a few hours before. "Am I boring you with all this?" I asked him.

"No, I'm fascinated, duckie."

"She was pregnant by then, but after he was found guilty and she learned of my involvement... ."

"How did she know that?" Chris interrupted.

"I told her myself."

"Why?"

"I felt I had to. If we were ever to have a life together, it couldn't be based on a hidden deceit."

"Big mistake, dear. Never admit to infidelity."

"It wasn't infidelity," I said.

"Okay, but you know what I'm getting at. She might never have learned."

"Her father would have told her. I was at the trial giving

evidence against him, remember? She refused to believe in his guilt and she wanted nothing more to do with me, child or no child. That was the end of it, she disappeared out of my life. I made efforts to trace her without success. So I felt there wasn't anything to stay on for in Germany, resigned my commission and came home. And here I am pouring out the story to you."

"Very Mrs Ibsen, dear. How will you ever know when the baby is born, if indeed it is born?"

"I won't, I don't suppose."

"I couldn't bear that," Chris said. "I'd have to know one way or the other. Can't you go back and make another search?"

"No, it's over."

"Nothing's over until the fat lady stops singing. I mean, it's such a fantastic story, dear, it's got to have an ending.

THIRTY FOUR

My friendship with Christopher, improbable though it was, gave me a different perspective on life, a glimpse into a hidden world. I sometimes wished I could emulate his cavalier attitude towards the slings and arrows that inevitably come our way. "Never look back, duckie, that's my philosophy. My dear, if I did I'd reach for the sleeping pills every night. I don't even look forward. Since Tony was killed, I've settled for one-night stands. Love ties you in reef knots." Even though, like many of his circle, he was terrified of exposure or blackmail, he still took risks. "One has to be on the lookout for Lily Law, dear, when going cottaging" – using camp vernacular for the police and excursions into public toilets – "two of my friends have had their collars felt last week for trying to pull good-looking members of the Old Bill." There were frequent witch hunts in the Press and calls for more draconian sentences. The casual promiscuity he sought seemed to me madness. Being on the perimeter of his world meant that I met a number of amenable and attractive young actresses, and although I was attracted, they brought home the loss of Lisa.

Lunches at Taylor's provided the only respite from my fruitless search for a suitable job; none of the positions I went after offered the answer I sought, for the prospect of a routine dreariness, a slow, sedentary suicide, filled me with dread. There appeared to be no clear passage through the minefield of my life. I envied the way in which actors were able to accept rejection, always living on the edge, knowing that for the most part their lot depended not on talent but on luck – being in the right place at the right time. They mocked the workings of the 'civilian' world in ribald shorthand as though, only by mocking it could they confirm that their insular world was superior.

True to his promise, Chris arranged a meeting with Roger Glennon but, although the interview went well, Glennon felt he needed somebody who knew his way around the show business jungle and could advance his career. Chris took my rejection personally. "She's got une grande tete, dear. So, fuck her."

While I longed for a kick start, an end to the agonies of a lost love, I was also concerned that, by now, my mother would be worried at not having heard from me for weeks. To eke out my diminishing funds I rationed myself to one meal a day, half a pint of beer and five cigarettes. Chris offered me a bed in his flat to save me paying rent to the Dranes. "I promise to keep my hands to myself despite every temptation. You probably don't believe it, but I can behave myself when I try."

"It's kind of you," I said, "but I can't sponge on you. I've given it my best shot as the Yanks say, and the time has come to go back to some home cooking."

"Will you promise to keep in touch? Please."

"Yes," I lied. Coming to terms with my own need for love was hard enough without taking on board another's wants. He came to the station to see me off and suddenly leaned forward and planted a kiss on my mouth.

"Take care of yourself, duckie. You're special. Like Tony." I saw he was crying.

I had sent a telegram to my parents telling them that I was back in circulation and returning home, preparing to tell them a fiction about having been on one last secret mission to account for my long silence. When I told it, I made light of the fact that I had resigned my commission.

"I'm sure they were sorry to lose you," was all my mother said. I don't think anything about my time in the Army got through to her, she was just so happy to have me home for good. She and my father had both aged since my last visit, my father in particular was more hunched, his face drawn and lined, his hair above the plimsoll line of sunburn, thinner.

"You did more than your bit, if you ask me," my father said.

"And you didn't come home with a German bride like some. We've lost our prisoners of war, they finally went back." He lit one of his cheroots and I noticed how twisted his fingers were as he cupped his hand around the match. "Until you decide what you want to do, I'd appreciate a bit of help around the place. I'm not trying to make up your mind for you, don't think that, it's just that I don't get around to things as fast as I used to, do I mother?"

"You do as well as anybody else," she replied, ever loyal.

"Of course," I said. "I need some exercise."

I couldn't sleep that first night I was home and in the small hours I crept down to the kitchen and made myself a cup of tea, using the iron kettle that stood on the blackened stove that was never allowed to go out. By the light of the paraffin lamp, I studied the room – the pine dresser stacked with odd pieces of crockery, the worn wooden chairs, the large zinc sink fed by a single cold water tap – and I wondered how my mother had managed all the years, seldom taking a holiday, she and my father always at the mercy of the elements, always tied, like jailers, to the needs of the animals. I tried to imagine them being in love when starting out in marriage. Thinking of them as they now were, settled into a placid companionship (when had I last seen them kiss?) I tried to trace the map of their love, but they had left me few signposts. Where, in which room, at what time, had they joined together to make me? Had my father come in sweated from the fields suddenly gripped with the urge to procreate, or had it been just an act of familiarity between two people who shared the same bed?

Awaking early and disorientated in my old bedroom the following morning, it was several minutes before I realised where I was. The room was bright, unlike the room I had rented from Mrs Drane; sunlight hit the wall opposite my bed, the shadows of leaves forming shifting patterns. There was a familiar smell of lavender polish and the bedclothes had a downy softness that came from being washed in rainwater. I lay listening for the familiar hum of traffic that had characterised my stay in London, but the only thing to break the silence was the insistent cry of a wood pigeon. Rising, I went to the open window. Beneath me half a dozen Rhode Island Reds were fluttering to escape as the rooster made repeated attempts to mount them; beyond, the flat landscape stretched to the horizon and the regular beat of a pumping station engine in a distant fen reached me in the still morning air. I felt rested and at peace.

After the ample fried breakfast my mother cooked for me, I parcelled up my demob suit and drove into Woodhall Spa. I parked in front of my old school where in the playground the children were at morning break, one group of small boys flicking cigarette cards against the wall, another group playing 'fives'. I was surprised how small the school building was, indeed how small all the neighbouring Victorian houses appeared. I watched the scene for a few minutes then walked to the general store. Pausing just inside the doorway I drank in familiar scents before going to the middle-aged woman behind the counter.

"Mrs Hundleberry?"

"Yes."

"Alex Seaton."

She clapped a hand to her mouth. "Good gracious. I'd never have recognised you. My, how you've grown. Are you home on leave?"

"No, I'm out for good at last." I put my parcel on the counter. "If you won't be offended I thought perhaps this suit might fit your Charlie. I seem to remember he was about my size."

"Bless you, my duck, but my Charlie's dead," she said. "He died in a Japanese prisoner of war camp."

"I didn't know. I'm so sorry, forgive me."

"Nothing to forgive, it was a kind thought and he'd have appreciated it. You were always good friends, you two. Up to all the mischief."

"Well, perhaps you can find a home for it elsewhere. Give it to anybody you like. How is Mrs Hundleberry?"

"He's gone too, my dear. Two years ago come March. Now there's only me keeping this going. Still, I manage."

"My parents didn't tell me. They're not good letter writers," I said lamely.

"No, well folks don't want to write bad news, do they? Enough of that around. We had the lovely Air Force boys stationed in the big house. I used to lie in bed at night counting the planes taking off, then counting them home again. Course some a lot didn't come back, more's the pity."

I felt compelled to buy something. "Do you still have any of those... what d'you call them? Pinafores? I thought I'd take one for my mother."

"I've got a few somewhere."

She disappeared into the dark recesses of the cluttered shop and came back with a selection of three flowered-patterned aprons. I chose the brightest. "What do I owe you? And how many coupons d'you want?"

"None from you, my duck. I don't bother with them stupid things."

"Well, don't get into trouble."

I gave her seven and six for the pinafore, and bought a bottle of whisky for my father.

Next I drove to the Kinema in the Woods, remembering as a child the excitement of the once weekly visit and where, if you paid the top price, you sat in deck chairs. The posters outside were advertising *The Seventh Veil* starring James Mason and Ann Todd. I mooched around the village for a while longer, reminding myself of old haunts, then drove home. In between aiding my father, this was the pattern I followed for the first week, sometimes venturing further afield, reminding myself of places and scenery that had once been the extent of my world. Many of the adjacent farms had the same air of neglect as ours: rusting equipment half buried in nettles, here and there a hay wagon with a wheel missing, everywhere evidence that the war had denuded the countryside of old skills. On the first Sunday after my return, I accompanied my parents to the evening service in the simple Wesleyan chapel that stood isolated on the road to Walcott Dales. A sudden cloudburst bounced noisily off the corrugated iron roof, drowning out the hymn singing while it lasted. I had no surge of religious belief but carried off a pretence for my mother's sake, kneeling in prayer, but not praying for a renewal of faith, just for some answer that would make sense of the rest of his life.

As the weeks went by the tempo of my day-to-day existence gradually changed. Working alone mending the gaps in the wire fences enclosing our land, or else mucking out the stables and fetching fresh hay for the two Shires, the unaccustomed physical exertion calmed my previous restlessness, and my bare arms acquired a tan, the muscles tautened and I enjoyed and a new feeling of well being. I slept well and let my beard grow, my skin softened from washing in rainwater taken from the butts. There was the long-forgotten pleasure of seeking out hidden nests in the hedgerows and bringing back a bowl of fat, brown eggs, but I found I still could not bring myself to wring a chicken's neck. I went into Spalding one Market day and came home with a black Labrador I named Harry.

"Funny name for a dog," his father said.

"I suppose so," I said, but volunteered no explanation.

Some nights we took shotguns and a torch and killed rats in the shed where giant Bramley apples were stored in a sea of chaff. I fell into the unhurried rhythm of the countryside where events were dictated by the weather, as though I had never left it. With every passing week geographical memories of Germany receded, though a day never went by when I did not think of Lisa and feel the pain of loss. Alone in the fields I sometimes stood still, seeing again the room she shared with Greta, seeing her face taut with rejection as I left for the last time.

When my father and I were working together it was always my job to fetch our lunches and a flask of tea. When I returned from the house on this particular day he was not where I had left him. I shouted for him but got no answer. I first looked in the stables then went to the Dutch barn, but there was no sign of him there. It was the dog who led me to him, zig-zagging ahead of me to the lean-to where the tractor was kept. As I turned the corner I saw my father lying with part of his body under the connected harrow. I went through the motions of feeling for a pulse on the side of the neck, and then opened his faded shirt and placed my hand over his heart, but I could not discern any sign of life. Although blood from a gash above one eyebrow had riveted down one cheek, I doubted if this had been the cause of death, it seemed more likely that he had suffered a massive coronary. Clenched between the first two fingers of the right hand, his last cigarette had burnt itself out, searing the callused skin. I prised the butt free and then eased the body clear of the harrow before closing his eyes. Drained by the suddenness of it all, I sank down, resting my head against the tractor's wheel arch, while I thought how I should break the news to my mother. I stayed there for quite a while and a rooster strutted into view and stood crowing as though incensed by finding another present. Harry stretched out on his belly at a distance and whined, sensing the presence of death. When, finally, I got up and walked to the house I found my mother in the diary, churning butter. I went to her and took her hands from the handle. "Come inside, Mum," I said, "I have to tell you something."

"I can't leave this now."

"Yes, leave it."

"What, what's happened?"

"Dad's had an accident. Come inside and sit down."

Her voice and expression changed. "No, tell me here. What sort of accident?"

"A bad one," I said.

She made a cry like a wounded animal. "How bad? Tell me. Show me where he is." Before I could stop her she ran out. I chased after and attempted to hold her back. It took all my strength to hold her. "There's nothing we can do," I said. "He's gone."

She struggled free and started to run across the yard, scattering the chickens. Seeing it was useless to try and stop her, I followed. When I caught up with her she was cradling his body and wiping the blood from his face with the edge of her apron. "He wouldn't have known anything," I said. "It must have happened instantly because he was fine when I left him, right as rain, talking about us all going to Skegness next week."

She rocked to and fro. "He always worked too hard," she said. "I told him time and time again, but he'd never listen."

"That was Dad," I said. "Always his own man."

"We can't leave him here."

"I'll call and get help."

"You make the calls, I'll stay with him."

"No, come back inside, please, Mum." I helped her to her feet and led her back to the house and seated her in a chair.

"The butter won't have churned," she said.

"Doesn't matter. You sit here." I made her a cup of tea with plenty of sugar then made the calls that had to be made. Two neighbours came and we brought my father body into the house and laid him out on the bed. Later our GP arrived, made his examination and signed the death certificate and afterwards took me outside.

"Will there have to be a post mortem?" I asked. "I hope not, for my mother's sake."

"I don't think so. See, there was a history, Alex. He had a chronic murmur. A couple of times in the past year I told him to ease off. I said to him, give up the fags and the whisky too, but I don't think he took any notice."

"Did my mother know?"

"Only if he told her. I certainly didn't give out any hints. He was a good man, it's just that this life gets you in the end."

I made another call when he had left and made arrangements for the funeral. My mother did not want the body to be removed to a chapel of rest and refused to go to bed but sat beside the body all that night. Her main concern was that he should be dressed in his best suit before being put into the coffin.

As the news travelled a succession of neighbours called the next day to give their condolences.

"Flowers," his mother said. "What sort of wreath would be right?"

"Did he have a favourite flower?"

"He used to buy me roses on our anniversaries."

"Well, roses would be perfect."

"Will you see to that?"

"Of course."

She never cried in front of me, but the shock and grief had visibly changed her, she seemed suddenly smaller. In the days before the funeral the house acquired an extra layer of silence such as descends on the land after a heavy snowfall. The funeral was well attended, the small chapel packed with friends, many of whom were strangers to me. I gave a short Address, frequently stumbling over the words as the finality of the occasion struck home. Afterwards we held a wake in the house, and then I and my mother were alone again.

"What will happen?" she said, fingering the cards she had removed from the wreaths. "What will happen to the farm?"

"Nothing. Nothing will happen. I shall stay and look after it."

"You couldn't manage it on your own."

"Then I'll hire some help. Don't worry about that now."

"You're sure? You told him you wanted to do something different before."

"Well, that was before. I'd changed my mind."

"Were you able to tell him before he died?" she said.

"Yes," I lied.

THIRTY FIVE

For the next two weeks after the funeral I concentrated on sorting out my father's affairs and preparing the information for probate. Save for a small legacy to the RAF Benevolent Fund, the simple Will passed on everything to my mother. He had kept a crude ledger in a school exercise book, everything meticulously noted in his sloping handwriting and the final balances married with the bank statements. A separate exercise book locked in a box listed the cash sales of surplus eggs, butter and bacon sold on the black market in the village. When all outstanding debts had been paid, the bank account was in credit for £3500. The mortgage on the house had been paid off, although there was an annual rent on a portion of the extra land he had leased at a later date. After doing the sums I calculated there was no immediate need to worry but obviously I had to ensure that the farm stayed solvent. I knew that I could not maintain it single-handed and would need help so my first priority was to find and hire a live-in waggoner.

Mrs Hundleberry's shop had always been the village pump where word of mouth quickly circulated, so I made my needs known to her. She came up with a name a week later, a widower named Jack Warrender whom I vaguely remembered. Warrender had been made redundant from his previous job and, as a result, had lost the tied cottage that went with it. In return for board and lodgings and a salary just over the going rate, the deal was struck. Warrender was able to turn his hand to most tasks, was good with animals, and had the experience that I lacked.

In the weeks that followed I began to enjoy the added responsibility, rising while it was still dark, lighting the boiler fire to warm the mash for the horses, feeding household swill to the pigs and attending to other necessary chores before going in for breakfast. That first season, the beet harvest commanded a good price, the sow reared a healthy brood and the potato yield was up on the previous year. I began to feel confident I could make a go of it. Using some of the increased funds, I traded up the old tractor for a later model, and when funds allowed, converted one of the upstairs rooms into a bathroom and inside toilet, something my mother had wanted for years.

No great conversationalist, Warrender had a taciturn nature, for he was that rare soul, a man content with his lot. He ate his meals with my mother and me, but for the most part kept to himself. On Sundays when he finished his chores he set his fishing lines along the river bank while he went to morning service and invariably returned to find a catch of bream. It was a simple life we all shared, light years away from what I had experienced in Germany and I went whole weeks without giving any thought to the past. It was only when, by myself, isolated under the wide sheltering sky, that a sudden longing for Lisa would stab me like a knife. Where was she now? Had she had my child? And the man in the cell, what of him? I had never talked of her to my mother and unless Warrender occasionally brought up the subject of the war, I never discussed my old life.

I had little free time and apart from driving my mother into Lincoln once a month for lunch and some shopping, my life was bounded by the demands of the farm. The only luxury I allowed myself was an – occasional visit to a pub. I found I smoked fewer cigarettes in the open air and slept the moment I put my celibate head on the pillow. Although I borrowed books from the mobile library that made the rounds every fortnight, they were often returned unread, for any spare time I had was spent in keeping the accounts up to date. The only connection with the past was a letter from Machell saying that he had finally been pensioned off and had moved to a seaside cottage in Norfolk where I would always be welcome. 'Let me have news of you if you feel like it," he wrote. 'Don't end up like me, bored out of your skull." I fully intended to reply but somehow never got around to it. For a while I also got a series of saucy postcards from Christopher, forwarded by Mrs Drane. One said: 'Safeguard your health, dear. Don't sleep with damp women', another, 'Modern fairy story: and they lived happily ever after someone else' and a third and final one which said: 'Abstinence is the thin edge of the wedge' to which was added a P.S. 'if only' followed by a row of XXXX.

The outside world seldom intruded. I found I had settled into the rhythms of life on the land and it was over a year before the dearth of any romance in my life surfaced to plague me. Not since the fighting in Normandy had I given much thought to my own mortality. I did my best to ape Warrender's phlegmatic acceptance of events beyond his control – Warrender, the born countryman who had long since acknowledged that you could do battle with Nature but never defeat it, it always had the last word. I relied on him to predict the weather, when the cow should be put to the bull, the best week to commence the harvest. I studied the tender way with which his assisted the birth of a calf, how he determined wither a pig runt would survive. At night I listened to the vixen's scream, resembling that of a child; then going out the next morning to find the mutilated hens, which brought home the realisation that death on the land was in the natural order of things and not for the squeamish; sentimentality was an unaffordable luxury. More and more as time went by, I contrasted the life I now led with the cynicism of the world I had left behind. I thought: what a long journey it had been, marking me forever. Often sleepless in the still small hours of the night when rats scurried in the eaves, images of Lisa came crowding back. Sometimes I walked myself through the empty rooms of the flat I had rented for love, reliving our last meeting.

Although my mother remained ignorant of Lisa, her maternal radar instinctively tracked me. "I wish you got out more, enjoyed yourself. Jack's able to take care of everything if you gave yourself a holiday now and then and met people of your own age. Never know, you might meet a nice girl."

"I'm not looking at the moment."

"You should. Plenty of girls would be happy to have you Being on your own like this, it's not natural."

"I'm fine, quite happy as I am."

"You don't want to leave it too late. I shan't be here forever, and I want to see you settled before I go."

"Don't talk like that. You're not going to go and I'm not on the shelf yet."

I did nothing and yet wondered why I did nothing. Physically, I had never felt fitter and yet even though the need to love and be loved was there, something had died in me.

Gradually the efforts I and Jack put in began to pay off. On the strength of another good harvest I was able to raise a loan from the bank and when finally power lines came as far as our land, I doubled the number of cows and installed electric milking machines. I constantly thought of ways to increase income, kept abreast of government regulations and attended the weekly market to exchange views and ideas with fellow farmers. One year, as an experiment, I planted a field of rape, finding the slash of vivid yellow I viewed every morning from my bedroom window a constant source of pleasure as well as a new source of income.

It was about this time that I began to notice changes in my mother; she started to neglect herself and her memory came and went like a lighthouse beacon, now illuminating what she trying to recall, now swinging away into blackness. The deterioration was most marked as she went about her normal household chores: the most mundane tasks confused her, she would make the tea with a kettle that had not boiled, lay the table with four places instead of three, addressing Warrender by my father's Christian name. Once, coming in after a day in the fields I found her making a bonfire of furniture in the yard. These uncharacteristic eccentricities caused me growing concern and I voiced my fears to the family GP.

"Your mother's seventy one. Not a great age, but it strikes some earlier than others," Doctor Cracknell said.

"What are we talking about?"

"Well, years ago we didn't give a name to it. People would just say, 'old so and sob's gone a bit funny in the head.' Now it's recognised as the onset of Alzheimer's which, sadly, can develop into senile dementia. Should your dear mother be one of the unlucky ones, she won't be with you any longer, she won't know you, or anything for that matter."

I watched my mother carefully, but there was no drastic change, or deterioration in her behaviour for several weeks until one day she slipped in the new bathroom, cracking her head against the toilet. Concussed and bleeding profusely she was taken to hospital and there she went downhill very rapidly. I visited her daily but was increasingly alarmed by the changes in her; the shock of the accident seemed to have accelerated her condition and now she was like a small, trapped, birdlike creature lying motionless in the white nest of the hospital bed. At times she treated me as a stranger; if I held her hand she pulled it away as though I was personally responsible for her condition. There were moments when I saw nothing in her face but anger. When her injury had healed it was thought best to find somewhere she would receive twenty four hour care.

The chosen nursing home was some thirty miles from the farm, and on my first visit there I was distressed to find that she was being constrained in an armchair with straps. The resident Matron said she had somehow walked out one night and had been found, semi-naked close to a main road.

The pattern was the same whenever I saw her: no glimmer of recognition and the only time she spoke she called me by my father's name. She was lost to me.

In addition to the upkeep of the farm, I did my best to tackle the household chores, learning to cook rudimentary meals for myself and Jack, but I found it all too much. Using Mrs Hundleberry's good offices again, I let her find me a housekeeper – a cheerful, robust spinster in her forties named Rebecca. Within a week she had put the house back in order, the smell of polish replacing the fug of stale cigarette smoke. "You men," she said, "you're hopeless," For the first time in weeks Jack and I sat down to proper meals at the end of a hard day.

When next I paid a visit to the nursing home, I found my mother had been moved into a different room, sharing it with two other unfortunates. "We thought the companionship would be good for her," the Matron told me, but it seemed to have made little difference, except there were now three ghosts in the room instead of one. A short time after my arrival a young woman came in and sat beside one of the other two beds. I had brought my mother a box of Cadbury's Dairy Milk chocolates, long her favourite. I offered her one and she opened her denture-less mouth and accepted without any change of expression, then let it drop out and onto her lap, all the time staring at me with a look that chilled.

I turned around and made a small grimace of despair to the young woman. She nodded and mouthed; "Your mother?"

"Yes," I said. "You too?"

She shook her head. "An aunt."

I made further attempts to communicate with my mother, loosening one hand tightly clutching the arm of her chair and stroking the loose, age-mottled skin towards the heart. "You're looking much better," I said with false conviction. "Much better. You'll be home soon," hoping that some fragment of comfort would penetrate the fog of her mind. It was hard for me to reconcile the silent immobilised creature with the person who had loved and nurtured me since birth. I talked to her as one would talk to a child until the visiting hour was over, then brushed the wispy white hair from her expressionless face and kissed her parchment forehead when I said goodbye.

In the corridor I hastened my step and caught up with the young woman. "These visits depress me," I said.

"Me, too."

"Because one can't do anything."

"Yes. That's the saddest part of it, being unable to make any contact. It must be especially heartbreaking for you, she being your mother."

I thought she had a beautiful mouth, faultless complexion and thick, luxurious hair that fell to her shoulders. It was so long since I had been in the company of a girl my own age: that and the shameful relief of having escaped from the sad room where my mother was confined, made me over-anxious. I had only one thought in my head and that was to keep her in conversation and get to know her. She was so devastatingly pretty. "Do you have to come far?" I asked, then added. "I'm Alex, by the way."

"From Lincoln. And I'm Kathleen. Where do you have to come from?" I didn't offer to shake hands for fear of breaking the spell with any formal gesture. Something told me she shared my keenness to linger.

"Woodhall Spa." There was a slight pause, then I

produced a convoluted invitation: "Look, you probably have to rush off, but I wondered, that is to say, would you like, I thought perhaps it would cheer us both up to have a drink somewhere before driving back?"

She hesitated, but only for a fraction, then said: "Yes, that sounds a good idea. It always takes me a while to throw off a feeling of depression when I come here."

"Or relief," I said. "Like I imagine prison visitors feel when they walk away. Good Samaritans, but happy to be on the outside."

We went to a quiet pub not too far from the care home and when we arrived, I chose a window seat away from the regulars. I felt a sense of something good about to happen.

"Has your mother been in there long?" she asked.

"About two months. Your aunt?"

"Much longer, almost a year."

"God! It's not the end we'd have wished for them, is it? For anybody, come to that."

Her mouth fascinated me as she sipped her gin and tonic and I fantasized what it would be like to kiss her. "You live in Lincoln, you say?"

She nodded. "We used to live in Harrogate, but my father moved to Lincoln during the war when was directed to work in an aircraft factory. Were you in the war?"

"Yes, in France and Germany. Now I farm. Can't you tell from my hands?" I held them out for inspection. "They're disgusting, aren't they? And that's after scrubbing."

"The result of honest toil."

"I never intended to be a farmer, but when my father died I had no choice."

"What did you want to be?"

"Oh, I never had a chance to make up my mind. Called up before I was eighteen, then nearly six years in the Army. At one point I thought I might make that my career. But I didn't. You, what d'you do?"

"Oh, nothing much, very dull. I serve in a chemist's. I was too young to be called up."

The conversation petered out until, with deliberate disingenuousness, I said: "Never know, perhaps we'll bump into each other again when you visit. Or" – this as casually as possible – "I have to come into Lincoln myself some weekends. We could have a meal together, perhaps?"

"I can't this weekend. I'm going to a wedding. But the week after I'm free."

"I don't know Lincoln that well, is there somewhere nice to eat?"

"People recommend the Majestic Hotel. I haven't tried it myself, but they say the food is good."

"Well, we could try it. Saturday week, you say?

"Yes."

"That's great. I'll book a table. Shall we say seven o'clock? Is that all right for you?"

"Yes, that's fine."

"I'll meet you there then." It all seemed too easy, something I hadn't expected.

I walked with her to our cars. Before we parted I said: "I'm not married, by the way."

"Nor me," Kathy said.

After waiting until she drove away, I sat behind the wheel of my own car for several minutes trying to think of the last time I had felt so happy.

THIRTY SIX

For one defining moment as I stared at my face in the bathroom mirror I found my father staring back: my father, scrubbed and clean-shaven, attired awkwardly in his Sunday best to go to Chapel. Now, having dressed carefully for my first date with Kathy, wearing the suit made for me in Berlin complete with new shirt and tie, I felt that I was looking at what I would eventually become instead of what I was.

I arrived at the rendezvous half an hour too early and went in search of the restaurant manager to ensure we had a decent table and order a bottle of wine in advance of Kathy's arrival. Then I went outside, anxiously scanning every car that pulled in. Kathy was punctual which I took as a good sign. I greeted her with: "You look so great.

"Do I? Thank you."

"And what's that perfume you're wearing?"

"A sample we were given at work."

"It's lovely on you. You should always wear it." When we were seated and the wine had been poured, I returned to the subject, happy to break the ice with an anecdote. "Tell you a funny story about perfume. When we finally drove the Nazis out of France, a Hurricane pilot had the brilliant idea of filling his extra fuel pod with concentrated Chanel No.5, fifty gallons of it, thinking he'd make a fortune selling it back home. Unfortunately he pranged the plane on landing and the fuel pod broke and split the whole lot on the runway. The released scent brought people running for miles."

"So what happened to him?"

"He was court marshalled, but went out smelling like a rose. It's probably apocryphal."

A waitress with a stained apron arrived at the table with the menus. With that cheerfulness British restaurant staff employ when relaying bad news, she immediately informed us that the speciality of the day was finished. "But Chef tells me the fish cakes are quite tasty."

"What fish is it?"

"Not sure. I'll check, " she said and left them.

"This place probably wasn't a good choice of mine," Kathy said.

"It's fine. How was your day?"

"Very fraught. I mixed up two prescriptions. Gave one customer eye lotion for gastric tummy and vice versa. The pharmacist said I could have killed them. Luckily it was discovered in time. How about you?"

"My day? Let me think. Oh, the usual exciting routine. Cleaning out the stables and pig pens. "

"The waitress returned. "Cod," she said. "Cod and halibut. Soup of the day's, leek. And there's two portions of chicken volley vant left."

"I'll have the soup and fish cakes," Kathy said.

"Likewise."

Even the lukewarm, watery soup could not dampen the growing attraction I felt for her. She was disarmingly frank about her life, admitting that she did not see eye to eye with her parents. "Daddy's a Mason and is paranoid about anything that runs contrary to his own rules, especially where I'm concerned."

"Does he allow you to have boy friends?" I asked lightly.

"Only if I bring home somebody on his wavelength."

"And have you?"

"Sorry?"

"Brought anybody home on his wavelength?"

"No."

"Would I pass muster? Maybe he'd relent if you let slip I held the rank of Captain in the Intelligence Corps." The moment the words left my lips I regretted saying them: I sounded boastful.

"It might, he's a snob about titles, likes to use his own rank."

"What rank? I thought he was in an aircraft factory during the war."

"He was, but he was also a Major in the Home Guard and still refers to it when he wants to impress. He wasn't a real soldier like you, but he has to feel important. Did you get on with your parents?"

"Yes and no. I don't think I got to know them until it was too late. Now, of course, I never will. They were very simple people. The time when I might have got closer to them, I had to leave home and go to the war. The chance never really came again." I paused while our main course was cleared away. "You haven't given me an answer. Would I pass muster with Daddy?"

"It wouldn't be his decision," she said, "It'd be mine. I'm over twenty one. He'll just have to accept it."

"Did you tell your parents you were meeting me tonight?"

"No, I said I was going out with a girl friend."

"Well, since I want to go on seeing you, I guess you'll have to come clean one day." I said. "That is if you want to go on seeing me. Do you?"

"Yes," she said.

Reaching across the table I touched her hand. "I want you to know I'm not involved with anybody else. You won't have to share me with anybody, past or present."

"Have you got a past?" she said.

"Not any longer. I wiped the slate clean when I left the Army." I thought, how glibly we lie. I squeezed her hand before relinquishing it. "I couldn't wait for this evening. I was frightened you might have a regular boy friend and were just being nice to me out of kindness."

"Why kindness?"

"Oh, I don't know, because of where we first met, because of my mother."

"No, it wasn't anything to do with that. I liked you. If I hadn't I wouldn't be sitting here."

We saw each other regularly after that, our meetings kept deliberately low key by me, the physical side limited to kissing, and it was several weeks before I asked whether her parents were aware we were seeing each other.

"Yes," she said, "and I suppose that one of these days I'll have to expose you to them. Can you face that?"

"Sure, you say when."

"I'll try and make it tea next Sunday. Tea, rather than dinner so it's not too prolonged for you. Daddy gets very argumentative after a few drinks."

On the day I went armed with a dozen eggs, butter and a ham. Her father fitted all my preconceptions: jowled, red-veined skin, thinning hair carefully brushed into place, a portly stomach challenging the limits of his waistcoat, conveying an immediate impression of middle-class complacency. He introduced me to his wife with the same enthusiasm he would use for a commercial traveller. Mrs Anderson, by comparison, greeted me warmly. Petite, with small, beautifully moulded features that gave me a foretaste of what Kathy might eventually look like, she seemed genuinely thrilled to receive my gifts.

"Goodness me," she said. "Thank you, what a feast. Just look at what Mr.Seaton's brought us, Frank."

"Well, we all know farmer's don't want for anything," Anderson replied."

Frowning at her husband's ungraciousness, she said: "I'm sure we're very grateful, Mr. Seaton. Let me put these somewhere safe, then get the tea. Kathy, come and give me a hand."

Kathy shot me a sympathetic look as I followed her father into the lounge. There was an ordered tidiness about everything – antimacassars on the chintz-covered armchairs and matching sofa, dried poppies in a vase by the side of the fireplace, a Westminster clock chiming the quarters on the mantelpiece, a framed print of The Monarch of The Glen over the sideboard, half a dozen silver cups displayed in a glass cabinet.

After an awkward silence Anderson said: "Wondering when we were going to meet you." Another pause. "My daughter tells me you made Captain in the war. What regiment?"

"I wasn't in a regiment. Intelligence Corps."

"Really? Reserved occupation myself, unfortunately, although it carried a heavy responsibility." He stood in front of the fireplace and shifted from leg to leg. "I thought perhaps, before the women join us, it might be as well to get a few things out in the open. Kathy being my only daughter I'm naturally concerned whom she sees. You seem to have sprung from nowhere." He fiddled with his cuff links.

"Perhaps because we met purely by chance. I'm sure she'd told you my mother's in the same nursing home as your relative. Kathy and I happened to be visiting on the same day and got into conversation. We were brought together by a common sadness, if I can put it that way, had a social drink together afterwards and it went on from there."

Anderson cleared his throat. "What does 'went from on there' infer?"

"We began a friendship, which developed into an attachment."

"Attachment? That doesn't tell me much, I'm afraid."

"Well, let me make it easier for you. Are you asking whether my intentions are serious?"

"Yes, that's more or less it. A father has to ask and in my case I should perhaps tell you that recently my name went forward to the Lord Chancellor for consideration as a Justice of the Peace. Should that be looked upon favourably, as I have every reason to believe it will, I'm sure you appreciate I have to be careful."

"In what way careful?" I asked, playing the ingenuous.

"About whoever has connections with my family," he continued. "I don't wish to be offensive, but can I ask did you leave the Army in the normal way?"

"By that, d'you mean did I get an honourable discharge? Yes. I resigned my commission for personal reasons. My father died and it was necessary for me to take over his farm."

"Right. Necessary to get that dealt with. Do you intend to go on farming?"

"As long as I can make a success of it." He seemed unable to proceed with his questioning. "To anticipate a question you haven't asked, I'm not married, but I hope that one day Kathy will do me the honour of becoming my wife." I discovered I was saying this to myself as much as to him. The statement seemed to take him by surprise.

"Quite so." Turning to the clock on the mantelpiece, opened the front and made a slight adjustment to the minute hand as Kathy and her mother returned with a tray of tea and cakes.

"Have you two men been having a nice chat?" Mrs Anderson asked.

"Just going over a few things," her husband said.

"What sort of things, Daddy? Nothing embarrassing, I hope?" Kathy sat opposite me on the sofa and gave me an enquiring look.

"These are home made," her mother said, offering a plate of small cakes, "but only with powdered eggs. Next time you come I shall use the proper ones you so kindly gave us."

"Oh, don't save them for me. I can always bring more."

"Strictly speaking, of course, they should go through the

Egg Marketing Board," Anderson commented.

Kathy flashed him a look. "Well, Daddy, you don't have to eat them if your conscience bothers you."

"Not a question of conscience, my dear. It's a question of abiding by the law of the land."

Kathy put her tea cup down. "Did you bring your cigarettes, Alex?" she asked. "I'm out."

I hesitated, then produced a packet.

"We don't usually smoke in here," Anderson said.

I went to put the packet back, but Kathy took it from me. "Well, I'm sure we can make an exception today, Daddy. And this is ridiculous. Alex knows full well he's here to be looked over, but that doesn't mean he has to suffer the third degree. We're both over age so nobody has to be coy about the situation. He's here because we've being seeing each other for weeks now and if he ever thinks of asking me to marry him, I shall say yes." She looked at me. "Do you want to ask me?"

"Will you marry me?" I said, just as surprised as her parents by her sudden command of the situation.

"Of course I will."

Stunned, Mrs Anderson looked for guidance from Her husband. When he did nothing she said: "Well, we're delighted for you both, dear. Aren't we, Frank?"

"Yes."

"Can we have a little more enthusiasm, Daddy? Aren't you happy for me?"

"Course I am."

"Then say so."

"Congratulations," he said grudgingly.

"Good, now we can all relax," Kathy said. "I couldn't bear it a minute longer, all of us sitting around as though in a doctor's waiting room. Life's too short."

"Just as long as you remember marriage is a solemn undertaking," her father said.

"I don't feel solemn, I feel liberated," Kathy replied.

THIRTY SEVEN

We were married two months later, not in 'unseemly haste' as Mr. Anderson privately pronounced – but because we saw little point in waiting and decided on a modest, registry office ceremony despite Mrs Anderson's disappointment at being deprived of a full, white wedding. "Alex doesn't have any family or close friends," Kathy argued, "it would be so one sided and unfair." She amazed me by the way in which she faced every problem positively.

Our brief honeymoon was spent at a boarding house in the seaside town of Weymouth. Whether because of my long abstinence or Kathy's inexperience, our first lovemaking left us both unfulfilled though, unlike me, she had nothing to compare it with. I wondered if I would ever put the ghost of Lisa to rest. That night I had a wounding, confused dream that remained with me the next morning when we took breakfast in the dining room that faced onto the sea front.

"Doesn't the tide go out a long way," Kathy said. "So far you think it's never going to come back."

"Yes. Have you ever swum in the sea?"

"Never. When I was at school we were taken to the public baths, but I hated the smell of the stuff they put into the pool."

"I used to swim in the river Withan when I was young. Haven't done it since."

"I wish I'd known you then. I bet you looked sweet."

"No. Hideous. Basin hair cut and lots of pimples."

"Have you got any snapshots?"

"There might be some amongst my mother's things. We'll look when we get home, though I can't think why you want to see them."

She suddenly looked anxious. "Was I a disappointment last night?"

"Of course you weren't. It was me. I was tired after such a long drive."

"I'll get better," she said. "I want to be as good as your other girls."

"There are no other girls now," I said.

After breakfast we walked along the edge of the sea, the wet sand clinging to the soles of our shoes. A scattering of hardy souls sat in deck chairs, the men with their trouser legs rolled up, while fractious children made and knocked over sandcastles. A solitary old donkey stood with head lowered as though praying for release from servitude. Why did I choose Weymouth? I thought; on days like this the English Channel must be one of the most uninviting stretches of water imaginable, sullen and grey.

"It's unforgiving," I said.

"What is?"

"This sea. One day I'll take you to France and show you the beaches where we invaded."

"I can't imagine what it must have been like. How brave you all were."

"Not me. I didn't land until the worst was over."

We stopped and kissed. "What d'you want to do for the rest of the day?" I asked.

"You decide. I'm happy to do anything."

"Why don't we have lunch somewhere then go back to bed and make a baby?"

She looked to make sure I was serious. "Do brilliant ideas like that just come to you?"

"Yes, it's a gift, he said modestly."

"It sounds so sinful to make love in the afternoon. Mummy and Daddy would have a fit."

"Well, I was thinking of sending them a postcard. Wish you were here. We're in bed conceiving a grandchild."

She put her arms around me. "You're so funny. Will it always be like this?"

"Not always, but most of the time I hope."

As we kissed again, a passing elderly couple gave us a disapproving look.

"It's quite legal," I called after them. "We're married."

We had lunch in a fish restaurant on the sea front, then went back to the boarding house. The one overworked maid still hadn't made up our room and so we forced to pass the time waiting in the cheerless lounge where half a dozen fellow guests dozed. When we were finally allowed up to our room, I whispered: "Isn't it peculiar how we British take our pleasures? Those characters down there are probably having their first holiday in years, and what do they do? They sit in that hideous room and go to sleep."

"Whereas?" Kathy said.

"Whereas you and I have other ideas. We are intent upon increasing the population."

"We won't get like them, will we?"

"Never."

We undressed in haste. "Are you disappointed I haven't got bigger breasts? Men like big breasts, don't they? Mine are ice cream cones."

"I happen to prefer ice cream cones to wafers."

I gently lowered her onto the candlewick bedspread and bent over her. She stared up at me, trying to read my expression. "What?" she said.

" I want to make up for last night," kissing first one small breast and then the other before slowly tracing a path to the dark triangle between her legs. She gradually relaxed as my tongue probed, and I brought her to a first climax before taking her with a slow, measured rhythm and this time she cried out as that unique, searing sensation consumed her. When our bodies relinquished each other, she said: "Tell me what time and what day it is, darling."

"Three thirty four, Wednesday September the tenth. Why?"

"If it's happened, I want to remember. D'you think it's happened?"

"I hope so."

She quickly fell into a contented sleep. I remained awake, staring up at the ceiling where watery sunlight shimmered. There are some places you return to in your mind time and time again. I thought: will I remember this room and this moment as often as I remember another room in Austria and a different kind of loving?

THIRTY EIGHT

There are no happy endings.

Had I kept a diary over the years, I might well have set down the secret thoughts of a disappointed man, somebody who lived in two eras, almost on two different planets and had to choose between love and conscience. I see now that the lethal dose I injected into the vein of that poor *Untermenschen* at Belsen, determined everything that followed. For a short while I glimpsed an image of happiness, but then another's past changed all my tomorrows. Now I see my life as a book borrowed from a library I have been forced to return before finishing it.

Our first child, a boy, was born nine months after our honeymoon, followed two years later by a second son, this time delivered by Caesarean section, but afterwards Kathy was told it would be too dangerous for her to conceive again. After much deliberation, I had a vasectomy and our relationship settled into an affectionate companionship rather than the great passion I had once experienced with Lisa. My mother was finally released from her nightmare of non-existence, and for the most part I lived a life protected from everything except my own regrets.

Maybe there never were any happy endings, nor can we trust that the past will remain forever buried.

It was on a shopping trip to Lincoln that the calm of the rest of my life was shattered. I had driven there with the family to purchase our first colour television. As the salesman extolled the virtues of the various models, a plethora of screens showed identical pictures from a news item about the Berlin Film Festival. Viewing them as I tried to make a choice, I was suddenly transfixed as multiple images of Lisa appeared: Lisa stepping out of a car accompanied by a pretty young girl; Lisa coming into close up, my Lisa whose face had fined down with the passing of the years, but still a face that stopped my heart. Now she and the young girl faced the battery of microphones, and a commentator was saying: "...tipped to win for her performance in the remake of *Frau Meine Traume,* is actress Lisa Manfred seen here with with her fifteen-year-old daughter."

At my elbow Kathy was saying, "Darling, are you concentrating? The boys are keen on that one, but I can't decide." When I did not answer, she said. "Hello? You still with us?"

"Yes, sorry. Which one?"

Kathy pointed. "They all look the same to me. You decide."

I tried to concentrate as Lisa and the young girl I knew must be my daughter disappeared from view, to be replaced by a commercial for Oxo cubes.

"Darling, you decide," Kathy repeated.

"I will," I said. "Give me a moment," turning away so that she would not see my crumpled face.